'There *must*

Angelica struck the arm of his chair in her exasperation. 'If you won't go to France yourself—'

'Did I say I wouldn't?' Benoît covered her hand with his, and she gasped as she suddenly realised how informally she had been behaving with him. She hesitated, unable to look away from his face. His gaze was strangely compelling, though she still couldn't decipher the expression in his guarded brown eyes. She was torn between a desire to snatch her hand away and a fugitive wish to prolong the moment. . .

Alice Thornton was born and brought up in the Sussex countryside. Her favourite subjects at school were English and History, and she has always made up stories for her own and other's amusement. She has a history degree from York University, and historical research is still what she enjoys most, next to writing. She works in London as a secretary in a large teaching hospital, and at present she has no children, pets, or a husband!

THE WOLF'S PROMISE

Alice Thornton

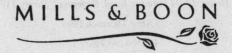

MILLS & BOON

To Phil and Irène—
and the authentic French phrases that didn't
get used!

*MILLS & BOON, the Rose Device and
LEGACY OF LOVE are trademarks of the publisher.
Harlequin Mills & Boon Limited,
Eton House, 18–24 Paradise Road, Richmond, Surrey TW9 1SR*

© Alice Thornton 1996

ISBN 0 263 79877 1

*Set in 10½ on 12 pt Linotron Times
04-9610-76158*

*Typeset in Great Britain by CentraCet, Cambridge
Printed in Great Britain by
BPC Paperbacks Ltd*

THE WOLF'S PROMISE

he quiet down, Sir William growled. If you
were any good at your job, neither the Earl nor I
would be wasting our time out this God-forsaken
beach. Well, they've given us time enough. We'll
follow them. Lead the way,

He handed the lantern back to the riding officer
and swung himself into

PROLOGUE

West Sussex 1793

IT WAS cold and dark on the beach. A black night
sky arched over the endless expanse of sand and
gusts of icy wind buffeted the Earl. He shivered and
turned up the collar of his greatcoat. He could hear
the crash of the incoming tide away to his right, but
he couldn't see much further than the circle of light
thrown by the lantern Sir William had snatched from
the riding officer.

'Damn it! The scurvy villain *lied* to me!' Sir
William exploded.

He was staring at the marks in the ridged, damp
sand where the kegs had been hauled up onto the
beach in a long daisy-chain of contraband.

'Or perhaps your informant was himself misled?'
the Earl of Ellewood suggested, stamping his feet to
keep warm.

It was quite clear what had happened. The smugglers' landing had been here, while Sir William's
small party had been lying in wait on an empty beach
two miles to the west.

'They're a cunning lot,' the riding officer began
nervously. It made him anxious to have the local
magistrate, two of the magistrate's men, and a visiting earl assisting him in his duty. 'It would be just
like them to feed you false. . .'

5

'Be quiet, damn you!' Sir William growled. 'If you were any good at your job, neither the Earl nor I would be wasting our time on this God-forsaken beach! Well, their tracks are clear enough. We'll follow them. Lead the way.'

He handed the lantern back to the riding officer and swung himself into his saddle.

'Yes, sir.' The riding officer shuttered his lantern until only a thin beam of light was visible. Then he climbed up onto to his horse and bent low in the saddle so that he could still see the smugglers' tracks. His lack of enthusiasm was very evident.

Sir William and his men followed the luckless riding officer, but Lord Ellewood did not immediately join them. He was frowning in the darkness.

'I think Bess has picked up a stone,' he called. 'I'll catch up with you in a minute.'

'As you wish.' Sir William's voice drifted back in the darkness. 'Damn sorry about this, Henry. I was hoping to show you some action tonight.'

'The night's still young,' the Earl replied.

He watched for a few seconds as the others rode away. Then he looked down at the dark, stirred-up sand and pinched his lower lip thoughtfully. The tide was coming in quickly; many of the smugglers' marks had already been washed away, but he was sure he'd seen the deep footprints of heavily laden men and horses going down *towards* the water—not away from it.

There was probably a reasonable explanation for that, and he knew so little about the smuggler's craft that he wasn't inclined to make a fool of himself by voicing his observations.

But it was certainly a fact that Sir William had been tricked into waiting on a beach two miles to the west, yet the very obvious tracks leading away from the landing point also headed in a westerly direction.

Lord Ellewood began to lead his mare east along the beach, keeping close to the tideline. There was no moon in the dark sky. It was hard to see what lay ahead, but the stars provided some light, and now that he was away from the riding officer's lantern the Earl's eyes adjusted to the darkness.

Two hundred yards along the beach he found what he was looking for. A track of damp, churned up sand leading inland from the sea. Horses and men had passed this way not long ago.

He felt a surge of gratified pleasure that he had guessed right, and his heart began to beat faster with excitement. There was no time to go back for Sir William. Without hesitation he followed the tracks up the beach towards the black shadows of the dunes.

The sea rumbled behind him; dried seaweed crackled beneath his salt-caked boots, and ahead of him he could hear the wind whistling through the thin, exposed grasses of the dunes—but he could barely see where he was going and he trod almost blindly towards his goal.

He was nearly among the dunes when the light of a lantern blazed suddenly in his eyes.

His heart thudded in startled alarm. He flung up a protective arm to his face, squinting into the glaring light and black darkness ahead, unable to see how many people confronted him. He had heard nothing to warn him of their presence.

He struggled to see beyond the lantern light, remembering all the stories Sir William had told him of smugglers beating or even killing anyone they believed to be a danger to them. Was he going to be battered to death without even seeing his attackers?

'I'm sorry, my lord,' said an apologetic voice, 'but I'm afraid I can't let you go any further.'

'What the hell do you think you're doing?' the Earl rasped, more angry than frightened. 'Who are you?'

He heard someone chuckle in the darkness behind the lantern.

'No one important.' The voice sounded like that of a young man—pleasant, educated and confident. 'In case you can't see it, my lord, I should warn you that there is a pistol levelled at your heart. It will be better for both of us if you don't make any sudden moves.'

'You damn murderer! You'll swing for this!' Lord Ellewood grated furiously.

'I haven't murdered anyone yet,' his opponent pointed out mildly. 'I would infinitely prefer it to remain that way—but the matter lies in your hands.'

The Earl's first moment of surprise and fear had passed and he began to relax. As far as he could tell, the other man was alone, and he didn't seem to have any immediate plans for violence.

'What do you intend to do with me?' he asked more temperately.

'Nothing,' said the young man. 'We could discuss the weather—it's remarkably dry for the time of year, don't you think? Or you could tell me the latest scandals from London—and when the conversation begins to pall, you will be free to go back to the Manor.'

'What if Sir William catches up with us first?' the Earl enquired politely.

His eyes were beginning to adjust to the lantern light which was not, in fact, all that bright, and he could discern the dim outline of his waylayer. The young man was bare-headed in the wind. He was also tall, but he seemed to be lightly built and Lord Ellewood felt confident that, if an opportunity arose, he would be able to turn the tables on his opponent.

'He won't,' said the young man confidently.

'What have you done to him?' the Earl demanded angrily, taking a hasty, unconsidered step forward as he spoke, suddenly afraid for his friend.

'Stand still!' Unexpected menace in the assured voice brought the Earl to an abrupt halt. 'Thank you. I believe I've already mentioned I'm not partial to murder.' After his initial sharpness, the young man sounded friendly again, and almost reassuring. 'But I've no doubt Sir William will find tonight's chase more exhilarating than the average foxhunt.'

The Earl drew in a deep breath, allowing the sudden tension to ease from his body.

'You've sent him on a wild-goose chase?' he said at last.

'As you say,' the youth agreed. 'Until your arrival I thought I'd lost the toss, but now I see I was mistaken,' he added politely.

The Earl grunted, unimpressed by the implied compliment.

'I'm sorry to detain you in such an inhospitable place, my lord,' said the young man apologetically. 'If you had gone with Sir William you would have been a great deal warmer! But I won't keep you much longer. If you wish, you can retrace your steps now.'

'That's hardly more enticing than my current situation!' Lord Ellewood retorted.

The young man laughed.

'I don't suppose it is,' he admitted. 'Allow me to make some amends.'

He put the lantern down, balancing it carefully between two tufts of grass half-way up a dune. The Earl's eyes narrowed speculatively, wondering if this would be a good moment to spring at his companion—but the pistol continued to point steadily at his heart. The young man was both watchful and cautious. It seemed increasingly unlikely that he would make a mistake.

He delved in his pocket with his free hand.

'Catch!' he said, and tossed something to the Earl.

Lord Ellewood barely had time to react. He fumbled the catch and nearly dropped the flask.

'Brandy?' he asked dryly, unscrewing it.

'What else? I'm not particularly fond of it myself, but it might compensate for the bitter wind around your ears,' the young man replied. 'You've had an unrewarding night, my lord.'

'I'm not so sure.' The Earl swallowed a mouthful of fiery spirit. 'At least I can claim to have bandied words with a smuggler. . .'

'Free trader,' the young man corrected him pleasantly. 'Sir William bandies words with us all the time—but not usually in circumstances of much benefit to him.'

A sudden gust of wind blew up a swirl of dry, gritty sand from the dunes. The mare snorted and reared backwards, lunging away into the darkness.

Startled, the young man turned his head—and the Earl seized the brief opportunity. He leapt towards the smuggler, knocking him to the ground without difficulty.

The pistol fired, but the Earl had already thrust it to one side. He was heavier than his opponent, and he'd had the element of surprise in his attack. He had no doubt that the youth had pulled the trigger involuntarily as he fell backwards.

They struggled among the dunes in an untidy confusion of flailing limbs. It was far too dark to see his opponent and Lord Ellewood fought by instinct, trying to subdue the youth without inflicting real damage. But the young man was strong, and agile as an eel. He twisted and broke free with a powerful lunge, disappearing among the shadows of the dunes.

The Earl sprang to his feet, drawing his sword instinctively as he glanced around, alert to any indication he was about to be attacked from the darkness.

The lantern was still resting undisturbed between the tufts of grass, sending its pale beam of light towards the sea. The wind hissed through the dunes, but the Earl could hear no other movement from the shadows surrounding him.

The mare had bolted, frightened by the pistol shot and the noise of the fight.

The Earl backed away, his boots crunching on the

shingle as he returned to the firm sand of the seashore. He wasn't a coward, but he had no desire to run on to an unseen blade among the dunes.

Then a dark shape rose silently from the shadows, sword in hand, and sprang towards him.

It was an untidy fight, illuminated only by the distant stars and the inadequate lantern. Twelve years earlier the Earl had served in the America Wars. He had both training and experience on his side, but his opponent was familiar with the ground and very, very fast.

Even so, the young man was soon outmatched. There was a sickening slither of steel, his sword was wrenched from his hand, and he found himself flat on his back in the sand.

'Now I'll see you!' the Earl growled, his blade at his defeated opponent's throat. 'Get up! But be warned—if you make one false move I'll run you through!'

The young man got to his feet displaying neither fear nor panic. He was breathing quickly from his exertions, but otherwise he was as much in control of himself now as he had ever been. The Earl smiled grimly in the darkness, aware of a certain measure of respect for his opponent. Smuggler or not, the youth had fought bravely and bore himself well in defeat.

'I must take a few more lessons before I cross swords with you again, my lord,' he said boldly.

'You'll not have the opportunity.'

The Earl picked up the lantern and shone it straight into the young man's face.

The youth had been expecting it, and he neither

flinched away nor threw up a hand to protect himself from the light. The tip of Lord Ellewood's sword was still grazing his throat; but his dark brown eyes stared fearlessly at the Earl from a lean, intelligent, and extremely youthful face.

'How old are you?' the Earl demanded sharply.

'Fourteen,' said the boy.

'My God!'

From his opponent's composure and self-confidence Lord Ellewood had assumed the youth to be a good deal older.

They stared at each other in silence for several tense moments, then the boy grinned impudently.

'Take care, my lord,' he said, glancing at the lantern the Earl was holding. 'It's an offence to show a light so close to the sea. If Sir William catches you, he may be obliged to clap you in irons.'

'You should be flogged at the cart's tail for your insolence!' the Earl growled, half angry, half amused by the boy's disrespectful boldness.

'Or hung in a gibbet until my dry bones fall through the iron cage as a warning to others?' the boy suggested softly.

'No!' Lord Ellewood exclaimed, startled.

He paused, considering the implications of the boy's comment. The lad's connection with the smugglers might be difficult to prove, but there was no doubt that he had waylaid—and attacked—the Earl; for that charge alone he could expect a heavy penalty if he ever stood in the dock. His youth would offer little protection.

'Do you intend to be a smuggler all your life?'

Lord Ellewood demanded abruptly. 'Or was this escapade just a moment of brief, high-spirited folly?'

'No.' The boy held the Earl's gaze for a few more seconds without attempting to clarify his ambiguous answer, then he turned away to look towards the sea, unheeding of the sword still held at his throat.

The first grey light of dawn was rising in the east and Lord Ellewood no longer needed the lantern to distinguish the boy's features. The youth was almost as tall as the Earl, and his black hair was wildly tousled by the cold, salty air—but his eyes looked steadily towards the distant, silvery horizon, almost as if he saw his future there.

Lord Ellewood smiled sardonically. Despite the threatening sword, his prisoner had obviously decided that the risk of being precipitously dispatched was minimal—but the Earl wasn't quite ready to confirm that assumption.

'Stand still!' he said harshly, thrusting the sword tip a little closer to the boy's neck. 'Don't give me an excuse to save the hangman work.'

'I am unarmed and at your mercy,' the boy pointed out calmly. 'I'm sure no man whom Sir William calls friend would take advantage of such a situation. What do you intend to do with me?' he added matter-of-factly.

'Damned if I know,' the Earl admitted frankly, although his sword didn't waver. 'You're too good for gallow's meat. Perhaps I ought to have you pressed. A few years of naval discipline might make a man of you!'

'A very courteous offer, but I have other plans,' the boy replied instantly.

'I daresay you have,' said the Earl dryly, 'but you should have thought of that before you held a pistol on me. You have the voice and manners of a gentleman, boy. News of this night's escapade might seriously damage your family's reputation and standing—don't you think?'

There was silence for several long moments. The boy's eyes were still fixed on the horizon and he did not look at the Earl. Lord Ellewood almost began to wonder if the youth had heard what he'd said. Then the boy replied,

'Yes, my lord.'

The Earl grunted and sheathed his sword. The boy turned his head sharply at the sound. For an instant he seemed poised for flight—but he didn't run; and there was a question in his eyes as he met Lord Ellewood's gaze.

'Which is the quickest way back to the Manor?' the Earl asked, without attempting to explain his actions.

The boy stared at him for a few moments, a frown in his dark eyes as he tried to decipher the Earl's intentions. Then he bent to pick up his own sword.

'I'll show you,' he said. 'We'll go along the beach. It's quicker and more comfortable for walking.'

'An important consideration, since I am now on foot,' Lord Ellewood agreed caustically. 'I suppose you don't have a horse hidden among the dunes?'

'I regret not, my lord,' the boy apologised.

'I imagine you must be well known to Sir William,' said the Earl, as they began to walk along the beach.

'We have met,' said the boy cautiously.

'Hm.' Lord Ellewood turned over several possible

ways of dealing with his erstwhile prisoner as they strode, almost companionably, along the damp sands.

'Why didn't you run when you had the chance?' he asked abruptly. 'You must know I couldn't catch you in the dunes.'

'You've seen my face,' said the boy simply. 'I'd like to know what you intend to do next. As you just implied, Sir William would certainly recognise my description.'

'I see,' said the Earl dryly. 'I dare say you could be long gone before he came in search of you.'

'But my family couldn't—as you also pointed out—and my father's practice would suffer. Inflict your punishment on me, my lord, whatever it is— but not on them.'

The boy turned as he spoke and looked squarely into the Earl's face. The force of his personality was reflected in his keen, dark eyes. Lord Ellewood was powerfully struck by the coiled spring of potential within the youth.

For a moment it seemed as if they were well matched: the shrewd-eyed, experienced man and the fearless, black-haired boy. They had more in common than the Earl would willingly choose to admit.

'I'll not betray your secret,' he said curtly. 'But I suggest you find more legitimate outlets for your ambition in future. The gibbet is a sorry place for anyone to end their days.'

'Thank you.' The boy spoke without over-emphasis, but the Earl caught the undercurrent of sincerity in the light voice.

'That way, my lord,' he said, turning to point inland. 'Follow the track for half a mile. Then turn right onto the lane. Turn left at the crossroads and Sir William's house is a mile further up on the right.'

'Thank you,' said the Earl.

He hesitated, suddenly reluctant to part from his companion. He was extremely curious about the boy but, in the circumstances, it probably wasn't advisable to try to pursue their acquaintance.

'My name is Benoît Faulkener, my lord,' said the boy, clearly and unhurriedly, surprising the Earl once again.

'Very French,' Lord Ellewood replied casually, not quite sure why the boy was sharing this information with him. 'I'd heard that most of the smugglers have contacts across the Channel.'

'My mother's French,' said Benoît. 'My father is the doctor in Arundel. My friends call me Ben. It seems unlikely that you will ever be my friend, my lord, or that you will ever need my services. But, if you do, I'll not forget what I owe you.'

The Earl stared at him in undisguised astonishment as he realised the implications of the boy's words.

'You're offering to repay me for my silence?' he exclaimed.

'At any time, and in any way you choose, my lord.' Benoît stepped back and bowed with something of a flourish.

The Earl laughed disbelievingly.

'Your effrontery is extraordinary!' he declared, unable to imagine any circumstances in which he might need the boy's help. 'Take care that one day you don't overreach yourself.'

Benoît grinned, the fresh dawn sunlight emphasising the distinctive contours of his dark face and the gleam of his strong white teeth as he returned the Earl's gaze.

'That may happen; but I'd rather try, and fail— than live knowing I'd never had the courage to try at all!' he declared boldly. 'Good day, my lord.'

He turned and strode away across the open fields which fronted the beach, leaving the Earl alone on the cold, windswept sands.

CHAPTER ONE

Early March 1809

THE pale winter's day was nearly over when Lady Angelica Lennard arrived at Holly House. She had been anxiously anticipating this moment for hours, but now she was here she was almost reluctant to climb down from the carriage.

'I'll knock on the door, my lady,' said her coachman.

'Thank you.'

As she waited for the door to open, Angelica glanced quickly around. It was too dark for her to see much, but she was acutely aware of how isolated the house was. It was situated a few miles south-west of Arundel, on the flat, windswept coastal plain of West Sussex. There wasn't another house within half a mile. It was an ideal place for a master smuggler to set up his headquarters.

Angelica suppressed a shiver. She was used to the teeming bustle of London and, even without the possibility that she was walking into a smuggler's lair, she would have found the absence of visible human life disturbing. There was not even a light showing from one of the windows to suggest the house was occupied.

It wasn't raining but there were heavy clouds in the sky, and an icy wind wrapped her skirts around

her legs and tugged at her bonnet. She did her best
to ignore the discomforts of the weather. She was
conscious of her maid's dour presence beside her.
Martha had made no secret of her disapproval of
this errand. Angelica was equally determined not to
reveal her own misgivings.

The front door opened and a maidservant looked
cautiously out into the gloom, lit from behind by a
pale light in the hallway. Angelica summoned up her
courage and stepped briskly forward.

'Good evening,' she said pleasantly. 'Am I correct
in believing that this is the residence of Mr Benoît
Faulkener?'

'Yes, m'm.' The girl looked at her suspiciously.

'Good! My name is Lady Angelica Lennard. I
would like to speak to your master, if you please,'
said Angelica firmly.

'The master's not at home. . .'

'Then perhaps you would be so kind as to allow
me to wait for him?' Angelica took another step
towards the girl. She'd come this far; she was determined not to be turned away when she was so close
to her goal.

'Oh, I don't know. . .'

'What is it, Tilly?' An older woman appeared
behind the maid, and the girl gladly gave way to her.

'Good evening, ma'am.' Angelica introduced herself again. 'I would be grateful if you would allow
me to wait for Mr Faulkener.'

'Is my son expecting you?' The woman spoke with
a hint of a French accent. She was in her early fifties,
and her dark hair was greying, but she studied
Angelica with shrewd brown eyes.

'No, ma'am.' Angelica replied steadily, although her heart was pounding a nervous tattoo within her chest. 'He does not know me. I have come to deliver a letter to him from my father. It is very important.'

Mrs Faulkener looked thoughtfully at her visitor for a few more seconds.

The shadowy bulk of the carriage rose up behind Angelica, but the light from the hall illuminated her face and picked out gold highlights in her blonde hair. She was very pale, and her expression seemed strained, but her candid blue eyes met Mrs Faulkener's gaze with an almost innocent steadfastness. The Frenchwoman nodded slightly.

'It must be important to have brought you all this way,' she said. 'Come in, my lady. Tilly, direct the coachman to the stables.'

'Thank you.' Overwhelmed with relief that she had so far been successful in her mission, Angelica followed her hostess into a sitting room at the back of the house.

'You must be cold, sit by the fire.' Mrs Faulkener spoke in a brisk but not unwelcoming voice. 'Would you like some tea?' She tugged on the bell pull .

'You are very kind,' Angelica said awkwardly. Now that the first moment of confrontation and relief was over, she was feeling increasingly ill at ease.

The sitting room was comfortable but unpretentious. It contained two armchairs on either side of the fireplace, a small, well-polished sideboard, and an occasional table beside one of the armchairs. The chairs were upholstered in rich, russet brown, but they were slightly shabby and old-fashioned. It was a

room for living in, not for show, and it offered a
welcome contrast to the bleak, dark, lonely fields
outside.

All the same, Angelica could not feel entirely
comfortable. It was clear from the neat pile of linen,
the scissors and pin-cushion that she had interrupted
Mrs Faulkener in the middle of doing her mending.
It was an unexpectedly mundane scene to discover
in a smuggler's house, and Angelica was thrown off
balance. It had never occurred to her when she set
out to find Benoît Faulkener that anyone else would
be involved in their meeting; or that she would be
forced to engage in social niceties with a member of
his family while awaiting his arrival.

'I'm so sorry to intrude upon you like this,' she
said impulsively. 'I really didn't mean to. It's just. . .'

'I met your father once, several years ago when he
was visiting Sir William,' said Mrs Faulkener calmly.
'My late husband was a doctor in Arundel. The Earl
is a very fine gentleman. Ah, Tilly—' she turned her
head as the maid came into the room '—Lady
Angelica will be spending the night with us. Please
prepare a room for her. We would like some tea,
and no doubt her maid is also hungry.'

'Yes, m'm.' Tilly glanced at Angelica curiously,
and then retreated with appropriate discretion.

'Oh, no!' Angelica leapt to her feet in agitation.
'I'm sure I needn't put you to so much trouble. I
only wish to speak to Mr Faulkener and then. . .'

'You came down from London, did you not?' Mrs
Faulkener raised an enquiring eyebrow. 'And Benoît
will not return home for several hours. You can
hardly travel back in the middle of the night.'

'But there must be an inn...' said Angelica helplessly.

'There are several,' said Mrs Faulkener equably. 'But you will be much more comfortable here.'

For a moment Angelica felt uncharacteristically daunted. She had been mistress of her father's household for several years since the death of her mother, she was used to being in command; but there was something rather disconcerting about the Frenchwoman's self-assurance.

Then Mrs Faulkener smiled, the expression softening the rather severe lines of her face.

'I will be glad to have your company at dinner,' she said. 'I doubt if Benoît will be back in time, and I get so bored when I have to eat alone.'

It was after nine o'clock when Benoît Faulkener finally returned to Holly House.

Contrary to her expectations, Angelica had enjoyed a surprisingly relaxed meal with Mrs Faulkener. The Frenchwoman had been a pleasant, undemanding hostess and, much to Angelica's relief, she had asked no awkward questions. But after dinner, when there was nothing to do but return to the sitting-room and wait for Benoît Faulkener, Angelica had become increasingly nervous.

She had to control a start when at last she heard a door bang and muffled voices in the hall. Mrs Faulkener nodded to her reassuringly and went quickly out of the room.

Angelica stood up instinctively and turned towards the door. Her mouth felt dry and she moistened her lower lip with her tongue before catching it nervously between her teeth.

Despite the cascading blonde curls, which had inspired her name as a baby, and which had never darkened as she grew older, there was nothing ethereal about her appearance. At the moment she was pale with anxiety, but under normal circumstances her cheeks were rosy and her blue eyes merry.

She was very well liked, but she had never been considered a classic beauty. Her personality was too forceful, her mouth was too wide and she laughed too readily. In addition, and most regretfully, her figure was considered a trifle too robust. It was true that she had a trim waist and long, slim legs, but she moved with an energy and determination which offered no concessions to the die-away airs fashionable among some of her contemporaries.

It was impossible to imagine that a zephyr of wind could carry her away like thistledown—or that she would find such an experience to her taste. Angelica preferred to keep her feet firmly on the ground.

She was dressed now in an elegant but suitably understated gown of soft blue silk which seemed unexpectedly vivid against the predominantly brown furnishings of the sitting-room. Martha had insisted on packing an adequate supply of clothes for her mistress's foolhardy mission, and now Angelica was grateful.

The dress had a modest neckline, but it was gathered in beneath her full breasts by a narrow ribbon which hinted at the voluptuous figure hidden by the demure folds of her skirts. She had thrown a long, fringed stole over her shoulders, and her glowing blonde hair was pinned up in a classical chignon of curls. Although she didn't know it, she shone like a candle in the shadows of the little room. All in all, she was as ready as she ever could be to confront a smuggler in his own home, but she felt uncharacteristically unsure of herself—and completely unprepared for the coming encounter.

She gasped as she remembered something, and snatched up her reticule. She dragged out two letters and cast the reticule aside, swinging hastily back to face the door as she heard footsteps approaching the room.

The door opened and the candles flickered in the sudden draught. Long dark shadows swooped up and down the walls as Benoît Faulkener entered the room. Angelica caught her breath, her hands gripping the letters painfully hard as she fixed all her attention on her host, trying desperately to divine what kind of man he was.

He closed the door quietly and returned her gaze with equal curiosity but considerably less intensity. He was tall, slightly over six foot, lean and sinewy, with a deceptive, whipcord strength. His hair was raven black and his skin tanned. He had high cheekbones and a slightly aquiline nose. There were small creases at the corners of his eyes, as if from squinting through bright sunlight and seaspray. His mouth was firm yet sensitive, but it gave away few secrets.

Apart from his white cravat and the frill of his shirt sleeves beneath his cuffs, he was dressed entirely in black, which emphasised his lean height and corresponded well with Angelica's somewhat exotic preconceptions of him. After her father's description of their dramatic encounter on the seashore, she had never expected Benoît Faulkener to look like an average gentleman—though what she had been anticipating she would have been hard pressed to say.

In fact, he looked more like a pirate than a smuggler. Her first, confused thought was that she wouldn't have been surprised if he'd been wearing a golden earring and a red kerchief, and carrying a cutlass. It was as if he had brought the briny expanse of the ocean into the small room with him. In his invigorating presence, the hitherto cosy chamber seemed to become claustrophobic and cramped.

Angelica's full lips parted slightly in amazement. She stared at him as if transfixed, still clutching the letters against her breast.

A hint of amusement appeared in Benoît's alert, watchful dark brown eyes. He had a mobile, intelligent face; his resemblance to his mother was elusive but unmistakable.

'Good evening, Lady Angelica,' he said politely, bowing slightly in her direction. 'I'm sorry you've had such a long wait for me. Had I known you were here, I would have returned sooner.'

Angelica blinked. After an evening spent with the still very French Mrs Faulkener, she had somehow expected Benoît to sound equally exotic. In fact his voice was pleasantly deep, but unambiguously English.

'I've brought you a letter from my father,' she said baldly. It wasn't what she'd intended to say, but her customary self-assurance had deserted her.

'So my mother said. Please, sit down again.' He gestured courteously towards a chair and then went over to the sideboard.

Angelica's gaze followed him. She knew she ought not to stare at him quite so intently but she couldn't help herself. Even if she hadn't already been so curious about him she would have felt compelled to watch him. He moved with a controlled, crisp grace which she found unaccountably rewarding to see. He was certainly the most assured man she had ever met; yet she sensed that his self-confidence wasn't founded on empty arrogance, but upon hard-won experience. Perhaps he really would be able to help her.

'Would you care for some brandy?' he asked courteously. 'You've come a long way today, and I don't imagine you are finding your errand an easy one.'

Angelica had been so preoccupied with her reflections on his potential character that, for a few moments, she barely understood what he'd just said to her. She glanced blankly at the decanter he was holding, and then a natural association of ideas popped unbidden into her mind.

'Is it smuggled?' she exclaimed, before she could stop herself.

He had been pouring the brandy, but at her comment he glanced sideways at her. There was a gleam in his dark eyes, and she saw a slow smile form on his lips. He was clearly amused by her gauche outburst. She blushed hotly, wondering furiously how she could have been so unsophisticated as to speak her thoughts aloud.

'I doubt if much of the spirit drunk in this county has had duty paid on it,' Benoît replied urbanely, completely unruffled by her question. 'Except for that in Sir William Hopwood's house, of course.'

'Thank you.' Angelica took the brandy he offered her, returning his gaze as calmly as she could.

She had already put herself at a disadvantage with him; she had no intention of allowing him to see the extent of her inner confusion.

'Of course, you must know Sir William,' said Benoît conversationally, as he sat down opposite Angelica and stretched out his long, black-clad legs across the hearth. 'He's one of your father's friends. But I don't believe you yourself have ever visited this part of the country before, have you?'

'No,' Angelica replied, more harshly than she realised. His words had conjured up an old, painful memory. 'We were going to visit Sir William one spring—but then my mother died,' she added.

She would not normally have said as much to a stranger, but she was thoroughly unsettled by the situation. Asking a favour from a man she didn't know, even one who owed such an enormous debt to her father, was turning out to be even harder than she'd anticipated.

'I'm sorry,' said Benoît quietly.

Angelica glanced at him quickly and then looked away, gazing into the fire as she tried to get a grip on herself. She knew she was being completely ridiculous. She had come to perform a simple errand and she was turning the whole thing into a foolish melodrama. After a moment she put the brandy glass down on a hearth stone with a firm click and lifted her head to look squarely into her host's eyes.

'Thank you, sir,' she said briskly, sounding much more like her normal self. 'But it happened several years ago, and I'm sure you are more interested in what I am doing here now.'

'I imagine you've come to reclaim my debt to your father,' said Benoît matter-of-factly, crossing one black-booted ankle over the other and taking a sip of his brandy. Unlike Angelica, he was completely relaxed. 'I confess I'm curious as to the exact nature of your request.'

'You do intend to keep your promise, then?' Angelica exclaimed, staring at him, her surprise audible in her voice. She had assumed he'd done no more than make a brash, boy's declaration all those years ago. She'd been quite certain that she would have to struggle to persuade him to keep his promise—perhaps even obliquely to threaten him.

Benoît looked up and met her eyes. He hadn't moved a muscle, but she was suddenly conscious of the immense force of his personality. Like a sleek black wolf slumbering by the winter fireside—he looked peaceful, but you roused him at your peril.

'I always keep my word, my lady,' he replied coldly. His voice was dangerously soft, and it contained an undercurrent of pure steel. 'But I do not yet know what service the Earl requires of me. Perhaps you would be good enough to give me his letter.'

He moved suddenly, leaning forward and stretching out an imperative hand towards her. Her heart leapt in momentary fright at his unexpected gesture and she instinctively hugged the letters against her breast.

'My lady,' he said impatiently, a hard gleam in his eyes. 'It would be foolish for you to come all this way and then refuse to give me the letter.'

Angelica hesitated, her gaze locked with his. She could see no apology in his eyes for having alarmed her—but neither did she have any intention of apologising for doubting his honour. She felt the same sense of apprehension, yet strange exhilaration, that sometimes gripped her at the sound of an approaching thunderstorm. The storm was unpredictable and uncontrollable, but after the endless silence that preceded it the noise and the lightning flashes could be so exciting.

'I know what's in it,' she said suddenly, still making no move to give it to him. 'Papa dictated it to me yesterday evening. It might be better if I try to explain.' She stood up restlessly, and took a few hasty steps, but there wasn't enough space in the small room to pace as she would have liked.

'Dictated it?' Benoît glanced at her, a slight frown in his eyes.

'Papa has been blind for more than a year,' she said curtly, the abruptness in her voice a measure of how painful she found it to make that admission.

'I'm sorry. He was a fine man.'

'*He still is!*'

Angelica spun around to confront Benoît in a swirl of flashing blue silk and dazzling, golden curls. Spots of colour glowed on her cheeks and her eyes burned like angry sapphires. Benoît's quiet words of sympathy had touched a raw nerve, jolting a far more vehement response from her than she might have wished.

'My father is a brave, noble man—not a common smuggler, a *thief*!' she blazed furiously. 'My God, he spared *your* life. How dare you speak of him as if he's *dead*!'

She broke off abruptly and turned her head away, blinking back treacherous tears as she tried to regain control of her emotions. She could not possibly explain to a stranger the bitter, black despondency which had consumed the Earl from the instant he'd realised he would never see again.

Lord Ellewood had lost far more than his sight when his carriage had overturned—and so had all those who loved him. Sometimes Angelica wondered despairingly if he would ever again be the same man she had loved and admired for so much of her life.

For a few moments after her outburst there was silence in the sitting-room. The clock ticked steadily on, and a log collapsed with a shower of sparks in the fireplace, but neither Angelica nor Benoît paid any attention to their surroundings.

Benoît was watching her with slightly narrowed eyes. He didn't seem to be particularly offended by her explosion of anger, but she had certainly succeeded in commanding his full attention.

He stood up almost lazily and went over to her, looking down at her thoughtfully. She glanced at him briefly, but she couldn't bring herself to meet his eyes. She was too afraid he would see the pain behind her anger, and she was ashamed on her father's behalf, as well as her own.

'I beg your pardon,' he said quietly. 'I had no

intention of insulting your father. I have no doubt
that he is still a fine and noble man. But he was also
a very active man—and the loss of his eyesight must
have hurt him grievously.'

'It has,' she whispered.

Benoît's unexpected understanding of her father's
plight disturbed her almost as much as his earlier
words had upset and angered her. She found she was
trembling with a mixture of confused emotions. She
didn't object when Benoît took her hand and led her
back to her chair. He picked up her brandy glass and
gave it to her, then sat down again himself.

'I hate to disappoint you,' he said lightly, once
more sounding completely relaxed and at ease, 'but
I haven't been actively involved in the smuggling
trade for nearly fifteen years. I am now an entirely
respectable and, I regret to admit it, unromantic
businessman.'

Angelica choked on the brandy and began to
cough, her eyes watering. She started to rummage in
her reticule, and then found that Benoît was present-
ing her with a spotless linen handkerchief.

'So I'm afraid you won't hear any ponies trotting
beneath your window tonight,' he continued, as she
dried her eyes, 'or see any mysterious lights shining
from the landing casement. In fact, you will probably
find your stay here as uneventful as a night under Sir
William's roof.

'Actually,' he added reflectively, 'you may find
your stay here rather more restful than it would be
with "Blunderbuss Billy". I believe he has a habit of
setting the whole household in an uproar whenever

he goes out to chase my erstwhile companions in crime.'

Angelica smiled, in spite of herself.

'I can imagine,' she said, trying to summon up her usual good-humoured composure. 'I'm sorry, sir. I had no right to speak to you so bitterly just now. Papa only told me about his meeting with you yesterday. I really wasn't sure what to expect of you—but I assure you I will keep your secret as faithfully as Papa has always done.'

'Thank you, my lady,' said Benoît gravely. 'Is your father well in every other respect?'

'Yes,' said Angelica, biting her lip. 'It was a carriage accident. The coach overturned and splinters of wood and glass went into his eyes,' she added, almost as if she felt impelled to do so, though Benoît hadn't asked for further details. 'He broke his arm and suffered a raging fever for several days, but now everything is mended except his eyes.'

She tried to sound matter-of-fact, but she couldn't disguise the bleakness in her voice. The Earl's body might have healed, but his spirit was still sorely wounded. Benoît watched her shrewdly, but he didn't comment.

Angelica glanced down, dragging her attention back to the business in hand, and was dimly surprised to realise that she was still holding the two letters. One of them had already been creased and stained; now they both looked the worse for wear. She tried to smooth them out in an instinctive, almost automatic gesture.

'So what is it your father wants me to do for him that he is no longer able to do for himself?' Benoît enquired, a trifle impatiently, as the silence lengthened.

Angelica looked up.

'To rescue my brother from Bitche,' she said simply.

Outside, the wind was growing stronger, and she could hear the patter of raindrops against the window. A storm was blowing up, isolating Holly House even further from the outside world. She had heard no movement from anyone else in the house for some time. It would be easy to imagine that she and Benoît were the only two people awake and breathing on the face of the earth. She certainly had the very real sense that he was the only person who could help her, and that this was the moment of truth.

'I see,' he said at last, his deep voice expressionless. 'You want me to travel through more than two hundred miles of French-occupied territory and then rescue your brother from one of Bonaparte's most notorious prisoner-of-war fortresses.'

'Papa spared you—and your family. Now we're asking for a life in return,' said Angelica with breathless urgency.

She leant towards him, her golden curls dancing, unconsciously holding out her hand to him in a pleading gesture, trying with every fibre of her being to compel him to agree.

She was desperately anxious for her brother to come home. She was sure the Earl's black moods were made worse by his unspoken fears for his son's safety. And Harry had always been so cheerful and lively. Perhaps *he* would be able to find a way of helping Lord Ellewood to come to terms with what he had lost—all Angelica's efforts had failed.

'A dramatic rescue is hardly necessary,' said Benoît dryly. He was still leaning back in his chair, dark and imperturbable, infuriatingly unresponsive to Angelica's beseeching blue eyes. 'All your brother—what's his name. . .?'

'Harry. He's a midshipman.'

'All Harry has to do is sit tight and behave himself, and he'll be exchanged in due course,' said Benoît. He took a sip of brandy, and watched Angelica over the rim of his glass. 'There's no need for all this melodrama over a perfectly straightforward situation.'

'But it's not straightforward!' said Angelica passionately. 'Maybe you haven't realised, but the French have stopped making automatic exchanges of their prisoners. When the war broke out again in 1803 they even detained civilians—women and children. Many of them are still being kept prisoner at Verdun. Papa says such infamy is in breach of every civilised code of war!'

'I'm sure many people think so,' said Benoît softly, still intently studying Angelica, an enigmatic expression in his eyes. 'But I also understand there is a school at Verdun, with several young midshipmen among its pupils. Why is Harry not one of them?'

'He wouldn't give his parole,' said Angelica flatly. 'He has already tried—and failed—to escape once. That's why they've sent him to Bitche. It a punishment depot, isn't it? You seem to know all about it.'

'Only what I hear,' said Benoît mildly.

His expression revealed nothing of his thoughts, but he was frowning slightly and Angelica at least had the satisfaction of knowing that he was giving the problem his full attention.

'The fortress was built by Vauban, I believe,' he said after a moment's reflection. 'It's situated on the summit of a great outcrop of rock. Not an easy place to escape from.'

'Harry's done it once already,' said Angelica proudly. 'Look!' She passed him the older of the two letters. 'We receivad this only yesterday from one of the *détenus* at Verdun.'

'Thank you.' Benoît put down his brandy glass, unfolded the crumpled paper and began to read.

'This paragraph here!' said Angelica impatiently, dropping onto her knees beside his chair, so that she could see the letter too.

Harry and his friends were at liberty for nearly three months. After many difficulties they reached the coast in safety, but they could not find a vessel to take them across the Channel. The French are strict in their surveillance of all boats at night; Harry was recaptured near Étaples and marched back to Verdun in shackles. . .

'You see, the main problem was finding a boat to get to England—that is why Papa thought of you!' Angelica exclaimed eagerly, her golden curls bouncing in her excitement. 'According to Sir William, the war hasn't made any difference to the smugglers.'

'But I'm not a smuggler any more,' Benoît reminded her, a gleam of appreciation in his eyes as he looked into her ardent face. 'Hush! Let me finish the letter,' he admonished her, as she opened her mouth to make a hasty retort.

She bit her lip in vexation and sat back on her heels in a rustle of impatient silk. She wasn't used to being spoken to like that, but she didn't want to alienate him if he might be able to help.

He smiled faintly, as if aware of her impatience, and carried on reading.

She watched him anxiously. If it was true he was no longer a smuggler, perhaps he couldn't help her. But he must still have relatives in France, and she retained the deep conviction that if he wanted to do something he could find a way.

The Earl's correspondent continued:

I saw Harry when he arrived here at Verdun, but I was only able to snatch a few words with him. Following his failed escape attempt he is regarded by the French as a *mauvais sujet*, criminal and the worst possible escape risk. He has been sent back to the fortress in Bitche, a punishment depot, but I am sure he will try to escape again as soon as the opportunity arises.

It is ironic, is it not, that if the French had offered him parole his own sense of honour would have held him more surely than any shackles? But the French don't really understand where mid-shipmen fit into the naval hierarchy. They often don't offer them the same privileges they allow commissioned officers. Of course, it might be different if they realised he was your son, but so far they don't seem to have discovered the connection. I remain your humble servant, James Corbett.

'You see!' Angelica declared, unable to remain silent any longer. 'It is a matter of life and death. Harry will surely try again, and next time he may be killed. I know that some of the prisoners have been killed trying to escape. All he needs is a little help. One small boat in the right place.'

She knelt up, gripping the arm of Benoît's chair in both hands.

'You don't even need to go to France,' she said earnestly, her lucid blue eyes fixed on Benoît's face as she concentrated all her powers of persuasion onto him. 'James Corbett sent his mistress over to England to carry out some business for him and she smuggled the letter out in her clothes—the French seem to be very lax in some respects—and she will be returning soon to Verdun.

'All we need is the name of someone Harry can safely approach to give him passage over the Channel. Fanny can take the information back to James Corbett.'

'And how will Corbett get a message through to Harry?' Benoît asked sceptically, raising one black eyebrow. 'And what happens if the name of the "safe person" falls into the wrong hands? What kind of tragedy would I be responsible for then, if I did as you suggest?'

Angelica bit back an angry retort. She knew Benoît's objections were valid; in her frustration and anxiety she wasn't thinking clearly. But his lack of a positive response to the problem aggravated her almost beyond bearing.

'There *must* be a way!' She struck the arm of his chair in her exasperation. If you won't go to France yourself—'

'Did I say I wouldn't?' Benoît covered her hand with his, and Angelica gasped as she suddenly realised how informally she had been behaving with him.

He was still sitting in the armchair, and she was kneeling on the floor beside him in a position which was neither dignified nor ladylike. In her wildest imagining she had never expected their interview would end up like this.

His hand was tanned, with strong but elegant fingers. She was instantly conscious of the warmth and potential power in his grip, and felt an answering spark at his touch which no other man had aroused within her.

She had been drilled in habits of strict decorum, but she also lived in a fashionable, glittering world in which flattery and flirtation were commonplace. She had received thousands of compliments during her few Seasons, and many eligible and not so eligible gentlemen had kissed her hand—but none of them had produced such an immediate response in her.

She hesitated, unable to look away from his face. His gaze was strangely compelling, though she still couldn't decipher the expression in his guarded brown eyes. She was torn between a desire to snatch her hand away and a fugitive wish to prolong the moment. Then she remembered it was her duty to

Harry—and her father—to do everything she could to persuade Benoît to help.

She smiled a trifle uncertainly at him, her anxiety and hope apparent in her candid blue eyes.

'You mean you will go to France?' she said, almost pleadingly.

'Perhaps.'

'*Perhaps*!' she exclaimed, drawing her hand away, consternation in her expression. 'But. . .'

'Let me have your father's letter,' said Benoît briskly.

'Why? I've told you everything it contains,' she said rebelliously.

'Nevertheless, I'd like to see it,' he replied equably. 'This one belongs to you.' He handed back James Corbett's letter and stood up.

Angelica was taken by surprise by his sudden action. She tried to stand up too, but she'd been sitting on her legs, and she was already stiff from the long hours in the coach. A flurry of pins and needles made her gasp and sink back to the floor.

Benoît reached down and took both of her hands in his, drawing her easily to her feet. She winced slightly as the tingling in her left leg made it extremely uncomfortable to put her full weight on her foot, and he steadied her with a light hand on her waist as she took an involuntary step sideways.

She looked up at him, very conscious of how close together they were standing, and the almost casual intimacy of their actions, which nevertheless did not seem entirely unnatural.

His brown eyes were as watchful as ever, but they didn't lack warmth.

'You're right,' he said, and he was so close his deep voice seemed to reverberate through her. 'I do owe your father a life—and that life would appear to be your brother's. But it will be best if you leave it up to me as to how I rescue him. I will write a reply to your father's letter and you may take it to him tomorrow.'

'But what are you going to *do*?' Angelica demanded. 'And when are you going to start?'

'That's my business,' Benoît retorted firmly. 'Does your father know you're here, by the way? He must have changed a great deal since my brief meeting with him if he allowed you to beard me in my den without a murmur.'

'Of course he knows!' Angelica exclaimed indignantly, stifling the uneasy awareness that she had informed the Earl of her intentions by the cowardly expedient of leaving him a note.

The Earl had wanted his secretary to bring his letter to Benoît, but Angelica had been deeply suspicious of asking a smuggler to rescue Harry. She hated doubting the Earl's judgement, but since his accident his decisions had often been erratic and even unreasonable. Harry's life was too important to entrust to a stranger on the strength of one brief meeting, sixteen years in the past. Angelica had been determined to discover what Benoît Faulkener was like for herself.

Benoît smiled. His dark face hung dizzyingly above Angelica's and she closed her eyes. The candle flames had begun to merge together in a glowing, misty haze. Now that she had finally put her case to

Benoît—and he had apparently agreed to help—she was suddenly overwhelmed with weariness.

She was dimly aware of an almost imperceptible touch on her hair, so light that she couldn't be sure it hadn't been a draught from the window disturbing her curls, then Benoît put his hand on her shoulder.

'You're swaying like an aspen tree in a summer gale,' he said, sounding amused. 'You've had a tiring day. I suggest you go to bed. You've done your part. Tomorrow you can safely return to your father.'

Angelica opened her eyes, insulted by the idea that she could be worn out by the carriage ride from London and irritated by Benoît's calmly amused dismissal of her.

'Don't patronise me, sir,' she said coldly. 'I am a little weary, but I am quite equal to my responsibilities. If your inordinately secretive disposition means that you prefer not to discuss you plans with me, so be it—but don't pretend it's because I'm not capable of understanding their complexities!'

Benoît stepped back and inclined his head in acknowledgement of her comment, but he didn't trouble to retaliate.

'After you, my lady,' he said, opening the door for her. 'I am sure we will all see things more clearly after a good night's sleep.'

Angelica gritted her teeth and walked out of the room with as much dignity as she could muster.

CHAPAPTER TWO

'WE'LL be going back to London today, my lady?' said Martha grimly as she brushed Angelica's hair.

She wasn't much more than thirty, but she'd cultivated an air of old-maidish disapproval from an early age.

'I expect so,' Angelica replied distractedly.

She had fallen asleep almost the moment she had climbed into bed the previous night. She'd had no time to reflect on her meeting with Benoît. She knew so little about him, and she wanted to be sure she was doing the right thing in entrusting Harry's safety to him.

Martha sniffed disparagingly.

'Nasty, damp, miserable, unfriendly place,' she said sourly. 'I don't know why we came here at all.'

That was, quite literally, true. Angelica hadn't thought it prudent to explain the whole story to her maid. She had simply said that Benoît Faulkener was an old acquaintance of the Earl, and that he might be able to help Harry.

'I came to deliver Papa's letter,' said Angelica calmly.

'No good will come of it,' said Martha grimly. 'It's an ungodly household. Comings and goings at all hours. Secretive servants. . . You mark my words, Sir William was right when he told the Earl Sussex was nothing but a nest of villainous—'

43

'What are you talking about?' Angelica interrupted quickly. 'What do you mean, comings and goings at all hours?'

'Far be it from me to talk ill of strangers,' said Martha, looking down her nose disdainfully, although her shrewd eyes watched Angelica closely in the mirror. Her mistress might not have told her everything, but Martha was quite capable of making her own deductions about the situation.

Angelica returned her maid's gaze suspiciously.

'What have you found out?' she demanded imperatively.

'They gave me a little attic room, overlooking the back of the house,' said Martha, her lips pursed with, for once, genuine distaste. 'The wind rattles through the casement something shocking—and the draught under the door. . . I got up to see if I could fix it and then I heard voices. Someone came to the house late last night, but they didn't come openly. There were no lights, just low voices.

'Then the Master himself went out. I saw him, and I heard the horses. You can be sure I didn't go to sleep after that. I waited for him to return, which he did. Two or three hours later, and on his own. But I'm asking you—what kind of a carry-on is that for a respectable household?'

'There might be a perfectly innocent explanation,' said Angelica slowly, not sure whether what she was hearing was good or bad news from her point of view.

'Oh, yes, and I'm a Chinaman,' said the maid scornfully. 'If it was all so innocent, why did they look at me as if I was mad this morning when I mentioned I'd heard visitors last night? "Oh, no," said the cook. "It must have been the sound of the wind you mistook, Miss Farley. You being more used to city life than the sounds of the countryside. No one came to the house last night."'

'I see,' said Angelica. 'I admit, it does sound suspicious.'

'That's what I've been telling you!' Martha exclaimed triumphantly, momentarily forgetting to be disapproving.

'But it may not be altogether a bad thing if what you suspect is true...'

'*What*?'

'Think! Martha!' Angelica twisted round in her chair to face the maid, seizing both the woman's hands in her eagerness. 'The reason Harry's escape failed was because he couldn't find a boat to bring him across the Channel. Who better than a smuggler...?'

Martha stared at her mistress for a moment, then she nodded grimly as if she wasn't entirely surprised.

'I guessed it might be something like that,' she said heavily. 'But how do you know they won't take your gold and then betray Lord Lennard to the French to make an extra profit on the deal?'

'I don't—yet,' Angelica replied. 'But it may be the best chance Harry has. I have to do everything I can...for Papa's sake...'

Martha pressed her lips together, accepting Angelica's argument, although she didn't like it very much. But she knew better than anyone how hard the past eighteen months had been for her mistress. No one had been able to break through Lord

Ellewood's morose mood. He had shut himself up in his Town house and refused to receive old friends.

For months Angelica had done little but read to her father and try to persuade him to take up his life again—but nothing had helped. If Lord Lennard's return could change all that, then Martha as well as her mistress would do anything to hasten it.

'Very well, my lady,' she said. 'Tell me what you want me to do.'

'Just keep listening for the moment, I think,' said Angelica, smiling ruefully. 'You've been more alert than I, so far.'

Martha sniffed disparagingly.

'Only because they put me in a room with half rotten window-frames,' she said caustically.

It was quite late when Angelica finally went downstairs. She was wearing a deep rose-pink travelling dress, with a soft shawl thrown around her shoulders in deference to the winter draughts.

Despite her uncertainty about the situation, she looked much brighter and less anxious than she had done the previous evening. There was a warm glow in her cheeks and a sparkle in her blue eyes. She moved with the vibrant sense of purpose which normally characterised her. Martha's gossip had intrigued rather than alarmed her, and for the first time in months she had something other than her father's problems to think about.

There were two doors at the front of the hall. She knew one led into the dining-room, and she was about to go over to it when she heard voices coming from the other room. The door had been left slightly ajar and she recognised Benoît's voice immediately. The other voice sounded familiar, but it was only when Benoît referred to him by name that she realised he was talking to Sir William Hopwood.

She caught her breath in horrified consternation. Her first thought was that her father had sent him to fetch her back, but then reason reasserted itself.

There would hardly have been time for the Earl to get a message to Sir William. Besides, her father had cut himself off from the rest of the world so thoroughly that he was unlikely to think of calling upon his old friend for such assistance.

Her second thought was that it would be extremely embarrassing if she did meet Sir William. It would be very difficult to provide an unexceptional explanation for her presence to him, and he was bound to be surprised and suspicious. She was about to hurry back upstairs when she suddenly realised that the subject of their conversation was of profound interest to her.

'My men are sure one of the ruffians escaped in this direction,' said Sir William gruffly. 'They're equally sure one of the others was hurt when he was thrown from his horse, but the fools lost track of them in the storm. Did you hear anything last night, Faulkener?'

'I regret not,' said Benoît coolly. 'Apart from the wind, of course.'

'Dammit! I wish I could believe you,' Sir William growled.

'Are you suggesting I'm *lying*, sir?' Benoît demanded, but he sounded more amused than outraged.

'You know damn well I am,' Sir William retorted. 'Not that it'll do me any good. There were times when I thought I'd caught Toby, fair and square—but somehow he always managed to outwit those porridge-brained men of mine. And you're as slippery as a greased pig.'

'What a flattering comparison,' said Benoît appreciatively. 'I'm sorry you don't find your men entirely to your satisfaction. I'm sure I could pick out some sharp-witted fellows to take their places.'

'I dare say you could,' said Sir William grimly. 'But I'll thank you not to interfere in my business.'

'I wouldn't dream of being so impertinent,' Benoît responded smoothly. 'Are you positive you won't take some refreshment?'

'Dammit! Faulkener! Why do you persist in siding with these villains?' Sir William burst out. 'If only a few of us made a stand, we could stamp out this infernal business in no time!'

'Who am I to go against tradition?' said Benoît lightly.

'*Tradition*!' Sir William exploded. 'A tradition of murder, terror, blackmail. . .*treason*!'

'Treason?'

'What do you call trading with the enemy? My God! I've even heard that smugglers row over to France from Dover with belts of guineas round their waists to pay for Bonaparte's armies. Don't you call that treason? When good English gold is being used to equip our enemies?'

'I won't argue with you on that point,' said Benoît coldly. 'But you might ask yourself, who supplies the guineas? Not the poor men who risk their lives in the Strait of Dover. It's merchants in the City—men who may never come within a mile of the coast—who send the gold to Napoleon. Why don't you discuss the subject of treason with them?'

'My God! Faulkener! How can you excuse the villainy of these base scoundrels by laying the blame on others?' Sir William demanded fiercely. 'If I had my way, every merchant or banker who sent gold to Bonaparte would be stripped of his possessions—but that doesn't justify what the local men do. They're lazy, workshy, and they'd rather spend the night dishonestly landing raw spirit than doing a decent day's work.'

'Perhaps if they were paid a decent day's wage for a decent day's work, they might not be so keen to risk their lives and their health on the beaches,' Benoît retorted sharply.

'By heaven, sir! I might have known you'd have a revolutionary spirit in you,' Sir William breathed, horrified. 'It's your French blood. Next you will be telling me that all men are equal and the government should be overturned. You're in league with the Frogs!'

Benoît laughed.

'My good sir,' he said, chuckling, 'when I take it into my head to overthrow His Majesty's government, you will be the first to know. In the meantime, I regret I cannot help you with your current problem.'

Angelica had been standing, transfixed, at the foot of the stairs, hardly able to believe what she was hearing. But now she suddenly realised Sir William was about to leave and she was in grave danger of being discovered. She hurried back upstairs, nearly tripping over her skirt, as Benoît and Sir William emerged into the hall.

She paused, just around the bend in the stairs, and listened to Sir William's departure. Her heart was beating rapidly with excitement and alarm, and she tried to still her breathing to a normal rate. It would never do if Benoît suspected she'd been eavesdropping.

His argument with Sir William had given her pause for thought. Asking the help of a smuggler was one thing—but what if he really was a traitor to England? He had made no greater attempt to deny that charge than he had to deny he was involved in smuggling.

She pressed her hand to her mouth in horror. What if Benoît really was a revolutionary? Some of the things he'd said certainly implied he had radical ideas. Until this moment the fact that he was half-French had seemed important only because it meant he might be in a better position to help Harry. She had met a number of *émigrés* in London, and most of them heartily loathed Napoleon. It had never occurred to her that Benoît might actually support the Corsican monster.

She heard the front door close behind Sir William and took a deep breath. She had a strong desire to run back up to her bedchamber, but she could hardly spend the rest of the day hiding there. The sooner she faced Benoît the better.

She draped her shawl more becomingly around her shoulders, and walked sedately downstairs. He had been about to return to the room he had occupied with Sir William, but he looked up at her approach.

'Good morning, my lady,' he said politely. 'I trust you slept well.' She thought she detected a glint of amusement in his brown eyes, but in the dimly lit hall it was hard to tell.

'Very well, thank you,' she replied calmly, although her heart was beating faster than she would have wished. 'My maid tells me there was quite a storm last night, but I'm afraid I was dead to the world.'

'I'm glad you were comfortable,' said Benoît. 'Come and have some breakfast.' He held open the dining-room door for her.

'Thank you.' Angelica went into the room, feeling a strange frisson of something that wasn't quite nervousness as she passed beside him.

For a man who could only have had a few hours sleep, he looked surprisingly vigorous. She was profoundly disturbed by what she'd just overheard—yet she couldn't suppress an unruly surge of excitement at being once more in his presence. There was a virile energy in his lean body which provoked an immediate response in her own ardent nature.

But she wasn't entirely comfortable with that piece of self-awareness, so she tried to distract herself with more mundane considerations. She noticed that he was once again dressed entirely in black—apart from the white cravat. She wondered vaguely if he took it off when he went out smuggling, or whether he just took good care to cover it up. She supposed it must be very convenient for him to be always dressed for business, whatever the hour of day or night.

There was no one in the dining-room, and Benoît pulled on the bell rope. Angelica hesitated. She was feeling extremely unsettled, and she knew if she sat down at the table she would feel trapped. The curtains were open so, partly out of curiosity, partly from a desire to appear at ease, she went over to the window.

The dining-room looked out to the front of the house. After the previous night's storm, the sky was a surprisingly bright and clear blue. She saw a holly tree close to the window, and in the distance some short-stemmed daffodils were dancing in a light breeze. They were the first she had seen that year.

'Spring is on its way,' said Benoît behind her, making her jump. She hadn't realised he was so close. 'You should have a relatively pleasant journey back to London.'

Angelica gasped, all coherent thought driven from her mind by his unexpected proximity. She was grateful she had her back to him and he couldn't see her confusion. It would never do to let him think he had her at a disadvantage.

She bit her lip, her eyes fixed on the daffodils, at a loss for an immediate reply. She had discharged her errand and she had no real grounds for refusing to go; but she didn't want to leave. She couldn't abandon Harry's fate in the hands of a man about whom she harboured such terrible suspicions.

'It certainly is a beautiful day,' she compromised, turning to face Benoît just as the maid came in.

It was a mistake. He was too close and she had no

avenue of retreat. He looked straight into her eyes for a few seconds, almost overwhelming her with the electric force of his personality. Angelica felt as if she had been stripped naked by the unexpected intimacy of that brief contact. She struggled to appear cool and unflustered, but her cheeks burned with embarrassment as she lifted her chin almost defiantly to meet his gaze.

He smiled, and turned his head to speak to the maid.

Angelica relaxed slightly, and discovered she'd been holding her breath. She controlled a desire to drag in a shaky lungful of air, and began to breathe normally again, berating herself for acting so foolishly. Surely she was far too sophisticated to be overawed by a provincial smuggler? But she couldn't resist the urge to watch Benoît as he spoke to the maid.

His black hair glinted blue in the bright sunlight. She could see the tiny lines around his eyes from all those times when he must have squinted to see in poorly lit conditions; but he was far more tanned than she would have expected of a man who spent most of his time working at night. For the first time it occurred to her to wonder how active a part in the smuggling trade he took. He surely wouldn't land the kegs and carry them up the beach himself?

He glanced at her, and she felt her cooling cheeks begin to flush again. A glint of amusement flickered in the intelligent brown eyes, almost as if he had guessed what she was thinking, then he said,

'Would you prefer tea or coffee with your breakfast, my lady?'

'Oh. . .coffee, please,' she stammered, suddenly remembering Sir William's strictures on the subject of smuggled tea, although she had a dim recollection that now the duty on tea had been so greatly reduced it was no longer an important item on the smugglers' inventory.

'I have written a letter to your father,' said Benoît, holding a chair for her to sit down. 'I will give it to you presently.'

'Thank you,' Angelica said vaguely.

Her errand was becoming far more complicated than she had ever anticipated. Not only did she have to face the possibility that Benoît might be a traitor; she also had to find a way of dealing with her own irrational attraction to him. She couldn't believe he had aroused such a strong response within her—no one else ever had. It was probably just a symptom of her anxiety over her father and Harry.

'You'll be sorry to learn that you've just missed seeing an old friend,' said Benoît pleasantly, sitting down opposite her.

'I have. . .I mean, have I?' Angelica stammered, flushing guiltily.

'Sir William Hopwood,' said Benoît helpfully.

'Oh, *Sir William*!' Angelica exclaimed, trying to sound suitably surprised. 'What a pity. . .I mean—'

'It would certainly have been entertaining watching you trying to explain your presence here to him,' Benoît observed, grinning. 'Your eloquence and his bewilderment—or perhaps I have that the wrong way round. As you no doubt know, the worthy baronet is seldom at a loss for words.'

Angelica bit her lip, wondering if Benoît suspected she had overheard his conversation with Sir William.

'I would have done my best not to embarrass you, sir,' she said stiffly. 'Obviously I would have been unable to give Sir William a true explanation for my visit. I am a person of honour—even if you are not.'

'But I'm not a nobleman's son,' Benoît pointed out, completely unruffled by her comment. 'No tradition of chivalry flows through my veins. I'm just the son of a poor, hardworking country doctor.'

'Which is how you come to live in such a large house and wear such fine clothes,' Angelica flashed, before she could stop herself.

'I earned those,' he replied, an enigmatic gleam in his eyes as he met her hot gaze.

'Yes! By illegal—' She broke off as Tilly came back into the room with a heavily laden tray.

'Thank you, Tilly,' said Benoît.

Angelica waited until the maid had left the room, almost grateful for the interruption. She found Benoît both disturbing and infuriating, but it was hard to imagine he was in league with his country's enemies. On the other hand, what did she really know of him?

'Do you deny that this house was purchased with the profits of smuggling?' she demanded, when they were alone again.

'I would do so with alacrity, if I didn't think the answer would disappoint you,' he answered immediately, a faint smile playing on his lips. 'I believe I told you before that I'm an unromantic businessman.'

'Are you suggesting I find anything. . .*attractive*

about the idea that you are a smuggler?' Angelica exclaimed, colouring angrily at the implication that she might find him attractive in any way at all.

'Well, obviously you do,' he pointed out reasonably. 'From your point of view, if I don't have any connections with the smugglers I'm unlikely to be able to help you. Your principles as a good, law-abiding citizen—the kind Sir William would welcome as a friend—are at war with your sisterly devotion. It's quite understandable if sisterly devotion wins the day.'

Angelica glared at him.

'I don't find this funny, even if you do,' she informed him through gritted teeth.

'Of course I find it amusing,' he retorted, grinning. 'I haven't been so entertained in months. On the one hand I have you, a monumentally respectable citizen under normal circumstances, I am sure, hoping and praying I am a dastardly smuggler—and on the other hand I have Sir William berating me for not taking a more active role in the suppression of the malevolent trade. How could I ever hope to satisfy both your expectations?'

'I don't wish you to be a smuggler,' Angelica denied grimly. 'I simply hoped you might have means of communicating with France...What do you mean—"monumentally"...?'

'A slip of the tongue,' Benoît assured her instantly, but she distrusted the gleam in his eye. 'I meant no disparagement of your character or figure. How old are you, by the way?'

'Really, sir!' she exclaimed, affronted. 'I don't see what business—'

'Not much more than five-and-twenty,' he mused, idly playing with a silver teaspoon. 'Not on the shelf yet.'

'I'm twenty-three,' she snapped.

He grinned and she flushed crossly, suddenly realising how easily she had allowed him to bait her, and with the most obvious ruse in the world. She had intended to learn more about him, but instead it was he who had prodded her into an unwary disclosure.

Before she could think of anything to say to retrieve her position, he stood up.

'I'll leave you to finish your breakfast in peace,' he said magnanimously. 'I wouldn't want any guest at Holly House to suffer from a disturbed digestion. Come into the library later. I'll give you the letter for your father.'

'The library?' said Angelica, raising her eyebrows in delicately disbelieving enquiry, as if wondering what a mere smuggler might know of books or learning.

'The room where you overheard me talking to Sir William,' Benoît explained helpfully. 'Enjoy your breakfast, Lady Angelica.'

Angelica was too hungry to allow her confused emotions to interfere with her breakfast. She had a healthy appetite which even Benoît's provocative manner couldn't disturb; but she was too distracted to pay much attention to what she was eating.

She kept remembering his conversation with Sir William, and the suggestion that perhaps his sympathies lay with the French.

He was in many ways an infuriating man, and one with whom she would never normally have exchanged a single word.

He had the appearance of a gentleman but, as he had reminded her himself, he was only the son of a provincial doctor. His handsome figure and quick wit might be enough to open the doors of her fashionable world but, unless he also had the wealth to support him, he was unlikely to make a permanent niche for himself there. Perhaps an ambitious, but nameless, man might well feel post-Revolutionary France did have more to offer him.

On the other hand, although she felt as if she'd been at an almost permanent disadvantage ever since she'd met him, he had treated her with a tolerable measure of courtesy—if you could discount that half-amused, half-mocking gleam in his brown eyes whenever he looked at her. It seemed incredible that he might actually be her enemy.

'Good morning, my lady.' Mrs Faulkener came quietly into the dining room, interrupting Angelica's speculations.

'Good morning.'

Angelica hadn't seen the Frenchwoman since her first meeting with Benoît. She wondered how much he'd told his mother about her reason for coming to Sussex—and what she ought to say to the woman. No mother could be happy at the possibility of her son undertaking such a difficult and potentially dangerous task; Angelica couldn't help feeling uncomfortable in Mrs Faulkener's presence.

'I hope you feel more rested this morning,' said Mrs Faulkener pleasantly, nothing in her manner revealing any underlying hostility towards her guest. 'Benoît tells me you will be going home today. Cook is preparing a basket of food for you. It's a long, weary drive back to London.'

'Thank you. You've been very kind!' Angelica exclaimed, touched by the Frenchwoman's thoughtfulness. 'I'm so sorry to have imposed myself upon you like this. I truly never intended. . .'

'All your thoughts were fixed on your goal,' said Mrs Faulkener calmly. 'That's only natural. I hope you have found the outcome of your visit satisfactory.'

Angelica stared at the Frenchwoman, wondering if there was some hidden meaning behind the words, but Mrs Faulkener seemed quite sincere.

'Has Mr Faulkener not explained why I came?' she asked curiously.

Mrs Faulkener smiled, a hint of quiet pride and amusement in her eyes.

'My son has never been one to betray someone else's secrets,' she said sedately. 'Even to me. If you came here seeking help, my lady, I am sure he will be able to provide it. Excuse me, I must see how Cook is getting on.'

Angelica gazed after her, deriving a degree of reassurance from her words. Mrs Faulkener clearly considered her son to be a man of honour, but she had also admitted that Benoît didn't tell her all his secrets—was he likely to tell her if he really was a French spy?

Angelica patted her lips with her napkin and stood up decisively. She wouldn't obtain any answers dawdling over her breakfast.

The door to the library was properly closed this time, but she turned the handle without hesitation. It was a larger room than she had anticipated, and she paused on the threshold, taken aback by its size and bright airiness. There were windows on two sides, and broad, clear beams of morning sunlight streamed in to illuminate the books and furnishings. A cheerful fire burned in the grate—but what caught her eye and completely arrested her attention was a picture over the chimney breast.

'That's not real!' she exclaimed, forgetful of everything else in her surprise.

Benoît had been sitting at a large desk, but he stood up at her entrance.

'I hate to contradict you,' he said, smiling, 'but I'm afraid it is.'

'But those colours...' Angelica stared at the picture. She guessed it portrayed a scene from somewhere in the Caribbean; she had seen many engravings of similar scenes. What had transfixed her were the colours. She couldn't imagine that the sky or the sea could ever be such vivid, vibrant hues.

'I was there when the artist painted it,' said Benoît, watching her fascinated, disbelieving expression. 'I can assure you that it's a faithful record of what he saw.'

Angelica went to stand beneath the picture, half raising her hand towards it. She still found it hard to credit that such lucid, brilliant colours could be real.

'Have you never left England, my lady?' Benoît asked quietly, coming to stand beside her.

She shook her head mutely, unable to take her eyes off the painting. After the dark gloom of an

English winter, and the bleak, anxious journey she had made the previous day, the vibrant colours seemed to sing within her, satisfying a hunger she hadn't even known she had had.

'The quality of the light is quite different,' said Benoît, 'even in the Mediterranean. And the Caribbean is a whole new world. How long was Harry at sea before he was captured?'

'A year,' said Angelica distantly. 'He was so eager to go. He was in a frigate on the way back from the West Indies when. . .'

'Then when you see him again, you must ask him to verify the truth of my picture,' said Benoît lightly.

Angelica turned slowly, still dazzled by what she had just seen and lifted her eyes to his face. With the splendour of the Caribbean sun behind her, she suddenly realised his tanned skin could owe nothing to a dark English winter. She had been so sure he was a smuggler that she had missed some obvious clues. When she had first laid eyes on him she'd even thought he looked more like a pirate than a smuggler, but then she'd dismissed the idea.

'If you're not a smuggler, what are you?' she blurted out, sounding completely disorientated.

He grinned, and she saw a flash of strong, white teeth against his dark skin. There was a glinting light in his eyes which was almost a challenge.

'I told you, my lady. I'm a respectable businessman.'

'I don't believe you,' she said flatly.

He laughed aloud, an unexpectedly full-bodied sound which only served to strengthen the image of piracy in her mind. She had a confused image of him standing on a quarterdeck, a cutlass in his hand, as his crew boarded a helpless merchantman.

'You're the second person to call me a liar this morning!' he remarked. 'Now Sir William knows I'm so lacking in the honourable qualities of a gentleman that I'm unlikely to call him to book for his words—but what about you, my lady? I can't *call* you out, but I could *turn* you out. Oh, no, you're leaving anyway so that threat lacks force. How would *you* suggest I obtain satisfaction?'

A familiar, slow smile played on his lips, and the challenging gleam in his dark eyes was very evident now. He was standing relaxed, yet poised, and there was no mistaking the provocative way in which his gaze lingered on her eyes, her hair and her rosy lips.

She gazed back at him, her blue eyes wide and questioning, her lips parted slightly in surprise. She had tried to convince herself that she had misinterpreted what had happened earlier; but the fiery spark of intimacy she had sensed between them in the dining room was even stronger now—and this time there was no maid to interrupt them.

Despite her attempt to remain cool and detached, Angelica's heart beat out an uncontrollable rhythm of excitement. Men had flirted with her before, but never like this—if Benoît was flirting. He had not uttered a single elegant compliment. But she could feel the virile power of his personality, even across the few feet of empty space which separated them. It half-frightened her, but it also made her blood sing.

She had spent the whole of her life comparing other men to her father—and none of them had ever measured up to him. She didn't know whether Benoît was a smuggler, though he was certainly involved in some shady business; he might even be a French spy—but dealing with him could never be boring.

She turned slightly away from him, resting her fingers gently on a large globe. She'd finally recovered her self-possession, and it was time he learnt that she couldn't be overawed by a quick tongue and a bold look. She was the Earl of Ellewood's daughter—not a giggling chambermaid.

'I don't know, sir,' she said lightly. 'I believe, in an affair of honour, it is the gentleman who receives the challenge who has the choice of weapons, is it not?'

'Are you suggesting you have already challenged me, my lady?' Benoît raised one quizzical black eyebrow. 'I thought it was the other way around.'

'Is it?' She paused, her hand poised delicately just above the globe, a faint smile on her lips. 'In that case, I will chose no weapons and thus you will have no opportunity to show me your mettle.'

'A very feminine solution to the problem,' he retorted. 'It ensures that you can accuse me of any dark deed you wish, secure in the knowledge that if I dispute your interpretation, you will refuse to pick up my gage.'

'If you were a gentleman. . .'

'But we have already established that I am not.'

'. . . you would not contradict a lady's opinion,' Angelica concluded serenely.

'But think how insulted you would feel if I were foolish enough to imply that you are incapable of understanding complex ideas,' he retaliated. 'I've made that mistake once already, my lady.'

'So you have.'

With a quick flick of her wrist, Angelica set the globe spinning. Oceans and continents flashed beneath her hand, merging into each other as the world revolved.

She had a giddy feeling that she had set much more in motion this morning than she fully realised. She didn't know how to stop it and she didn't know if she wanted to do so. She hadn't realised just how frustrated she had become with the enclosed life she'd led for the past eighteen months.

Benoît reached past her and stilled the globe with a deft touch.

'I've always had an ambition to circumnavigate the world, but perhaps not at quite such a breakneck speed,' he observed dryly.

'You mean you haven't already done so!' Angelica exclaimed in mock amazement, seizing gratefully on the change of topic.

'Not yet. As I believe I've mentioned several times, I've been earning a living. But one day I fully intend to sail in the wake of Vasco de Gama.' Benoît turned the globe slowly beneath his hands, lightly tracing his planned course over the surface of the polished wood.

Angelica glanced at his face. For a few moments his features were in repose, neither challenging nor concealing anything. His eyes rested on the world as if he thought it was a wondrous place—and life an endless adventure.

She looked at the picture on the chimney breast

and wondered, a little wistfully, if she would ever have the opportunity to see the colours of that glowing world with her own eyes. Harry had, and she knew her father had, but it had never occurred to the Earl to tell her about them—and now he was blind.

Benoît reached over and picked up a letter from the desk. He offered it to her.

'This is for your father,' he prompted her, when she didn't immediately take it.

'What does it say?' she asked, receiving it rather reluctantly and noticing that it was already sealed.

'My lady!' Benoît exclaimed. 'Do you make a habit of enquiring into other people's private correspondence?'

'Papa will ask me to read it to him, I might as well know what it says now,' Angelica replied, a dull note in her voice.

Some of the brightness seemed to have gone out of the day. Ahead of her lay only a weary journey back to London, an unpleasant interview with her father explaining what she'd done—and then a long wait to find out if Harry really would be be rescued.

'That's his privilege,' Benoît agreed, unperturbed. 'He sent me a letter and I have replied directly to him. That's my privilege. It might also make him feel less humiliated by the situation if he has the opportunity to break my seal himself.'

'Yes, perhaps,' Angelica replied almost inaudibly. She doubted if her father would appreciate Benoît's tact. He loathed his dependence too much to be consoled by such courteous gestures.

She weighed the letter in her hand, remembering

her earlier doubts about Benoît She found it almost inconceivable that he might be intending to betray Harry to the French—what good would it do him? The information that Harry wanted to escape was hardly going to be news to his captors. But she did wish he had given her firmer assurance about what he meant to do.

She looked up and found that he was watching her, a half-smile, and perhaps a question, in his eyes.

'You were right, sir,' she said slowly, 'it was a very tiring journey yesterday. It's lucky the storm didn't break earlier in the day. We had enough trouble jolting over the ruts and boggy places in the road as it was.'

She went over to the front window, looking out at the driveway and the bobbing, yellow daffodils. There were one or two shallow puddles on the ground, reflecting the blue sky above.

'I confess, I am a little daunted at the prospect of setting out again so soon,' she said hesitantly, as if reluctant to admit a weakness.

'Come now, Lady Angelica,' Benoît said bracingly. 'This doesn't sound like you. What happened to being "equal to your responsibilities"? I'm sure you won't let a little discomfort stand in the way of your duty. Besides, the Earl's carriage is very well upholstered.'

Angelica bit her lip. She disliked intensely the role she had created for herself, but she couldn't think of any better excuse to stay at Holly House another day.

'I'm sure the journey to London must seem infinitesimal to a man who has sailed halfway round the world,' she said grittily, 'but to me it is not so. I do not enjoy having to admit such foolish sensibility to a stranger, but the prospect of climbing into the coach again this morning fills me with horror.'

'Now that I can believe,' Benoît said appreciatively. 'It's always best, when telling lies, to stick as close to the truth as possible.'

Angelica swung round indignantly, sparks in her blue eyes.

'Were you planning to challenge me?' he asked softly, before she could speak. 'I warn you, my lady, I will pick up the gage.'

He was standing beside the desk with the still vigour which characterised him, simultaneously relaxed yet alert. There was an intelligent, amused understanding in his brown eyes which was very disconcerting.

Angelica hesitated, thinking better of what she'd been going to say. She knew she was on shaky ground. Her own nature would not allow her to play the part of a nervous, vapourish female, even if she wanted to do so; sooner or later she would betray herself.

'Nevertheless, I would be grateful if you would allow me to intrude upon you another night,' she said, as serenely as she could. 'If the weather remains dry the roads will be in much better condition tomorrow. It will be easier for the horses.'

'Of course, we must consider the horses,' Benoît agreed smoothly, a gleam in his eye. 'But how long will the Earl tolerate the absence of his daughter? I should hate to have Sir William come storming in here accusing me of kidnapping you. He might

suspect me of trying to hold the Earl to ransom for
your safe return.'

Angelica gasped. Not once, in all the time she
since had decided to deliver her father's letter herself, had that possibility occurred to her.

'You wouldn't!' she exclaimed, caught between
indignation and disbelief.

'I might, under certain circumstances,' Benoît said
reflectively, startling her even further. He smiled at
her expression. 'No, my lady, you're quite safe with
me,' he assured her. 'But I think we might send a
message to your father that you're still here. He
must be more aware than most of the possibility of
accidents on the road.'

Angelica nodded, unable to argue with Benoît's
suggestion. For all his black moods, she knew the
Earl was probably desperate with worry for her. It
upset her that she was causing him so much distress.
But it was an unbelievable relief to have escaped
briefly from the dark, gloom-enshrouded house in
Berkeley Square. One more day could not hurt.

'I'll tell my mother you are staying while you write
a note to the Earl,' said Benoît briskly. 'Feel free to
use the desk. We'll send him my letter at the same
time.'

'Oh. . .' Angelica wanted to protest, but she
couldn't think of an unexceptional way to resist his
eminently reasonable suggestion.

'You will have to curb your curiosity in that
respect a while longer,' said Benoît, with dry amusement, removing it neatly from between her fingers.
'Excuse me, my lady.'

He went out, leaving Angelica alone. She looked

around, her eyes drawn once more to the brilliant painting over the fireplace. She was staying for Harry's sake, she told herself. There was a great deal about Benoît Faulkener that still needed investigation before she could finally trust her brother's life to him.

But was there also something here for her? She spun the globe idly, and then noticed for the first time the model of a ship standing alone on its own table. It was beautifully made, with a well-polished hull, delicate spars and intricate rigging. She went over to it, hardly daring to touch it. It was resting on a wooden plinth, but the sails billowed as if it were scudding through the waves, free and unrestrained.

For eighteen months the Earl had rarely left the familiarity of his own home. For the first time she wondered if he would be happier if they travelled; if he could feel the wind on his face even though he could no longer see it bending the trees? It had to be so.

When Harry came home they would *make* Lord Ellewood emerge from his self-made prison. They would take him out so that he could sense the teeming world all around him, and they would *make* him start living again. Because if they didn't, she could not bear to contemplate what the future would be like.

She remembered suddenly that she was supposed to be writing him a note, and hurried back to the desk, half afraid that Benoît would be back before she had finished.

CHAPTER THREE

'WELL, my lady,' said Benoît, when a messenger had been dispatched with two letters for the Earl, 'how would you like to spend the day of repose you have won for yourself? In a comfortable chair by the fire—or perhaps you'd rather lie down for a few hours?'

'You are very considerate, sir,' Angelica replied coolly, trying not to let him provoke her, 'but I think I could endure a little more activity than that. Perhaps you might permit me to look at some of the books in this well-stocked library.'

Benoît inclined his head politely, an ironic gleam in his eyes.

'Be my guest,' he said graciously. 'Are you very fond of reading, my lady? If you tell me your taste, I may be able to select just the thing for you.'

'I have read a great deal to Papa,' said Angelica.

She wandered over to the nearest shelves, idly running her fingers along the leather spines of the books. Then she paused, her hand resting lightly on the edge of the shelf as she looked up at the rows and rows of books.

'You haven't read all these?' she said suspiciously.

'By no means,' Benoît replied urbanely. 'Most of them belonged to old Mr Fanshaw, the previous owner. He had very eclectic tastes, not all of which I share. But there are also my father's medical books, and I have added others on subjects which interest me.'

'The Great Discoverers—the New World?' Angelica guessed, glancing at him for confirmation of her suggestion.

'Among other things.' Benoît watched, smiling slightly, as Angelica looked back at the shelves.

Her dusky pink gown was more subdued than the blue she had worn the previous evening, but nothing could dim the vivid glory of her hair. Her full-breasted figure radiated energy and a barely contained zest for life. She didn't belong in front of rows of dusty books.

Then she sighed, clearly unaware that she had done so, and Benoît frowned, his eyes narrowing a trifle as he studied her.

Angelica had just realised that she was sick of books and everything they stood for. There had been too many days and nights when she had read endlessly to her father from texts that she didn't understand or that didn't interest her.

Books had become the only substitute for life the Earl was prepared to accept. He was more willing to listen to the words of long-dead philosophers than the voices of old, and once-valued, friends. Angelica turned abruptly away from the shelves.

'On the other hand,' said Benoît smoothly, before she could speak, 'if you don't feel too bruised from your journey yesterday, perhaps you might like to explore some of the surrounding countryside.'

Angelica glanced at him, startled and not quite sure of his meaning.

'I take it you do ride?' he said, lifting an enquiring eyebrow.

'Of course, but—'

'Then since this is your first visit to this part of the country, I would be honoured to show you around,' he offered politely.

He spoke in the unexceptional tone of a good host doing his best to entertain a difficult guest, but there was an amused glint in his eyes as if he had read Angelica's mind and knew exactly how she felt about a day spent in the library.

'The scenery isn't spectacular, but we're quite close to the sea,' he added encouragingly.

'I know,' Angelica replied dryly, wondering why he always managed to make her feel at a disadvantage.

He grinned, unabashed at her implicit allusion to smuggling.

'What do you say?' he asked, the challenging light in his eyes almost daring her to decline his offer.

She hesitated, meeting his gaze with fearless, lucid blue eyes. She already knew she was going to go riding with him—it would be far too craven-hearted to refuse his implicit challenge—but she couldn't help wondering, briefly, about the propriety of his suggestion. She stifled her conscience with the thought that she was extremely unlikely to meet anyone she knew.

Above all, the prospect of riding freely in the crisp open air was irresistible, and she was suddenly filled with exuberant anticipation. She smiled, her expression lighting up with unexpected radiance, her blue eyes almost dazzling with luminous excitement.

She met his gaze without reservation, unaware of the impact her happiness might have on him.

'I would be delighted, sir,' she said eagerly. 'Oh!' Her face fell. 'Unfortunately I didn't foresee the need to bring a riding habit. I'm afraid. . .'

Benoît had been watching her internal struggle to justify riding with him with an appreciative half-smile. But now he was gazing at her with an arrested expression in his eyes, almost as if he had been taken by surprise by something. He seemed to absorb her last, disappointed words with an effort, but then he responded with his customary competence.

'I dare say my mother will be able to make good that deficiency,' he said briskly, ringing the bell. 'I will have a couple of horses saddled and we will set out as soon as you are ready, my lady.'

Angelica had no time to reflect on the wisdom of her decision. Besides, she was too excited at the unexpected treat in store for her to worry overmuch about propriety. She dressed as quickly as she could in the old-fashioned riding habit Mrs Faulkener lent her, eager to get out of the house and anxious not to keep Benoît waiting.

'Well, it's not what I like to see you wearing, and it's to be thanked that no one we know will see you in it, but it will do,' said Martha grudgingly, although she was secretly pleased to see the renewed glow of life in Angelica's eyes.

Angelica's preoccupation with her father's problems—and her increasing anxiety about him—had worried Martha. But she had been unable to think of any advice which might help.

'Oh, Martha, it's fine!' Angelica protested buoy-antly, hastily checking her appearance in the mirror.

The riding dress was charcoal grey, severely cut and very plain. It was a trifle too loose around her waist, and it fitted very snugly across her bust, but it was undoubtedly smart. The doctor's wife had had style—still did have, Angelica reflected. There was nothing of the vulgar, provincial housewife about Mrs Faulkener.

Angelica cast one more glance at the mirror and turned to leave the room, but at the last minute she paused. She picked up her reticule and took out the letter from James Corbett, slipping it safely into a concealed pocket in the capacious riding skirts. It was the most valuable thing she possessed, and somehow it seemed to bring her closer to Harry. Besides, if it came to an argument with Benoît about how he was going to rescue her brother, she wanted to have all the facts at her fingertips.

It was wonderful to be outside in the fresh air. There wasn't much warmth in the March sunshine, but the sky was still a clear blue. The damp cobble-stones in the stableyard glistened in the bright morn-ing light and the horses were glossy and sleek. Angelica hadn't been riding for a long time, and she could hardly contain a thrill of anticipation at the prospect ahead of her.

'It's a beautiful day!' she exclaimed, almost danc-ing in her sudden light-heartedness.

'I can't argue with that,' said Benoît more sedately, but smiling at the vivid picture she made in the sunlight. 'This is Billy,' he added, rubbing the silky nose of a neat bay gelding. 'My mother named him. She said she perceived a resemblance to Sir William in his countenance.'

'Oh, no!' Angelica protested instinctively. 'I mean. . .'

The bay turned its head at the sound of her voice, flicking his ears disapprovingly. Then he struck the cobblestones a couple of times with an impatient forefoot and pulled against the groom's restraining hand.

Angelica laughed. 'I think I can see what she means,' she confessed.

The groom grinned and spoke chidingly to the horse.

'And this is Dorcas,' said Benoît, patting the shoulder of a quiet chestnut. 'She's my mother's mare. Allow me to put you up, my lady.'

He was standing right beside her, and she was suddenly deeply conscious of his nearness. Her heart began to beat faster and she knew she was blushing.

'Thank you,' she said in a muffled voice.

She was grateful that her face was turned away from him, and that she could blame any colour in her cheeks on the exertion of mounting.

He tossed her up with an easy, confident strength which landed her securely in the saddle. He stepped back and watched as she gathered up the reins. She was very aware that she was under observation and tried to compose herself, as well as her mount.

She told herself fiercely that she mustn't allow her natural excitement at this welcome moment of freedom to blind her to the more serious issues at stake. And she certainly mustn't let Benoît Faulkener use his undoubted charm and quick wits to put her at a disadvantage.

Despite that, she had to resist the urge to fidget under his gaze, and she knew she was blushing even more rosily than before. She was unbelievably relieved when at last he nodded, as if satisfied, and swung himself up onto the bay.

'Thank you, Thomas,' he said.

The groom stepped back and watched them ride out of the stableyard.

Angelica was suddenly aware that she was going to be quite alone with Benoît. In the past a groom had always acoompanied her whenever she went riding, but Benoît had apparently given no thought to the matter.

She wondered for a brief, almost panic-stricken moment whether she should insist that her coachman accompany them. In the circumstances it would be a perfectly reasonable request, but she decided against it almost immediately. Benoît might do his best to disconcert her, but she had no real fear that he might molest her—and it would be easier to find out more about him if no one else was within earshot.

She glanced at him surreptitiously. He was sitting erect yet relaxed in the saddle, holding the reins in one hand, his other hand resting lightly on his lean, well-muscled thigh. He hadn't troubled to wear a hat, and his raven hair glinted in the winter sunlight. He was gazing south over the water meadows, his deep set eyes resting on the horizon, momentarily forgetful of her presence.

She could easily imagine him on the deck of his ship, looking out across the sea-swell. Her heart stirred within her at the picture she had conjured up, and she realised in stunned disbelief that she felt sad that it was a sight she would never see in real life.

'What is your respectable business?' she asked abruptly, trying to banish the disturbing vision.

Her question recalled his attention to her, and he flicked a quick look in her direction. There was a humorous gleam in his brown eyes, and a tantalising smile played on his lips.

'I would tell you anything you want to know, my lady,' he declared, 'but are you not afraid that once I have done so we will have nothing left to talk about?'

'Don't be ridiculous!' she snapped, flushing, determined not to let him make fun of her. 'This situation may be amusing to you, sir—but it isn't to me! My brother's life is very important to me. I'm not prepared to entrust it to someone I know so little about.'

He turned his head towards her, one black eyebrow raised interrogatively. There was a direct, challenging glint in his eyes which she found very disturbing.

'Are you suggesting you no longer want my help in rescuing Harry?' he enquired silkily, and she could sense the sleeping wolf within him beginning to stir.

Her thoughts were thrown into chaos, for she had not expected such an uncompromising response to her hasty remark. She glanced away, trying to regain her composure, and then looked up to meet his eyes.

'I don't wish to offend you,' she said steadily, 'but you have given me little reason to trust you. You're right, I did, quite unintentionally, overhear some of your conversation with Sir William this morning. He must have known you for many years, and if he has doubts...' her voice faltered slightly '...doubts about...'

'Ah, yes, if Sir William harbours doubts about me I must be a treacherous, blackhearted scoundrel,' Benoît interrupted smoothly, a disquieting smile on his lips. 'What exactly do you fear, my lady? That I am not equal to the task of rescuing Harry? Or that, having done so, I might sell him back to the French? I presume from a comment Corbett makes in his letter that they don't know he is the Earl's son. I might be able to get a very good price for him— although I dare say I could force a higher one from your father.'

Angelica bit her lip, unable to face the expression of aloof contempt in his eyes. There was an under-current of fierce inflexibility in his voice which she had heard once before, and which was very difficult to confront. She had inadvertently angered him far more with her cautiously worded doubts than Sir William had with his intemperate accusations. She lifted her head, flags of bright colour flying in her cheeks, confusion in her wide blue eyes.

'Why are you so offended by my natural apprehension?' she demanded hotly. 'Sir William called you a liar and you laughed out loud! All I know about you is that you were once a smuggler and that you will tell me nothing of how you intend to help Harry—and you act as if I have bitterly insulted you by asking a few questions! If you were in my place wouldn't you want some indication of your good faith?'

Silence followed her impassioned words. The blue dome of the sky arched above them, and a strong breeze whispered through the damp grass beneath the horses hooves. It was a very flat, open landscape. Even in the bright sunlight it could not be called cosy, and it was easy to imagine how a grey sky and biting wind could transform it into a bleak, desolate wilderness.

There was a frown in Benoît's eyes, and his lean, aquiline face seemed particularly hawk-like as he turned his head to meet Angelica's heated gaze.

'It hadn't occurred to me that you might try to sell Harry to Papa,' she added bitterly.

'I know,' said Benoît coldly. 'You are not very consistent in your anxieties, my lady.'

'That's because I'm not used to thinking ill of other people!' Angelica flared back at him. 'You force me to be suspicious because you're so secretive.'

'On the contrary,' Benoît retaliated, an edge of steel in his voice. 'You came to Sussex with such deeply embedded preconceptions about me that you have shown no willingness to accept the truth. I told you last night that I haven't been actively involved in smuggling for fifteen years—but you still refuse to believe me!'

'What do you expect when you receive secret visitations in the night, and then tell Sir William you didn't hear anything but the wind!' Angelica demanded wildly, abandoning all caution.

To her surprise, Benoît didn't seem particularly disturbed by her accusation. She had expected an angry denial, but instead he stared frowningly between his horse's ears for a few moments.

'That must have been your maid,' he said curtly. 'Your room faces the front, but she slept in the attic. I heard she'd been asking a lot of questions this morning.'

'How do you explain that, sir?' Angelica challenged him, her chin lifted defiantly.

Her heart was beating uncomfortably fast, and her agitation communicated itself to the mare who tossed her head nervously, but Angelica was determined not to be overawed by her companion.

'I don't intend to explain it at all,' Benoît replied evenly. His expression was distant and uncommunicative. 'What happens in my house is my business, my lady.'

Angelica shook her head in frustration, her golden curls trembling beneath the brim of the hat Mrs Faulkener had lent her.

'Then we are back where we started,' she said in angry exasperation. 'You will not explain, and my doubts will not be satisfied until I receive some earnest of your good intentions.'

'My word should be good enough for that,' said Benoît chillingly. 'You would not make such a demand of your father—or of Sir William.'

'But you have already proved yourself to be a liar!' Angelica exclaimed, firing up instantly. 'If you can lie to Sir William, why not to me? You don't need to remind me that you don't have honourable blood in your veins—you've proved that already!'

Benoît pressed his lips together in a thin, furious line. Beneath his tan he was very pale, and his hand gripped the reins almost convulsively. Angelica was light-headed with the effects of her own anger, but she was dimly satisfied that she had finally provoked a strong emotional response from him. He wasn't laughing at her any more.

'I wonder if you really understand the meaning of the word honour, my lady,' he said harshly. 'Do you? Tell me—is it to risk the lives of men, whose names you don't even know, in a search for vain-glory? Or to call out and kill a passing acquaintance for some supposed slight? Or does it mean betraying men who have known and trusted you all your life to satisfy one man's momentary frustration? Is that what it means, my lady? *Tell me*!'

His eyes, as they met hers, were granite-hard and uncompromising. He was icily furious and he was allowing her no quarter in their argument.

No one had ever confronted Angelica like this. Her social status and sex meant that on inconsequential matters she was used to having her opinion politely deferred to; and she had rarely had an opportunity to discuss more profound matters with anyone—even her father. The Earl had always indulged his daughter, but he would never have considered it appropriate to enter into a serious debate with her. Benoît's obvious willingness to do so was a new experience for her.

'No,' she said faintly, feeling very shaken, but unable, in all honesty, to disagree with him. 'Of course not.'

Benoît stared at her for a long, unyielding moment. She looked away, unable to meet his flinty gaze.

'Do you suppose that Sir William really wanted me to tell him the truth, this morning?' Benoît said at last, some of the uncharacteristic roughness smoothed from of his deep voice.

'What else. . .?' Angelica looked at him in bewilderment, grateful that he was no longer so freezingly angry. 'He was furious with you.'

'He very often is,' Benoît said equably. 'But he'd never have spoken to me again if I'd told him what he wanted to know—he respects loyalty, if nothing else. And I don't imagine you would have had much time for me either if I'd turned informer.'

Angelica's eyes fell beneath his sardonic gaze. She knew there was an element of truth in what he'd just said.

'We live in a complicated world, my lady,' he said more gently. 'It is not always easy for even the wisest man to decide on the best course of action.'

'I know that!' Angelica's temper flared up again at the almost indulgent tone in his voice. She hadn't enjoyed being challenged by him, but she preferred it to being treated as a child. 'Don't patronise me, sir! I am not a fool! And my original point still remains. I do not know anything about you except that you were once rash enough to put yourself at my father's mercy. I would like to know exactly how you intend to rescue my brother.'

'Since I do not yet know myself, you are likely to have to wait some time for that information, Lady Angelica,' Benoît replied blandly. He seemed to have his own temper well in hand now.

'My God! You're insufferable!' Angelica exclaimed. 'I have never known a more conceited, arrogant, cocksure. . .' Words failed her as she tried to describe his infamy.

'Have you run out of insults already?' He grinned wolfishly. 'I'm sure there's a dictionary in the library at home. You will have to look up some more.'

For the last few minutes the horses had been ambling along a narrow, tree-lined lane, but Angelica had been too engrossed in their argument to pay much attention to her surroundings. Suddenly the lane petered out and the beach opened up before them, stretching out to east and west in a long, smooth expanse of shimmering sand.

Angelica was taken completely by surprise, and Benoît smiled faintly at her obvious amazement. She sat and gazed about her, utterly forgetful of his last provocative comment. Her riding skirts rippled in the sea breeze, and she could taste the salt in the air. It wasn't the first time she had seen the sea. She had visited Brighton several times with the Earl, but their family estates were in the midlands, and her first glimpse of the sea after such a long absence was an exciting experience for her.

She slipped her foot free of the stirrup and slid down to the ground, almost without realising what she was doing, and let Benoît take the reins from her without a murmur of protest. She picked up her skirts and crunched down over the large round pebbles onto the firm sand, her eyes fixed wonderingly on the horizon.

In some small, logical part of her brain she knew there were places on the south coast where France was closer than London—but staring out to the horizon it didn't seem so. It seemed as if the glittering expanse of water might go on for ever.

She could see the white wings of seagulls as they soared above the waves and then dipped down with raucous calls to the surface of the water. She could smell the dried seaweed on the stones, crisp with salt and sand, and hear the rolling murmur of the waves. The sea was going out, and wading birds crowded the tideline, hurrying back and forth in a never-ending quest for food. The glistening wet sand was ridged and furrowed with the regular pattern of the waves, and here and there a pool of seawater reflected the light of the sky above.

She walked down the beach, heedless of the wind tugging at her skirts and whipping her hair into her face. She'd almost forgotten Benoît, and he made no effort to remind her of his presence as he followed her, leading the two horses.

Then the wind snatched her borrowed hat, bowling it along the shining sands at a brisk pace.

'Oh!'

She clutched ineffectually after it, and then picked up her skirts, intending to run after it.

'Leave it!' Benoît caught her by her upper arm, swinging her around to face him, laughing at her consternation.

'But I can't lose your mother's hat!' she protested. 'She's been so kind to me.'

'I doubt if it will be wearable, covered in salt,' Benoît pointed out, grinning. 'It won't be difficult to replace.'

'I suppose not,' said Angelica doubtfully.

She was acutely conscious of his grip on her arm.

It was cold on the beach, but the warmth of his hand seemed to burn through the sleeve of her habit. He was standing very close to her, and the wind whipped her skirts against his legs, almost as if to bind them together. She knew she ought to withdraw herself gracefully from his grasp, but she looked up and met his eyes and couldn't quite bring herself to do so.

A few minutes ago she had been arguing with him more fiercely than she had ever quarrelled with anyone except her brother, but there was no anger in his expression now. There was an unfamiliar but exquisitely disturbing warmth in his brown eyes as they rested on her face. He dropped the reins and lifted his other hand to her waist.

'The horses will run away,' she said, hardly recognising her own voice. A pulse was beating rapidly in her throat. She could scarcely breathe with the pressure of unfamiliar anticipation.

'They'd go back to the stable if I told them to,' said Benoît, with soft confidence. 'But they won't run away.'

'Just the kind of trick a smuggler would teach his horse,' Angelica said breathlessly, still trying to maintain some resemblance of normality, as he drew her a little closer towards him.

'Blame Thomas, not me,' Benoît replied, smiling. 'He gets bored when I'm at sea. He even taught Billy to count.'

'*What*—?'

Angelica's surprised exclamation was cut short as Benoît drew her neatly into his arms. He held her breast to breast, his dark face dizzyingly close to hers for an electrifying moment.

'This time there's no doubt your eyes are open,' he said, half-humorously. 'Remember that, when you next accuse me of not being a gentleman.'

'I don't. . .'

Benoît's mouth covered her parted lips and stifled whatever it was she had been going to say. Shock held her rigid for several seconds. She had never been kissed like this before, and nothing in her previous experience had prepared her for dealing with such a situation.

The wind wrapped her skirts around them, locking them together. She could feel the heat of his body burning through her clothes. He was holding her firmly in his arms. She was acutely aware of the power in his lean, hard-muscled body, but his lips were gentle and persuasive on hers. Her heart was racing; strange, exotic warmth slowly filled her veins. Her empty hands opened once or twice in vague uncertainty then, almost of their own volition, they slid up over the ridged black cloth of his sleeves to rest on his shoulders.

She felt his tongue stroke her lower lip in sensuous exploration, and a fresh wave of burning sensation flooded her. She closed her eyes, feeling disorientated and exhilarated. She had nothing to compare this experience with, and no way of moderating her response to him.

His hold on her tightened. He slid one hand sensuously up her back to bury it in her windswept golden curls, dislodging a few hairpins as he did so. She trembled at his touch, clutching erratically his shoulders. Her legs felt weak and she leant against him, needing his support.

The muted roar of the sea and the harsh cry of the gulls receded to the edge of her awareness. Benoît filled the whole of her consciousness. Her lips were swollen and throbbing with the desire he had aroused in her—and then he slipped his tongue gently between them and she felt as if her heart stood still.

Nothing had prepared her for the intimacy of this moment. His tongue confidently explored her mouth, gently probing, overwhelming all her senses. Part of her wanted to pull away and protest at the liberty he was taking, but another part of her wanted to surrender completely to his love-making.

Her arms slipped around his neck and she clung to him, her lips parted to allow him the soul-shattering intimacy he sought, not actively returning his kiss, but not denying him either.

It was Benoît who at last drew back, and she could hear his ragged breathing as he continued to hold her against him, her face resting against his shoulder. Her heart was hammering in her ears, she was deaf and blind to the world around her. She was content to remain in his arms for a several long moments before reality finally reasserted itself.

Then she lifted her head in horror as she realised what had happened and tried to wrench herself out of his grasp. He held onto her firmly.

'We'll both fall over if you do that,' he murmured provocatively. 'Which might be quite pleasant, but I'm sure it's not what you have in mind.'

Angelica gasped in embarrassed, furious indignation and helped him unwind her traitorous skirts.

Then she stepped back quickly and lifted her burning eyes to his face.

He grinned at her, a rakish light in his eyes. He was slightly flushed beneath his tan, but he was once more his customary controlled self.

'Don't blame me, my lady,' he said before she could speak, an unexpectedly humorous lilt in his deep voice. 'I only meant to snatch a quick kiss. It was your own passionate nature that betrayed you.'

'How *dare* you?'

Sudden fury blazed through Angelica. Her over-excited emotions were in a complete turmoil, and she was too keyed up to think clearly. The only thing she knew for sure was that it was all Benoît's fault. Without stopping to think, she struck out wildly at him.

He caught her wrist before her hand connected with his cheek.

'Let me go!' she spat at him, pulling away from him and nearly stumbling over her skirts.

'No.'

She tried to wrench her arm out of his grasp with a vicious twist and his hold on her tightened until she winced.

'Stand still, Angelica,' he said sharply, almost as if he was talking to a naughty child.

She obeyed him, partly through surprise at his tone, and partly because she was startled by the use of her name.

'I haven't hurt you, and I'm not going to hurt you,' he said calmly, releasing her wrist. 'Believe it or not, both your morals and your person are quite safe in my hands—so don't attack me because your ideas about yourself have been thrown into confusion.'

She stepped back, rubbing her wrist absent-mindedly as she glared at him.

'Look!' He reached out and spun her round by her shoulders, moving so fast that she didn't have time to protest 'There's a whole world out there.' He faced her towards the horizon. 'Different people with different cultures and even different ideas of honour. Don't accept everything you've been told about life without question. Make up your own mind.'

He was standing behind her, his hands firm and insistent upon her shoulders, his words ringing in her ears.

She didn't pull away from him. She stared out to sea, feeling her hair whip about her face. The waves kept rolling up the beach, slightly further away now than they had been before. The sky seemed huge, it filled her vision; small white clouds had appeared in the distance.

'Papa always said—*says* you need good information to make a good decision,' she said at last.

'The Earl is a wise man.'

'So how am I supposed to make up my mind about you when I don't have any information?' she demanded, turning to face him.

He smiled almost gently, and reached out to tuck an errant curl behind her ear.

'You have a lot of information, my lady,' he corrected her gently. 'More than most, I might add. You just don't know how to fit it all together.'

'It *is* my brother's life we're talking about,' she said, almost pleadingly.

'Is it?' he asked, an enigmatic gleam in his brown eyes. 'Come along, my lady,' he added, before she could speak. 'The horses have been standing in the wind long enough, and there's something you might be interested to see further along the beach.'

She let him put her into the saddle without a word. She was deeply bewildered by what had happened, and more unsure of herself than she could ever remember being. He had challenged her preconceptions on several levels and she needed time to think.

She gathered up the reins and followed Benoît down towards the tideline. They turned east and Benoît urged Billy into a brisk walk across the wet sands. Disturbed sea birds flew up in raucous flurries, scattering and then returning to their foraging in the glittering water as soon as the horses had passed by.

'Where are you taking me?' Angelica asked, struggling to sound as if nothing exceptional had happened.

'Can't you guess?' Benoît shot her a glinting, almost mocking glance.

'No. How should I know?' she replied crossly. 'I hate guessing games.'

'Then you shouldn't have embarked upon one, my lady,' he replied, his voice carried to her on the wind blowing in across the sea. 'Shall we see how well you can put Dorcas through her paces?'

Angelica didn't hesitate. She leant forward, all her concentration instantly centred on showing Benoît just what she was capable of. The mare sprang forward eagerly and the bay matched her instantly.

The two horses raced along the bright sands while the seagulls wheeled in the sky above them, shrieking their disapproval of such unmannerly disturbance.

There was a wild joy for Angelica in the sudden burst of speed. After the complications of the past two days this moment of untrammelled freedom was pure pleasure. She knew that when they stopped she would once again have to face all the growing complexities of her situation—but not just yet.

The horses matched paces, and Angelica made no attempt to outdistance Benoît. There had been too many challenges between them already; she did not want even a hint of competition to tarnish this perfect interlude. It was comforting to allow herself the brief illusion that he was merely an undemanding companion, and not. . .what was he? A friend or an enemy—or a chance met stranger she would never see again after today?

At last the horses slowed, falling back into a canter, a trot and then a walk. Angelica had time to look around and, for the first time, to become aware that she must have left most of her hairpins scattered behind her along the beach. She lifted a hand to her tangled, salt-sticky hair in mild consternation.

Benoît observed her gesture and grinned.

'That's a sorry sight to present to your long-suffering maid,' he teased her. 'She'll probably take one look at you and hand in her notice.'

Angelica opened her mouth indignantly, but then her sense of humour overcame her and she smiled wryly.

'She'll certainly have something to say about it,'

she admitted ruefully. 'And she'll be horrified I lost your mother's hat. I just hope we don't meet anyone.'

'Sir William,' Benoît suggested wickedly. 'I believe he often rides on the beach.'

'Oh, my God!' Angelica let go of the reins with both hands and reached up to run her fingers through her unruly hair.

Blonde tresses which fell almost to her waist were blowing in unrestrained glory around her shoulders, shining like spun gold in the bright sunlight.

'What am I going to do?' she exclaimed in distress as the full enormity of her situation dawned on her. 'I'll never be able to find all my hairpins. I can't ride round the countryside looking like a hoyden!'

Dorcas had come to a natural stop, and Billy followed suit. Benoît dismounted and looked up at her, resting his left hand lightly on Dorcas's withers.

'Come down, my lady,' he commanded her softly, the light in his dark eyes daring her to refuse.

Her breath caught in her throat as she found herself snared in the compelling intensity of his gaze.

'I can't do much about your plight when you're perched several feet above me,' he pointed out reasonably, although there was a smile playing on his lips which made the blood tingle in Angelica's veins.

'I don't see what you can do anyway,' she objected, trying not to let him see how powerfully he was affecting her. 'Not unless you've any experience as a lady's maid.'

'None at all,' he said cheerfully, 'but I've plaited a few horsetails in my time.'

For some reason Angelica found his unflattering comparison reassuring, and she unhooked her leg from around the pommel and slipped down into his waiting arms. He set her neatly on her feet, but continued to rest his hands on her waist for a few seconds. She looked up at him with uncertain blue eyes, not quite sure what he intended, and he smiled crookedly.

'If you don't want a repeat of what happened the last time you looked up at me like that, I suggest you turn around,' he said softly.

Angelica gasped and turned so quickly she nearly tripped over her flowing skirts.

Benoît chuckled and drew her hair gently over her shoulders. She was standing on the lee side of Dorcas, and it was relatively easy to smooth the wild tresses into a manageable handful.

'You turned your back with unflattering haste, my lady,' he chided her, his hands light and unbelievably stimulating in her hair. 'My manly sensitivities are deeply wounded. I had no idea you found my attentions quite so objectionable.'

Angelica gripped the stirrup leather for support and closed her eyes. She felt trapped between the mare and Benoît. She wanted to step briskly away from Benoît's hands and declare that she could fix her hair for herself. But she remained standing where she was, caught under the spell of his seductive touch which sent delightful shivers running up and down her spine.

Despite the tangles in her sea-blown hair he managed to divide it into three relatively equal portions without causing her too much discomfort.

Then he plaited it neatly and Angelica was almost disappointed when she realised he had finished.

'Hold that.' He put the heavy braid over her shoulder and she obeyed without question. She heard a faint ripping sound and glanced round in surprise to see him tearing a strip from his handkerchief.

He grinned and she caught a glimpse of his strong white teeth.

'You may not appreciate my love-making, but you can't deny I'm resourceful,' he said outrageously.

She blushed and turned her head away as he took back the braid and tied it firmly at the end. Then he folded it under and tied it again at the top of the braid, creating a relatively neat club of hair at the nape of her neck.

'Not bad,' he said judiciously. 'Although I don't think you maid is going to be afraid of the competition.'

'I don't know how I'm going to explain it,' said Angelica as she turned to face him, desperately trying to strike a normal note. 'First your mother's hat, now this.'

'You can blame it on me, if you like,' Benoît offered generously. 'You can tell them I pulled out most of the pins when I kissed you.'

'*What*?' Angelica pressed her hands against her burning cheeks, a victim of so many conflicting emotions she didn't know which one to give voice to first.

'I could pretend that nothing untoward happened between us earlier,' Benoît said deliberately. 'No doubt that would be the gentlemanly thing to do.'

He met her disturbed gaze with a half-mocking, half-challenging light in his brown eyes. 'But the sooner you get used to the idea that I did kiss you—and that there's a very strong likelihood that I'm going to do so again before long—the better we shall proceed.'

'Oh!' Angelica whirled away from him. 'How can you be so *unfeeling*? I came to see you in good faith—to ask for your help. And you. . .you. . .'

'Took advantage of your innocence?' Benoît supplied helpfully when words failed her. 'Abused your trust? But you didn't come to Sussex entirely in good faith, did you? You're a strange mixture of trust and suspicion, my lady. On the one hand you question my motives and my integrity at every turn—and on the other you are content to wheedle an extra night under my roof and ride out with me alone as if you have no fears for your safety in my company. Should I be flattered or insulted?'

Angelica shot him a quick glance, feeling quite unable to answer his question. She drew in a deep breath, trying to regain her self-control.

'I believe you were going to show me something, sir,' she said, with as much dignity as she could muster. 'Or was I mistaken?'

'No, you weren't mistaken.' From the dark gleam in his eye she knew she wouldn't be permitted to continue with her evasion indefinitely, but at least she had won herself some respite.

'Take a look around and see if you can guess where we are,' he said.

She glanced at him frowningly and then stepped away from the horses, not really sure what she was

supposed to recognise. The beach hardly seemed any
different than it had done further west. The tide was
still going out behind her, the wet sand gleamed, and
whispering, thin-grassed sand dunes rose up before
her.

'I don't. . .it was *here*!' she exclaimed as light
suddenly dawned. '*This* is where Papa had you at his
mercy!'

'As you say,' said Benoît dryly, although there was
a hint of appreciative amusement in his eyes at her
phraseology. He wasn't naïve enough to suppose her
unflattering description of the incident had been
entirely accidental.

'Tell me what happened!' she demanded.

'Your father came along the tideline, just as we
have done,' said Benoît, apparently quite willing to
tell the tale. 'He knew the tide was coming in, and
he guessed we'd used it to cover our tracks and send
Sir William off on a wild-goose chase.'

'He was a match for your devious schemes,'
Angelica declared proudly, her blue eyes shining.

'Obviously,' said Benoît, grinning at her evident
satisfaction. 'When he got to about there—' he
indicated a point a few more yards down the beach
'—he found the tracks going inland, so he followed
them. I was waiting to intercept anyone who did so.'

'And he vanquished you!' said Angelica, with
relish.

'Although I don't remember him taking such an
unholy pleasure in his victory as you are doing,'
Benoît remarked dryly. 'But it's true he didn't have
a kiss to avenge.'

'You never give up, do you?' said Angelica wrathfully. 'Since I have not the slightest intention of allowing the incident to be repeated, it would be more courteous—and more tactful—if you would let the matter drop.'

'That sounds remarkably like a challenge, my lady,' he said good-humouredly.

There was a bright, unreadable light in his eyes, and she caught her breath as he took a step towards her. She was convinced he was going to kiss her. But he went past her and picked up the mare's reins.

'We should be moving on, my lady,' he said politely. 'The day is passing, and I wouldn't want you to exhaust yourself before your gruelling journey home tomorrow.'

'You are very thoughtful,' said Angelica through gritted teeth, wondering why she suddenly felt so deflated.

'Just trying to be a good host,' he replied self-deprecatingly. 'I've never had a member of the aristocracy grace my home with their presence before. I want to take good care of you.'

Angelica bit her lip, not sure whether to be amused or indignant. He met her gaze, a hint of warm understanding as well as the familiar, glinting humour in his brown eyes, and she felt reassured. He held out his hand and she went over to him immediately, letting him lift her once more into the saddle.

It was impossible to feel entirely relaxed in his company, he was too unpredictable. But he wasn't boring and she did, instinctively, trust him. He was unconventional and frequently disconcerting in his manner, but if he'd wanted to take advantage of her she'd given him the perfect opportunity—and he hadn't made use of it.

By imperceptible degrees, her opinion of him was rising. It might well be reasonable to entrust Harry's safety to him. She still refused to entertain the notion that she had any other reason for being interested in Benoît Faulkener.

CHAPTER FOUR

'LOOK.' Benoît interrupted her thoughts. 'It's the mouth of the Arun,' he explained, as Angelica glanced at him questioningly.

He had led her a few more yards along the beach while she'd been reflecting on his personality.

'Over there—' he pointed diagonally inland, across the river '—is Littlehampton. Arundel is three or four miles north—as the crow flies, not as the river bends. And there—' he gestured across to a construction on the east river bank '—is the battery which is supposed to defend us from Napoleon's invading hordes.'

'Won't it?' Angelica asked, catching the note of dismissal in his voice.

'It might,' said Benoît sceptically. 'It used to be armed with ten eighteen-pound guns, but they replaced them with several thirty-six pounders a few years ago. It's not in the best state of repair, but it does command both the entrance to the river and the eastern shoreline. Anyone stupid enough to sail within range is liable to get a good hammering— always supposing that it is sufficiently well manned and that the gunners are awake.'

'But if there was any danger of such an attack it would be adequately manned, wouldn't it?' Angelica persisted.

The invasion scares of earlier years had pretty

much passed her by. It was only standing here, on the exposed foreshore, that she suddenly realised how vulnerable England might be to a seaborne offensive.

'Possibly,' Benoît conceded, throwing a quick glance in her direction. 'But it's almost irrelevant. The best way of gaining control of the river would be to land a party of marines on *this* bank. They'd be protected from the guns by the dunes. They could work their way inland and eventually attack the battery from behind. Once it was taken, the French would have free passage up the Arun.'

'My God!' Angelica exclaimed in horror. 'You make it sound so easy!'

'Make no mistake, my lady,' said Benoît calmly, 'it would be easy. I would engage to do it with a handful of men.'

'Then why isn't something done?' Angelica demanded forcefully.

'Because they'd have to fortify this bank,' said Benoît reasonably. 'Which would take money and a determined effort by the Board of Ordnance. It's not that they don't know the dangers—they just don't have the resources to tackle them.'

Angelica looked around almost wildly, as if she half-expected to see hordes of armed Frenchmen emerging from the dunes.

'They won't come tonight,' said Benoît confidently, seeing the alarm in her expression.

'How can you be so sure?' she exclaimed nervously.

In London, safe within the security of the Earl's town house, the dangers of the war had seemed very remote. She had been afraid for Harry serving in one of the King's ships, but she had never experienced any personal sense of threat. Even Sir John Moore's devastating, three-hundred-mile retreat, which had ended in the Battle of Corunna less than two months ago, had had little impact upon her enclosed world.

Benoît grinned at her obvious alarm.

'Instinct,' he said unhelpfully. 'Don't worry, my lady,' he added more gently. 'I think there's very little danger of Napoleon landing an army on English soil.'

Angelica frowned, reassured by his words, but irritated that he hadn't bothered to explain further. It was annoying that he should assume a brief comment from him would be enough to calm her anxieties. She coiled a few strands of Dorcas's mane idly around her finger.

'It's hard to make up my own mind when I have so little information to work with,' she said slowly. 'Why not?'

'Because even Frenchmen can't walk on water.'

'What?' She looked at him suspiciously, afraid he was laughing at her, but there was no indication in his expression that he was mocking her.

'It's not easy to transport and disembark an army,' he enlarged upon his answer. 'It took a week or more for Wellesley to disembark of our troops in Mondego Bay last year—and they didn't have to contend with an attacking local militia while they were recovering from seasickness and reassembling their guns.'

'*Would* the local people fight?' Angelica said

doubtfully. 'Wouldn't they run away? Sir William says the county is riddled with lazy, disaffected. . .'

'Possibly,' said Benoît dryly. 'But the same men who take up cudgels to protect their livelihood from Sir William, might show equally little respect to anyone trying to invade their homes—don't you think?'

They had begun to ride slowly back along the beach, retracing their path, although the sea had further retreated and they no longer disturbed the wading birds at the water's edge.

'Think of the logistics of organising a full-scale invasion,' Benoît continued as Angelica frowned, trying to get to grips with what he was saying. 'Even supposing Napoleon has enough seaworthy vessels suitable for transporting a reasonably sized army—and I doubt very much if he does—he doesn't have enough skilled seamen to sail them. The French navy has never recovered from its losses at Trafalgar.

'It may be relatively easy for individual boats to slip back and forth across the Channel, but can you imagine the chaos of two or three hundred transports all sailing on the same tide—scattering, colliding and foundering in the unfamiliar waters along our coast? No, Napoleon may dream of marching on London, but I'm sure he's putting more faith in the destructive power of the Decrees he issued at Berlin and Milan.'

He paused then, shooting a quick glance at Angelica out of the corner of his eye before allowing his attention to rest on the shoreline ahead, as if there was nothing more to say.

Angelica waited for him to explain what the

Decrees were, realised he wasn't going to do so without prompting, and drew in a deep, rather exasperated breath. It was not so much that she wasn't interested in what he was saying, but she was slightly humiliated to discover how little she knew, and at how much of a disadvantage her ignorance placed her.

'Ah, yes,' she said brightly. 'I remember hearing something about Napoleon's Decrees, although I can't quite remember...'

'At Berlin he outlawed all trade between England and French-controlled lands, whether in English or neutral ships,' said Benoît, only a slight twitch of his lips indicating that he was aware of her feelings. 'That was in November of 1807, and it effectively cut us off from the European carrying trade. Then at Milan, about fourteen months ago, he issued a new set of Decrees which outlawed any neutral vessel which submitted to a British search or touched at a British port.'

'But surely, if our navy is so superior...!' Angelica protested, shocked. 'How can he hope to enforce—?'

'Ultimately, I don't believe he can,' Benoît replied grimly. 'But the Decrees have certainly had serious consequences for British shipping and manufacturies. The cotton weavers of Manchester rioted last year because the disruption of their industry had reduced them to starvation.'

Angelica stared blindly ahead, heedless of the increasing chill in the wind. Manchester was as remote from her experience as the Caribbean, but it was dawning on her that the war involved far more

than the well-publicised battles fought on land or
sea.

'We have retaliated, of course,' said Benoît,
relenting from the black picture he had been painting as he saw her disturbed response to it. 'After the
Berlin Decrees, England blockaded all European
ports from which she was excluded, and only allowed
neutral ships to use them if they also touched at a
British port and paid a reshipment duty on their
cargo.

'And don't forget that the French are suffering
from the effects of Napoleon's blockade as well. All
those goods they've come to rely on—sugar, coffee,
cotton, spices, dyes, tobacco—are now in short
supply. Unless they resort to accepting smuggled
goods,' he added blandly.

Angelica looked at him sharply.

'Is that how you justify smuggling?' she demanded,
momentarily wondering if that was what all this
information had been leading up to.

'I'm not a smuggler,' said Benoît flatly, his face
expressionless.

Angelica bit her lip. There had been no hostility
in his tone, but she felt as if a door had clanged
shut in her face. It was quite clear that, however
much general information he was prepared to vol-
unteer, he wasn't going to be provoked into
revealing more personal details by such a clumsy
sally.

'You certainly seem to know a great deal about
the subject,' she said, forcing herself to smile
unconcernedly.

'Any man who reads the newspapers and keeps

himself reasonably well informed would know as much,' he replied, and she saw the gleam of his white teeth as he grinned.

She was reminded, once again, of his elusive resemblance to a great black wolf. He revealed only what he wanted to reveal, and his response was always unpredictable.

'We will win, won't we?' she asked suddenly. It was the first time it had ever occurred to her to wonder.

'Oh, yes,' he said confidently.

'How can you be so sure?' she demanded.

'Because however many markets Napoleon closes to us in the Old World, we will always be able to open up more in the New World,' he replied, with absolute certainty. 'It has already begun with the islands we've taken from our enemies in the West Indies. We will survive for as long as we maintain control of the sea—and we will win as soon as we can put an army on continental soil that's capable of consistently defeating the French.'

'And when will that be?' Angelica asked curiously.

Benoît shrugged. 'I'm not a soldier,' he replied. 'I cannot give an informed opinion on that. All I can say is that, although we took a beating last year in Spain and Portugal, we also won a couple of victories that prove once and for all that Napoleon's army is not invincible. Further than that, we shall just have to wait and see.'

Angelica sighed. It wasn't an entirely satisfactory answer, but there didn't seem to be much she could say to it. She glanced around, noting, with mild surprise, that Benoît had turned inland before they'd reached the same track they had originally followed to the beach.

'It's quicker,' he said, answering her unspoken question. 'The day is losing its bloom and you must be getting cold, my lady. I wouldn't want to be accused of giving you a chill. Besides, we mustn't overtax your strength—you've got a long journey ahead of you tomorrow!'

Angelica swallowed a hasty retort, aware that she was being deliberately provoked and determined not to rise to it.

'What do you mean, Thomas has taught Billy to count?' she asked, remembering something he'd said earlier, although carefully blocking from her mind the context in which he'd said it. 'Surely the most accomplished horse would have difficulty. . .?'

Benoît laughed. 'When we get back, I will arrange a demonstration,' he promised her. 'I'm sure you'll be impressed, my lady.'

It took a long time for Martha to restore Angelica's hair to some kind of order, and she grumbled at her mistress throughout the ordeal.

'How could you be so heedless. . .so lacking in common decency. . .to go stravaging around the countryside without a hat on your head and your hair looking like a bird's nest?' she exclaimed, as she tried to untangle the knots. 'You're not a gypsy, my lady! What would the Earl say if he knew about this?'

'I don't know,' said Angelica, a hint of rebellion in her voice, 'but since he's never going to find out it doesn't matter, does it?'

'And how could it have happened?' Martha persisted, ignoring Angelica's words, although she had no intention of ever betraying her mistress's lack of conduct to anyone, least of all the Earl. 'Your hat blowing away I can understand—this wicked wind—but your hair! I always take care to fix it firmly. I know how you bounce about when you're excited. You've never managed to achieve the elegant carriage suitable for a lady in your position. Who did it up again?'

'Mr Faulkener,' said Angelica, boldly meeting her maid's eyes and desperately trying not to let a blush betray her.

'Did he, indeed?' said Martha dryly, her eyes resting thoughtfully on Angelica's glowing cheeks. 'I suppose letting your hair down was part of your ploy to discover more about him, was it? You ought to be ashamed of yourself, my lady!'

Angelica coloured uncomfortably; very little escaped Martha's sharp gaze and Angelica wondered just how much her maid had guessed about her ride with Benoît.

'So how have *your* investigations been going?' she asked brightly, trying to change the subject. 'Is this house a haven for smugglers, or is there an innocent explanation for what happened last night?'

Martha sniffed disapprovingly.

'To think that a respectable woman like me should have to stoop to such devious behaviour,' she said sourly. 'I'll have you know that I'm not accustomed to playing the part of a spy, my lady. It's not what I'm used to.'

'Oh, Martha!' Angelica exclaimed, caught between

laughter and exasperation. 'You're used to doing whatever it takes to keep Harry and me out of trouble. You know you are!'

Martha smiled austerely as she finally succeeded in dragging a comb through Angelica's tangled hair.

'There can't be much regular smuggling organised from this house,' she said, as disapprovingly as if she'd just announced it was a den of iniquity, 'not by the master, at all accounts. He doesn't spend enough time here.'

'What do you mean?' Angelica said quickly. 'I know he's recently returned from the West Indies, but—'

'This is the first time he's spent more than a few weeks at home since his father died, two years ago,' Martha continued, as if she hadn't heard Angelica's interruption. 'According to what I hear, he's worked his way up from ship's boy to junior partner in a shipowning business. Very proud of him below stairs, they are.'

Angelica stared at her maid, quite speechless for several moments. Martha smiled with grim satisfaction at her mistress's astonishment.

'It seems he went to sea when he was fourteen years old,' she said. 'By the time he was twenty-one he was master of a merchantman trading to the West Indies. He was employed by a man called Josiah Crabtree, who had a fleet of four ships. Very fond of Mr Faulkener the old man is, seemingly. Mind you, he has good reason to be—Mr Faulkener brought his ship safely through a hurricane after he'd only been in command a few months.'

'He did?' said Angelica breathlessly.

Her eyes were shining with excitement at Martha's tale. It was easy to imagine Benoît on the bridge of his ship, waves crashing all around, the wind shrieking and timbers creaking as he fought the elements themselves in his determination to bring his vessel safely home.

'So I'm told,' said Martha dryly, her eyes on Angelica's glowing face. 'When he thought he'd learnt as much as he could, he left Mr Crabtree and bought a ship of his own—started up an independent business. He's got three ships now—and last year Mr Crabtree suggested they go into partnership. From what I hear, Mr Crabtree's still got a soft spot for Mr Faulkener—like as not he'll make him his heir.'

'Good heavens!' said Angelica faintly.

In a matter of minutes, Benoît had been transformed in her eyes from little more than a pirate adventurer to a man of substance. It was true she had realised some time ago that he didn't earn his living from smuggling, but her notions of what he had become instead had been extremely hazy.

She had taken it for granted that he had captained his own ship, but she hadn't given much thought to the capacity in which he had done so. She had still tended towards the idea that he must be involved in some illegal or semi-legitimate business—perhaps as a privateer, licensed by letters of marque to prey upon enemy shipping. It was hard to believe he might really be as respectable as he had claimed to be yesterday evening.

'How did you find out all this?' she asked wonderingly, thinking about her own lack of success in discovering more about her host.

'His people are very proud of him,' said Martha repressively, as if she were revealing a discreditable secret. 'It wasn't hard to get them to boast about his achievements.'

'What about last night?' Angelica said. 'Did you find out any more about that?'

'No.' Martha frowned with dissatisfaction. 'Close as clams on that subject, they were,' she said irritably.

'Never mind,' said Angelica, suddenly feeling very cheerful. 'At least we're making progress.'

'And how do you work that out, my lady?' said Martha dourly. 'You came here in the hope he was a smuggler, and therefore in a good position to rescue Lord Lennard. We've just found out that he's spent the best part of the last fifteen years at sea. Hardly the best news from your point of view, is it?'

'I suppose not. On the other hand. . .' Angelica's words trailed off.

She was remembering that, although Benoît had refused to explain what had happened the previous night, he had as good as admitted that his visitor had been one of the men Sir William was searching for— men who had known and trusted Benoît all his life. He might not still be actively involved in smuggling, but he knew men who were.

'Thank you, Martha,' she said. 'I knew you wouldn't let me down.'

Not long later, Angelica ran lightly downstairs and burst into the library. Benoît had been sitting at his desk, writing, but he looked up at her arrival and grinned.

'So much energy, my lady,' he teased her. 'I was sure you would need to rest upon your bed for several hours before you would feel strong enough to rise for dinner.'

'Oh!' Angelica stopped short in confusion, suddenly remembering that she ought to make at least a pretence of being fatigued.

Benoît stood up and went behind her to close the door. She revolved on the spot so that she could keep him under observation. He made her nervous when she couldn't see him.

'Or perhaps you came to find a soothing text to lull you to sleep,' he suggested, a familiar half-mocking, half-humorous gleam in his eyes.

She met his gaze and her heart skipped a beat. Until a few minutes ago she had been so sure that he was completely ineligible that she had done everything she could to suppress the attraction she felt for him. But now it turned out that he was, after all, relatively respectable—although obviously not a suitable match for her father's daughter.

She tried to tell herself that it didn't matter to her what he was; she would be gone tomorrow. But it did matter—and she was beginning to realise and accept that fact.

'Why didn't you tell me you were a shipowner?' she demanded impetuously.

Benoît grinned and she remembered the wolf in him.

'Your maid obviously took the lesson about the persuasive powers of the sun and the wind more deeply to heart that you have done,' he observed dryly, although the mockery in his eyes was quite gentle.

'What do you mean?' Angelica exclaimed breathlessly, confused by his words and disconcerted by the expression in his eyes.

'Despite her forbidding appearance, I understand she can display a warm and charming nature when the occasion warrants it,' Benoît explained helpfully. 'She certainly seems to have made a favourable impression on Thomas. Apparently she even got him to show her some of the tricks he's taught the horses. He's very taken with her.'

'Good heavens!' Angelica's attention was briefly seized by the incredible and fascinating picture of Martha sweet-talking the groom.

'Alas, my lady,' said Benoît, with laughing, teasing regret in his eyes. 'If you'd only pursued the same technique with me, think how much you might know about me by now.'

'What?' Angelica stared up at him with enormous, startled eyes, her lips parted in genuine surprise.

She saw the expression in his dark eyes change, and threw up her hand instinctively to ward him off, taking a hasty step backwards as she did so.

'No!' she exclaimed.

He grinned.

'You disappoint me, my lady,' he taunted her gently. 'With so much at stake, are you really not prepared to make a small sacrifice for your brother?'

Angelica swallowed. It was dangerous to keep looking into his eyes. What she saw there made her feel light-headed with excitement, and barely able to control her emotions. This wasn't how Martha had done it, surely?

'You mean if I. . .if I let you. . .' Her voice failed her and she tried again. 'If I. . .you'll tell me how you're going to rescue Harry.'

He smiled and her heart turned over.

'You could always try the experiment,' he suggested softly.

'That's. . .that's *blackmail*!' she protested breathlessly.

Benoît's smile broadened.

'But at least you'll have the consolation of knowing you did it for Harry's sake,' he consoled her, the enticingly wicked gleam in his eyes almost irresistible.

'Oh, dear!' said Angelica faintly, as he took her in his arms. 'Perhaps you ought to tell me first, sir.' She made one last attempt to remain in control. 'Then I could decide whether. . .'

Benoît laughed softly.

'You should have thought of that before, my lady,' he advised her.

It was too late to protest, and perhaps she didn't really want to. She lifted her face quite willingly to his, closing her eyes instinctively as his lips found hers. She'd believed that she was at least partially prepared for the experience, but she discovered almost instantly that she'd overestimated her new-found sophistication.

Last time he had kissed her they had been standing on a windswept beach and she had been dressed for the weather in a heavy cloth riding habit. This time she was wearing only a light muslin gown. She could feel every button on his waistcoat, every ridge of his clothes—and all the muscular strength in his body—in devastating intimacy.

She gasped, startled and a little disturbed, and pushed ineffectually against his shoulders. His hold on her relaxed slightly. He scattered gentle, feather-light kisses on her lips, her cheeks, and even her eyelids, until the tension ebbed from her body. Slowly, she began to feel more secure. Warm, billowing clouds of golden sunlight seemed to cocoon her in pleasure.

She slipped her arms around his neck, running her fingers through his crisp black hair in an unconsciously sensuous gesture. His lips became more insistent upon hers, tempting her with the promise of even greater delight to come if she allowed him the intimacy he demanded. She resisted briefly, half-afraid of what might happen if she capitulated. Then her lips parted beneath his and she surrendered completely to his kiss.

Instantly the spark of desire between them erupted into flames of scorching passion. The potent, surging energy within Benoît's whipcord body was matched by an ardent, unfettered response from Angelica which was quite beyond her power to control. Her zest for life found a natural outlet in the arms of a man who commanded both her respect and admiration.

She responded to him with an innocent, unselfconscious eagerness which startled, then enthralled him.

His hand slipped down her back, following the graceful curve of her spine, electrifying her senses with his seductive touch. She clung to him as he explored the voluptuous swell of her hip, before pressing her body closely against him.

She was standing thigh to thigh with him. She could feel his taut, powerful muscles against her softer flesh; and the hard, urgent desire in his body burned through her thin muslin dress. She was dimly aware that she was playing with very dangerous fire indeed, but she didn't have the strength to resist him.

He had burst into her confined, claustrophobic life like a whirlwind. Now she was riding on the back of the storm, exhilarated by the life-affirming passion they had unleashed between them.

He slid his hands up behind her shoulders and bent to kiss her throat, teasing her soft skin to even greater heights of sensitivity. She let her head fall back, leaning against his supportive hands as his lips left a fiery trail across her collar bone.

She was breathing in short, quick gasps, but her heart was drumming so loudly in her ears she couldn't hear the sound of her own excitement. She was consumed by conflicting sensations. Her legs felt too weak to support her, yet pulsating life scintillated through her body. She was full of glowing, warm languor—yet she was on fire with impatient anticipation.

Then Benoît straightened up, still holding her against, him, but in an enforcedly neutral embrace.

'My God!' he said hoarsely, his eyes dark with barely controlled passion. *'Ma douce séductrice!*

You've come very close to completely unmanning me!'

Angelica felt the sudden rigid tension in his muscles and her eyes flew open in confused alarm. She fluttered in his arms, seeking reassurance more than escape. He was still fighting to contain his own fierce emotions, but he lifted his hand instantly to stroke her hair in a soothing gesture.

'Hush.' He held her against him. He was breathing very quickly. She was aware of his uncharacteristic lack of composure, but he still managed to sound wryly amused when he spoke. 'I promised I wouldn't hurt you, and I meant it. I just hadn't allowed for the effect of that passionate nature of yours.'

'Oh!' Angelica pushed herself away from him, taking refuge in indignation because she was too bewildered to know how else to react.

Her lips were bruised and swollen. Her skin still tingled from his kisses, and her body throbbed with the sensations his embrace had aroused within her.

She took a couple of irresolute steps, stumbling slightly because her legs no longer seemed to obey her wishes. She thought she would feel more in control if she put some distance between them, but away from the support of his arms she felt bereft and cold. She looked up at him, painful confusion in her lucid blue eyes.

He smiled crookedly, and reached out to stroke her cheek. She closed her eyes briefly at the sensations his gentle touch aroused within her.

'I think, perhaps, we have played this dangerous game long enough,' he said quietly. 'You will return to London tomorrow, my lady, and I've no wish for you to go back to your father hurt or distressed by what has happened to you here. It would be a poor reward for all I owe him, wouldn't it?'

Angelica stared at him, her blue eyes troubled and uncertain.

'I don't know what you mean,' she whispered.

'No?' He looked at her thoughtfully, an enigmatic gleam in his eyes. Apart from the unusual depth of colour in his tanned cheeks he seemed to be almost his normal, coolly controlled self—but Angelica could sense the ruthlessly suppressed energy in his lean body. 'Why aren't you married?' he asked suddenly.

'*What?*'

'You're twenty-three years old. Beautiful, desirable, a lady from the top of your golden curls to the soles of your elegant feet and—I suspect—something of an heiress to boot. So. . .why aren't you married, or at least betrothed?'

Angelica pressed her hands against her burning cheeks, suspecting at first he was mocking her, and then seeing from the steady expression in his eyes that he wasn't.

'I. . .Papa needs me,' she said with difficulty.

'He needs you now—he didn't need you two years ago,' Benoît reminded her. 'How long have you been out?'

'Since I was seventeen,' she replied, in a constricted voice.

'Five whole years for someone to catch your heart—or at least your interest,' he mused lightly, but there was an intent expression in his brown eyes. 'Didn't anyone light a spark within you?'

Angelica stared at him for a moment. Finally, after a desperate struggle, she succeeded in regaining some of her composure.

'I don't think that's any of your business,' she said steadily, managing to inject a cool note into her voice.

'Well, I'm not sure,' said Benoît slowly. He smiled suddenly. 'Even with my coaching, you're not very efficient at extracting information, are you?' he said provocatively. 'You should have demanded your fee long ago. I think I may invoke a time forfeit.'

Angelica blinked, momentarily confused.

'You were going to tell me how you're going to rescue Harry!' she exclaimed, remembering.

'Well, no,' he corrected her, a glint in his eye. 'I suggested you might find the experiment of kissing me worthwhile—but I didn't guarantee that I'd tell you about Harry.'

Angelica opened her mouth, drawing in a deep, indignant breath as she realised she'd been tricked.

'You devious, unscrupulous, ungentlemanly. . .' She glared at him with hot burning eyes, because she suddenly realised that what she felt was not indignant but hurt and betrayed. How could he have made such heartless use of her innocence?

Tears filled her eyes before she could stop them, glittering on her long eyelashes, and she turned away, humiliated that he should see her cry.

He was beside her in two long strides, gently turning her into the comforting circle of his arms.

'Don't!' She tried to push him away.

'Shush.' He stroked her hair gently, making no demands upon her with his embrace. 'I didn't trick you that badly, *ma chérie*. And if you'd remembered to ask me, I wouldn't have teased you about it.'

Angelica knew she ought not to allow him to comfort her, but it was beyond her strength to push him away. His hands were soothing and his arms very protective. She had a brief, enticing vision of what it would be like if there was always someone there to turn to when she was hurt or afraid. It was a long time since she'd been able to turn to the Earl for support.

'That wasn't very gentlemanly of you,' she said at last, a catch in her voice, as she lifted her head to look at him.

'But I'm not a gentleman, *mignonne*,' he reminded her softly. 'We established that very early in our acquaintance.'

He paused; he was looking at Angelica, but there was a distant expression in his frowning eyes, and she could sense that he wasn't seeing her.

'My grandfather was a brickmaker who could neither read nor write,' he said abruptly, 'but he was determined his sons would do better in life than he had done, and he made enormous sacrifices to ensure that they did.'

He let Angelica go and went over to the globe, spinning it idly with his tanned, supple fingers.

'I don't think the old man ever travelled more than ten miles from his home in his life,' he said over his shoulder. 'He died soon after I went to sea.'

'He must have been very proud of you,' said Angelica almost hesitantly, recognising that she was being offered a rare insight into the making of Benoît Faulkener.

'He was proud of my father,' said Benoît. 'Yes, he was proud of me,' he added, as he saw her expression. 'But he didn't like it when we visited him, and he never consented to visit my parents in Arundel—less than twenty miles from his home. He said it wouldn't do to remind my father's patients that he was the son of a common brickmaker.'

Angelica bit her lip. She'd lived all her life in a privileged and sheltered world, taking for granted the advantages that had been bestowed on her. Now she was being confronted with an entirely different world, one which she'd only been dimly aware of until this moment. She realised that it must be hard for Benoît to speak so openly.

Benoît glanced at her, a sudden tension in his long limbs at her prolonged silence. What he saw in her face seemed to reassure him, and he added more lightly, 'Actually, I think the member of my family you'd find most interesting is Toby.'

'Toby?' The name sounded vaguely familiar but Angelica couldn't place it.

'My father's older brother,' Benoît explained. 'If it was Grandfather who had a dream of what his sons and grandson could achieve, it was Toby who ultimately made it possible. He learnt to read and write, and then got himself apprenticed to a blacksmith in Chichester. But he knew what was really needed to make the old man's dream come true was money. So he set about making some. It was Toby who paid for my father's training, his books and his instruments—and his first suit of clothes to impress his future patients. And it was Toby's inheritance which allowed me to buy my first ship. But he was still only a blacksmith in Chichester when he died.'

Angelica stared at him, her lips silently forming the word 'how', but she already knew and, even if she hadn't guessed, Benoît's wolfish smile would have informed her.

'He smuggled tea,' said Benoît, 'among other things. It was very profitable until they reduced the duty in the 1780s. We were running brandy the night I met your father. So you were right, my lady,' he concluded, a challenging glint in his eyes, 'this house is ultimately built on the profits of smuggling—or free trading, as Toby preferred to call it.'

Angelica gazed at him. She knew he wasn't ashamed of his antecedents; that, on the contrary, he was extremely proud af his determined and enterprising relatives. All the same, it couldn't have been easy to tell the tale and risk her possible ridicule. She was deeply impressed by both his moral courage in doing so, and his faith in her ability to understand.

'Why did you tell me this?' she said slowly.

He glanced at her, an intent, almost questioning look in his eyes, then shrugged dismissively.

'I cannot tell you how I will get Harry out of France, much less how I shall extricate him from Bitche,' he replied. 'Even if I knew, which at this point I don't, it wouldn't be wise. But I'd rather you didn't spend the next few weeks imagining me everything from a French spy to an extortionist. You may take this information as a—what did you call it this morning?—ah, yes, an earnest of my good faith.'

Angelica lowered her eyes, considerably shaken that he had remembered and finally responded to her angry demands. Then something occurred to her and she looked up, a spark kindling in her blue eyes.

'I don't believe I accused you of being a spy?' she protested indignantly.

'Bearing in mind what Sir William said to me this morning, and the vivid powers of your imagination — I'd be very surprised if that hadn't been among your suspicions,' Benoît retorted.

She saw the white gleam of his teeth as he grinned at her startled reaction, and surprisingly she felt reassured by his gentle mockery. It was hard to know exactly how she felt about Benoît Faulkener, but it was inexplicably comforting to know that, however quickly some aspects of their relationship changed, others remained the same.

'It was a perfectly reasonable concern on my part,' she said with dignity. 'And if you hadn't provoked Sir William into losing his temper, it would never have occurred to me!'

'Poor Sir William,' said Benoît appreciatively. 'It doesn't take much to enrage him. Do you know, he spent more than twenty years trying to get the better of Toby, but he never let his horses be shod by anyone else? He was very upset when Toby died.'

'You mean he liked him?' said Angelica wonderingly.

'They were, in a strange way, friends,' Benoît replied. 'Toby was a hard man, but he imposed a ruthless discipline on those who worked for him. For the twenty-five years or more he controlled the smuggling on this part of the coast there were none of the atrocities which have occurred in other parts of the county. The situation is far more unstable and unpredictable now that he's gone. There are several gangs vying with each other—' Benoît broke off, shrugging. 'Not that any of this is of interest to you,' he said briskly.

'It might be,' Angelica replied tentatively.

Benoît glanced at her sharply, then smiled faintly.

'No, it isn't,' he said firmly. 'Because none of this makes the slightest difference to Harry's rescue.'

'But if you no longer. . .' Angelica began.

Benoît laughed.

'My lady, you are so used to looking at the problem from Harry's point of view that you don't have a clear view of the picture,' he declared. 'It's true that Harry's main stumbling block was the Channel, but that's the least of *my* worries. I'm much more concerned about how I'm going to establish communications with him in the first place, and get him out of Bitche in the second.'

Angelica bit her lip. 'He's already done it once,' she said.

'Which will make it that much harder next time,' Benoît pointed out. 'Don't worry, my lady,' he added reassuringly, seeing her anxious expression. 'We will find a way.'

CHAPTER FIVE

ANGELICA was very quiet as she let Martha dress her for dinner. She'd had little time for reflection since her arrival at Holly House, yet so much had happened to her in the last twenty-four hours. Some of her most deeply held assumptions had been challenged. Even the familiar Martha had been revealed in a new and startling light. Did she feel frustrated by the limitations of her life as a lady's maid? Benoît had given Angelica so much to think about.

She touched her slender fingers briefly to her lips as she thought of how he'd kissed her. Her body stirred with the memory of his embrace, and the excitement he had aroused in her. He'd asked her if anyone had ever previously kindled a spark in her and she'd refused to answer—but she knew that, until today, they hadn't.

Five years ago she had gone out into society hoping to find someone to stir her heart, but every man she had ever met had been a pale, sickly shadow compared to the Earl. At first she had been disappointed, then resigned to the situation; and when the Earl had been hurt it had ceased to matter. He needed her, and depended on her, and she had done her best to be what he wanted her to be—if only she knew what that was.

But Benoît had changed everything. She wondered how easy it would be to go back to reading dusty books to her father, sharing the bitter limitations of the Earl's life since his accident, yet knowing there was so much more on the other side of the wall.

After tonight she might never see Benoît again!

This evening she would dine with him, tomorrow morning she would say a polite farewell to him, and that would be the end of her brief adventure.

She stared blindly at herself in the mirror, startled and rather dismayed by the powerful sense of loss which swept over her. She barely saw the huge, distressed blue eyes which gazed back at her out of a pale, troubled face. It was Benoît's eyes she saw, and Benoît's voice she could hear—teasing her, exasperating her, soothing her—and talking to her about things that mattered to him, confident that she was capable of understanding and responding to what he said.

Did he feel as sorry as she did that this brief interlude was nearly over? It hardly seemed likely. He had seen so much more of the world than she had—he must have known many women who interested or excited him. She felt an unexpected stab of an emotion which could almost have been jealousy and her hands clenched in her lap.

'Stand up, my lady, it's time you were dressed,' Martha interrupted her thoughts.

Angelica obeyed automatically, hardly aware of what she was doing, and allowed Martha to button her into a shimmering gown of pale ivory satin.

The long, softly gleaming skirt fell in a smooth, elegant line from just beneath her bosom to her feet, skimming discreetly past the curves of her waist and hips without entirely concealing them. The dress had a deep, square neckline which revealed the soft, creamy skin of her shoulders and throat, and a long train which whispered richly across the carpet whenever she moved.

Angelica frowned as she slowly became aware of what Martha was doing. For the first time she noticed that her maid had caught up her shining curls in a glittering diamond and sapphire comb, and that there were matching jewels in her ears.

'No!' she protested quickly, throwing up a hand and stepping back as she saw the pendant Martha was holding out. 'I can't go downstairs like this! It's a quiet dinner in the country—not a ball at Carlton House!'

'That's as may be,' said Martha quietly. 'But I think it's time he was reminded exactly who he's dealing with—and perhaps you need reminding too, my lady.'

Angelica stared at her maid for several long seconds, her skirts still caught up in one hand from when she'd stepped backwards so quickly, her other hand held almost protectively at her throat. She seemed vibrant with suppressed energy. The only colour about her came from the golden glow of her hair, the soft pink of her lips and cheeks, and the vivid blue of her eyes which was matched, but not overshadowed, by the sapphires in her hair and ears.

She didn't bother to ask who Martha meant by 'he' because she already knew. She stared at her maid, wondering how much Martha had guessed, and trying to read her thoughts in her expressionless face—but it was impossible.

'It that all you're going to say?' she asked at last.

'Yes, my lady.'

'I see.'

Angelica had been startled out of her preoccupation with Benoît more effectively by Martha's brief, elliptical comment than she would ever have been by the maid's more familiar grumbling. She glanced at the sapphire in Martha's hand and remembered her momentary jealousy at the thought of Benoît's other women.

Perhaps Martha was right. Perhaps it was time to remind Benoît he wasn't dealing with an unsophisticated country wench, but with the daughter of a noble and long-established family. She made no further objection as Martha fastened the pendant around her neck.

'I never told you to bring any of my jewels,' she observed, as the cool silver of the necklace caressed her warm skin, 'much less this dress. Why did you do it?'

'You never know when you might need to show your quality,' said Martha grimly, stepping back to look at her handiwork. 'Clothes are a useful reminder. And you can be sure I took care to hide your jewels from prying eyes.'

'You don't think there's much danger of me being robbed in this house then,' said Angelica, a half-smile on her lips.

But Martha might not have heard for all the notice she took of Angelica's remark. She studied her mistress intently, then nodded slightly, with evident reluctance.

'You'll do,' she said sourly.

Angelica hesitated as she approached the drawing-room door. Despite her earlier resolution she felt nervous and overdressed. She wondered if she'd made a crass and insulting mistake. There was nothing pretentious about the Faulkeners. In defer-ence to their guest, Mrs Faulkener had had the fire lit in a larger room than the one she had occupied the previous evening, but it was still furnished very simply, with more regard for comfort than elegance.

Angelica was suddenly afraid that Mrs Faulkener would think she was showing off; and that Benoît would believe she was deliberately parading her consequence before him in direct response to what he had told her about his humble origins. That hadn't been her intention at all. She almost turned and fled back to her room, but it was too late. She turned the door handle and went into the room with as much nonchalance as she could muster.

She noticed, almost with relief, that Mrs Faulkener was not yet present—then she gave all her attention to Benoît. He had risen politely at her entrance, but she saw a flicker of startled, warm appreciation in his eyes as they rested on her face. Her heart skipped a beat because surely that first, unguarded reaction to her appearance had been very revealing.

He recovered his composure quickly, looking her up and down with a coolly amused expression on his face. At last his gaze came to rest on the jewel around her neck, and his eyes narrowed almost imperceptibly.

'You are looking very magnificent tonight, my lady,' he said politely.

'It was Martha!' Angelica said breathlessly, hearing the cool note in his voice, and afraid that her fears had been well-founded. She lifted her hand instinctively to touch, and perhaps hide, the sapphire and diamonds at her throat.

'She insisted...' Her voice trailed off as she realised how impossible it was to explain what Martha had said. She looked at Benoît with luminous blue eyes which contained an unconscious appeal for understanding.

Benoît smiled, the warmth springing back into his brown eyes as he strolled towards her, moving with the controlled grace and latent power of the wolf he so frequently reminded her of.

'Martha is a formidable woman,' he said dryly. 'I must make sure I make her acquaintance before you leave, my lady. In the meantime, you may tell her that I have understood her message.'

'I don't understand,' Angelica said, in some confusion, although she was almost certain that she did.

How could she ever have been foolish enough to suppose Benoît would be too unsophisticated to comprehend the significance of her finery? She wondered briefly whether she truly understood it herself. Was she trying to disconcert him with her magnificence—or captivate him with her glamour?

Either way, she seemed to have met her match.

For the first time since she had known Benoît, he was not dressed entirely in black. He wore a dark blue, double-breasted tail coat which fitted his broad shoulders admirably. A snowy white cravat fell in soft folds beneath his chin, emphasising his dark tan, His breeches were buckled just below his knees, and close-fitting white stockings revealed his well-muscled calves.

It was Angelica's turn to be surprised. She had protested to Martha that she wasn't attending a ball in Carlton House, but Benoît would certainly not have been out of place in such a setting. He bent low to kiss her hand with elegant assurance, and she could feel the warm pressure of his fingers through her long gloves. She looked down at his crisp black hair, feeling strangely close to him, yet at the same time very unsure of herself.

'Come and sit down,' he said. 'My mother will be with us shortly, but she was delayed by a minor domestic crisis. The cook's late brother—he was killed last year in Portugal—turns out to have been a bigamist.'

'What?' The force of Angelica's disbelieving exclamation owed much more to her chaotic feelings than to what Benoît had just said, but at least he had provided her with an excuse for her obvious confusion.

'Oh, it's quite true,' he assured her, grinning, as he took the chair opposite hers. 'According to my mother, the first bereaved widow arrived on the doorstep a couple of months ago, and the second one came this afternoon. Apparently she gave quite a dramatic performance—I'm almost sorry I missed it.'

'You're not serious?' Angelica didn't know

whether to be appalled or entertained at what he'd said.

'That she came—or that I'm sorry I missed the show?' Benoît enquired, a wicked gleam in his brown eyes. 'You're right, I doubt very much whether I would have found it as rewarding as a day spent in your company.'

Angelica blushed and turned her face away, uncertain how to respond to him. His directness always disconcerted her, and it was almost a relief when Mrs Faulkener came quietly into the room.

Dinner was an exquisite torment for Angelica. It was the first time she had ever spoken to Benoît in company, and she was acutely conscious of Mrs Faulkener's observant eyes as she tried to maintain a flow of light-hearted conversation.

But the Faulkeners were very easy and entertaining companions. Mother and son shared a similar sense of humour, and they had a relaxed respect for each other which impressed Angelica. She wondered if Benoît would show equal respect to his wife. Then she blushed and suppressed the fugitive thought as quickly and guiltily as if Benoît could read her mind. It was hardly any concern of hers how he treated his wife.

At last the two women left Benoît to enjoy his port alone and retired to the drawing room.

'You have been so kind to me,' said Angelica warmly. 'I cannot tell you how much I appreciate your hospitality. I feel so guilty for imposing on you a second night.'

Mrs Faulkener smiled as she sat down opposite Angelica.

'On the contrary,' she replied cordially, 'I am grateful for your company, my lady. We don't often have visitors. I'm only sorry that you must leave so soon.'

'Thank you,' said Angelica, uncomfortably aware that she had been so preoccupied with Benoît that she had spared very little thought for her hostess.

It would hardly be surprising if Mrs Faulkener did feel lonely, living in such an isolated spot and with Benoît away so often. Angelica resolved to be a more entertaining guest for the limited time she had left. She felt vaguely that it was important Mrs Faulkener should like her, although she didn't analyse why.

'Perhaps, in the summer, you could persuade your father to visit Sir William,' Mrs Faulkener suggested. 'It's a long time since the Earl came to Sussex, and I'm sure Sir William would appreciate it.'

'I will certainly try,' Angelica agreed, snatching at the idea eagerly. 'It would be such a relief! He hasn't left the house for months. . .' Her voice trailed away as she realised how close she was to openly criticising her father.

'It must be very painful for him,' said Mrs Faulkener quietly. 'And for you. It is hard to live in the shadow of someone else's unhappiness—particularly when you love them.'

Angelica looked down at her hands gripped together in her lap, seeing them through suddenly misty eyes. She was afraid if she spoke her voice would reveal how close she was to tears, so she didn't say anything, and in a moment Mrs Faulkener began to tell the story of the cook's bigamous brother.

When Benoît joined them, a few minutes later, Angelica had her feelings well under control. Even so, the sight of him after his brief absence caused her heart to leap into her throat and left her temporarily bereft of words. She couldn't believe she was acting so foolishly; anyone would think she was still in the schoolroom! Yet she had been mistress of her father's household for several years.

Her thoughts were interrupted by the maid who came into the room, looking a little flustered, and delivered a letter to Benoît.

'Thank you, Tilly.' He took it and broke open the seal, reading it quickly. A frown creased his forehead as he nodded his dismissal to the maid.

'There'll be no reply,' he said curtly, standing up.

'What is it, Benoît?' Mrs Faulkener asked calmly.

He glanced at his mother and smiled, his expression clearing as he did so.

'Nothing serious,' he said lightly. 'It's from Sir William. He thinks he's caught a smuggler, but the man is claiming his innocence and says I can provide him with an alibi. It could wait till morning, but you know how excitable Sir William gets. It's probably best if I don't keep him waiting.'

Mrs Faulkener nodded, although there was a flash of annoyance in her eyes.

'Sir William is a good man,' she said with some asperity, 'but I wish he wasn't so prone to turn other people's lives upside down in his quest for the truth!'

Benoît laughed and turned to Angelica with a hint of apology in his eyes.

'I'm sorry, my lady,' he said sincerely. 'I hate to abandon you like this, but I will see you before you leave in the morning; and I will certainly keep my promise to the Earl.'

Angelica stood up instinctively, her hands gripped together anxiously.

'Do you know the man? Can you provide him with an alibi?' she asked, more bluntly than she'd intended.

She was remembering Benoît's absence the previous night, and wondering whether Sir William's letter had made more dangerous accusations than Benoît had chosen to reveal. She was suddenly frightened for him, although that was ridiculous. It was impossible to imagine that Benoît wasn't equal to any threat Sir William might pose to his security.

Benoît smiled as he took her hand, squeezing it reassuringly as he bowed with his customary grace.

'I certainly know the man,' he said easily. 'And it doesn't sound as if Sir William has much in the way of evidence. I think he's just so exasperated that he's trying to frighten the poor fellow. It shouldn't be difficult to sort out. Good evening, my lady.'

Angelica watched him leave the room with an anxious expression in her eyes. For a moment she had completely forgotten Mrs Faulkener's presence.

'Don't worry, my lady,' said the Frenchwoman cheerfully. 'Whatever may have happened, Sir William is no match for my son. I'm sure everything will be all right—but I'm sorry he has broken up our evening!'

'It is a pity.' Angelica sat down again, reassured by Mrs Faulkener's unquestioning confidence in Benoît.

But now that he had gone she felt deflated and at a loss. The evening which had offered so much promise seemed to stretch emptily before her, and the weariness which she had falsely claimed that morning finally caught up with her.

It was months since she had been riding and her muscles were stiff and sore from the unaccustomed exercise. Until that moment she hadn't even been aware of her tiredness, but now all she wanted to do was lie down on her bed and sleep.

'My lady?' said Mrs Faulkener enquiringly.

'I'm sorry.' Angelica roused herself to smile at her hostess. 'I haven't been riding for so long—I suddenly feel very tired. Perhaps I ought to have another cup of tea.'

'Perhaps you ought to go to bed,' Mrs Faulkener suggested gently. 'I hate to remind you, but tomorrow you'll have to spend several hours in the coach.'

A flicker of reluctance crossed Angelica's face, partly because the idea of being jolted around in the carriage was unpleasant, but mainly because she didn't like the idea of leaving.

Although it hadn't occurred to her, her response to Mrs Faulkener's remark was giving credence to the hasty excuse she had made to Benoît that morning for staying another day at Holly House.

Her father's accident had never made her fearful of travelling, but Mrs Faulkener didn't know that. The Frenchwoman had a very clear memory of how strained and anxious Angelica had been when she first arrived. She found it easy to believe that Angelica was reluctant to travel more than fifty miles over bad, winter roads on her own.

'My lady, when Benoît returns, I will ask him if he'll take you back to London himself,' said Mrs Faulkener suddenly.

'What?' Angelica exclaimed, looking up in astonishment.

'He will be able to speak to the Earl in person, and you need have no fear that an accident might occur while he is with you,' Mrs Faulkener continued, warming to her theme.

'Oh, but. . .' Angelica began to demure, then hesitated.

There was no reason why Benoît shouldn't come to London to speak to her father. She wondered why the idea hadn't occurred to her before—and why Benoît hadn't suggested it himself. Surely it would be the natural thing for him to do?

'Good!' said Mrs Faulkener briskly, taking Angelica's consent for granted. 'I'm sure you will sleep much better tonight, my lady, now that's decided—and so shall I. I didn't like the idea of you travelling so far alone—even though I know you've got your maid and your coachman with you. But Benoît will take good care of you.'

She stood up, and Angelica followed suit.

'Good night, my lady,' said Mrs Faulkener. 'Now I really must go and talk to the cook. She was terribly upset this afternoon. She burnt the soup twice!'

* * *

Angelica began to walk slowly upstairs. Some of her tiredness had vanished, although she was trying not to admit to herself how much she owed her improved spirits to Mrs Faulkener's suggestion. If Benoît came to London. . .

She heard a quick, light tread on the stairs above her and looked up to see him coming down towards her, two steps at a time. Her heart gave a great bound in her breast and she caught her breath.

'I thought you'd gone,' she said foolishly, hoping against hope that he didn't know how powerfully his unexpected appearance had affected her.

He grinned.

'I'm on my way,' he said. 'But I think even Sir William at his most impatient would understand my reluctance to ride around the countryside in full evening dress!'

'Yes, of course!' Angelica exclaimed, wondering why she hadn't thought of that for herself.

Benoît was once again dressed in the familiar black riding coat and breeches which he had worn at their first meeting.

She hesitated, looking up at him as she wondered whether to mention his mother's idea to him.

'What is it, my lady?' he asked.

'Nothing.' The suggestion would sound better coming from Mrs Faulkener. 'I hope you're able to placate Sir William,' she said.

'Have no fear of that.' He touched her cheek lightly, and then, almost as if it was against his better judgement, he bent his head and kissed her quickly on the lips.

She half lifted her hand towards him, but he was already stepping back.

'Good night, Angelica,' he said softly. 'Sleep well.'

She turned and watched him run lightly down the rest of the stairs, her hand pressed against her tingling lips, wishing she knew what was in his mind.

Then a look of puzzlement stole into her eyes. There had been something different about him. He'd been dressed in black as before, but something. . .if only she could think what. . .something had been—

He'd been wearing a black cravat!

In fact, he'd been dressed entirely in black, without even the white shirt frills at his cuffs to relieve the sombre impression.

Angelica's eyes narrowed as she remembered her earlier suspicions about why he chose to wear black—and her idle curiosity as to how he might conceal his white cravat when he was trying to avoid detection.

Now she knew. And surely he wouldn't dress in such a funereal fashion just to visit Sir William?

She stood stock-still for several seconds, then picked up her skirts and ran pell-mell upstairs. She burst into her room and tugged energetically on the bell pull, before struggling to extricate herself as quickly as she could from the formal satin gown. The tiny buttons resisted her attempts at speed and she pulled impatiently at the fastenings, hearing the fabric tear beneath her hands.

'My lady, what is it?' Martha arrived breathlessly. 'Are you ill?'

'Get me out of this dress,' Angelica said urgently. 'Hurry.'

'Why?'

'Don't argue, just do it!'

Martha did as she was bid, her lips pressed together in a thin, anxious line.

'Where's the riding habit?' Angelica spun around. 'Good.'

She almost snatched it from Martha in her impatience.

'Where are you going?' Martha demanded.

'I don't know,' Angelica replied briefly.

She seized up a dark shawl and wrapped it around her head, covering the bright golden curls.

'Come with me,' she said imperatively to Martha. 'I might need you to distract the groom.' A brief, reckless smile lit up her face. 'I understand you're good at it,' she added.

They ran downstairs, Angelica in the lead, cautious in her haste, but there was no one in sight. Mrs Faulkener was presumably consoling the cook in the kitchen, and Benoît had already left. They let themselves quietly out of the front door and hurried round to the stables, careful to keep in the shadows.

'What—?' Martha began.

'Shush!' Angelica silenced her quickly.

She flattened herself against the wall of the house, hardly daring to breath as she heard hooves striking on the cobblestones. Benoît exchanged a couple of words with his groom, and then she saw him ride past, less than twenty feet away, his dark shape silhouetted against the paler night sky. He was riding one horse and leading another, and Angelica was sure her instinctive suspicions had been correct. There might be a perfectly innocent explanation for why he should need to take a spare horse to Sir William, but she couldn't think of one.

'Come on!' she whispered to Martha.

'What's going on?' Martha whispered back.

'I don't know, but I'm going to find out!' Angelica declared in a low voice. 'You keep Thomas occupied while I saddle the mare!'

'*My lady!*' Martha's protest was no less vehement for being uttered in a tone that wouldn't have been audible from two feet away.

'Are you telling me you can't do it?' Angelica challenged her.

'Of course I can, but. . .' Martha realised she was voicing her protests to empty air and abandoned her attempt to make Angelica see reason.

'Wait here,' she said as she caught up with her mistress.

'You'll have to get the saddle out of the tackroom while I distract Thomas. Be careful how you lead the mare over the cobbles or he'll hear her.'

Angelica huddled in the shadows and watched as her maid sauntered out into the stableyard. There was something subtly different about Martha, she even moved differently from the grim, sour-faced woman Angelica was so familiar with.

Even in the grip of the urgent excitement which filled her, Angelica was reminded of how much she had taken for granted before she came to Sussex. The world around her was changing shape before her eyes. Was that Benoît's influence?

'Good evening, Thomas,' said Martha.

'Miss Farley!' The groom turned as she spoke to

him, unmistakable pleasure in his voice. 'Doesn't her ladyship need you?'

'She's asleep in bed,' Martha replied, a hint of laughter in her voice. 'She hasn't been riding for nearly a year—the exercise fairly tired her out.'

'I'd never have known. She looks good in the saddle,' said Thomas appreciatively.

'She should—the Earl spent hours teaching her,' said Martha indulgently.

She was standing very close to Thomas, and Angelica was sure she heard the groom's quick intake of breath as he looked down at her.

'I'd like to see *you* in the saddle,' said Thomas hoarsely. 'Are you really leaving tomorrow?'

'I'm afraid so,' said Martha regretfully. 'Unless I can think of a way to persuade her ladyship to stay. Do you have any suggestions?' She smiled up at Thomas, moving slightly so that to look at her he had to turn his back on Angelica.

Angelica stared at Martha in disbelief for a moment. Then she collected her wits and darted silently behind Thomas.

The tackroom was lit by a single lantern and Angelica spotted the lady's saddle immediately. She found a bridle, lifted the saddle down, careful not to let the tack jingle together, and slipped out of the tackroom and into the stables.

By the time she found the mare her arms were tense with the strain of carrying the saddle in complete silence. She'd had no choice but to allow her skirts to drag on the ground. Fortunately, Thomas had hung a lantern on a hook when he'd saddled the horses for Benoît, and there was enough light for Angelica to see what she was doing.

She heard voices outside, and knew that Martha had led her eager suitor into the tackroom. She hoped he wouldn't notice the missing saddle, then decided he was too entranced by Martha to notice anything else.

She spoke softly to Dorcas and slipped the bridle neatly over her head. It occurred to her briefly, and incongruously, that she had less trouble dressing the mare than she did herself.

As a child, she had spent far more time in the stables than her mother had thought suitable, and she had been fascinated by all aspects of horsemanship. Now she was grateful for that early training. She saddled the mare as quickly as she could and led her out of the stables. Dorcas's hooves seemed to ring loudly on the cobblestones and Angelica's heart leapt in her mouth at the possibility that someone might surprise her—but the tackroom door remained firmly closed.

She paused by the mounting block and clambered into the saddle, hoping she had tightened the girths sufficiently to hold it firmly in place. The mare tossed her head, but made no other protest to the eccentric behaviour of her rider, and Angelica followed in the direction she had seen Benoît take.

He'd had several minutes' head start over her, but he hadn't been hurrying, and she was almost certain he was going towards the sea. Where else *could* he be going? She had a good sense of direction, and it wasn't too difficult for her to retrace their steps of that morning, but she was anxious in case she missed him—or overtook him unexpectedly.

She tied the shawl firmly under her chin and looked around at the dark, shadowy landscape. In this flat country surely she ought to be able to see him in the distance—but she might have been alone beneath the lofty stars.

It was very cold. The wind which had seemed almost invigorating that morning was now icy and hostile, cutting through her riding habit and chilling her bones. It sliced through the dank, winter grass beneath the mare's hooves and snatched Angelica's breath from her mouth.

She began to wonder if she was crazy. How could she hope to find Benoît in strange country in the middle of the night when, in truth, she had no idea where he was going? She only assumed he was heading towards the sea. And if she did find him, what was she going to do? Spy on him? Why?

She had acted without thinking, her pent-up and confused emotions finding release in a flurry of furious activity. At best she had made herself look foolish; at worst she might seriously jeopardise her friendship with Benoît—but she was desperately curious to know more about him.

Was he smuggling? Or was he involved in something else? She looked around at the dark, shadowy landscape. Her eyes were unable to pierce the gloom for more than a few yards, and she suddenly felt afraid.

She remembered their talk of a French invasion earlier that day—and all the stories Sir William had told of smugglers terrorising or murdering people who had inadvertently surprised them at their work. Her heart began to beat faster as she realised she might have done a great deal more than simply make herself look foolish with this impulsive escapade.

She almost turned the mare for home then and there, but a tiny core of stubbornness within her refused to give up.

She rode on cautiously, glancing nervously around at the shadows. The sound of the mare's hooves suddenly seemed very loud, and she was uncomfortably conscious of how conspicuous she was perched on top of a tall horse in such flat countryside.

She had been a fool. It was time to turn back and hope no one would ever be the wiser—

Suddenly a dark shape loomed out of a nearby thicket, and a man lunged towards her.

Shocked, icy fear clutched at Angelica's stomach. Images of smugglers and wild-eyed French invaders filled her mind. She dragged on the reins, putting her heel to the mare's side in an unthinking, desperate attempt to get away—but the man seized the bridle and Dorcas submitted to his low-voiced command.

Angelica clung to the saddle like a panic-stricken limpet. Terrified thoughts of rape and murder drove every other consideration from her mind. She was determined not to let him haul her down. As long as she remained on Dorcas's back she should be able to get away—*if only he'd let go of the bridle!*

She slashed fiercely at her assailant with her riding crop, her actions made vicious by desperation. The mare snorted and tried to shy away—Angelica was jolted and bruised against the saddle pommel. The man moved fast in the darkness. She could hardly see him, and she'd had no warning of his intentions when he grabbed the crop and wrenched it out of her hand. Pain speared up her arm, startling her into an unwary cry of distress. Panic threatened to overwhelm her as she realised she was now almost defenceless.

'Angelica! Get down!' Benoît commanded in a furious undertone, barely controlled anger throbbing in his words.

She gasped in sobbing relief as his voice penetrated her terror and slid down into his arms, her legs all but giving way as her feet touched the ground. He half lifted, half dragged her into the shadows of the thicket, leading Dorcas with them. The other two horses were already there, standing like statues, though Angelica was in no condition to notice that fact.

'Quiet!' he whispered urgently in her ear.

He was holding her tightly from behind, one arm locked around her waist. As she drew breath to speak he clamped his other hand over her mouth. She was already thoroughly alarmed and now she experienced an irrational fear that he was going to suffocate her. Her heart hammered with fright. She'd known he was strong, but his strength had never been used against her before, and she was terrifyingly aware of how helpless she was in his arms. She struggled desperately, trying to kick back at his shin, but her long skirts impeded her.

'Quiet!' he commanded again, in the same imperative undertone, but his hold on her relaxed slightly, and Angelica's panic began to subside.

She became aware of the silence of the horses,

and the tense expectancy in Benoît's body. Then she heard the muffled sound of hooves and realised that a sunken lane passed by on the other side of the thicket.

Benoît lifted her slightly in his arms and turned so that he could look in the direction from which the sounds were coming. Hidden in the shadows, staring out at an oblique angle towards the lane, Angelica could just see the dim silhouettes of ponies and men pass by.

There were more than fifty men in the gang, some of them carrying staves across their shoulders. They marched through the dark night in confident silence, as if they had an inalienable right to do so. Angelica knew that if they were surprised by Sir William they would fight; at least one of the magistrate's men had been seriously injured in a battle against smugglers — and another had been killed.

She closed her eyes, chill with horror as she realised that, if Benoît hadn't intercepted her, she would have ridden straight across the smugglers' path. What would they have done to her?

'What the hell are you doing here?' Benoît demanded furiously, when there was no longer any danger of them being overheard.

'I... You were wearing a black cravat,' said Angelica lamely, in a small voice.

She was still badly shaken by the realisation of how stupid she had been and in no condition to deal with his fury.

'For God's sake!' he exploded, his anger no less potent because it was so quiet and so controlled. 'What the devil did you think you were going to achieve? Do you know what might have happened to you if I hadn't been here? That gang has at least two murders to its credit already!'

Angelica bit her lip, tears filling her eyes. It was hard to defend herself because she knew she was in the wrong, but it was equally hard to apologise when he was so angry with her. The situation was made even worse because she couldn't see his face—all she could feel was his rigid, furious grip on his arm.

'I can take care of myself,' she declared, trying to put a spark of spirit into her voice and dismally failing.

'Not out here,' said Benoît categorically. 'What the hell am I going to do with you?'

'I was right, you aren't visiting Sir William, are you?' Angelica accused him, instinctively deciding attack was the best form of defence. 'You have no business scolding others when you make such a habit of lying yourself!'

'You little vixen!' said Benoît tautly. 'That's the last pert answer I'm prepared to take from you—lady or not! If you're going to trail around the countryside after me like a bitch in heat, then it's time you learnt to take the consequences!'

'How *dare* you?' Angelica struck out blindly at him, infuriated and bitterly insulted by his words.

She landed a glancing blow on the side of his face, then he dragged her into his arms. She struggled, pummelling at his chest and shoulders, and his hold on her tightened until she could barely move. She couldn't see his face, and she felt trapped by the black shadows of the thicket and the unyielding force of his arms.

'Let me go!' she commanded in a low, throbbing voice.

'No.'

She tried to wrench herself out of his arms, but it was impossible. She tried to kick him, but her long skirts and his well-made leather boots protected him from any harm.

'*Let me go!* You have no right—'

'Haven't I?' he interrupted harshly. 'It's too late to play the part of an aloof noblewoman, Angelica. I've made allowances for your innocence and your loneliness. But if you want to be treated like a lady, then you shouldn't act like a trollop following an army!'

'I didn't. . .!' she gasped, more shocked and hurt by his words than offended.

'For God's sake!' he ground out. 'Is this what you came looking for? Because if it is—by God you can have it!'

She caught her breath in protest as his lips found hers with ruthless efficiency in the darkness. Her arms were still trapped against his chest. He was holding her so tightly that she couldn't move and she could barely breathe. Shadows encircled them and the wind tugged at their clothes. His kiss was rough and almost punishing and offered her no escape. She struggled to resist him, appalled at the overwhelming surge of passion and anger she had unwittingly aroused in him.

She could feel the rigid tension in his body. She was dimly aware that his fury had very little to do with the fact that she had been trying to spy on him—or even that she'd accused him of lying to her.

Then, somehow, the nature of his kiss seemed to change. From being fierce and unforgiving on hers, his lips become warm and passionate. He was still holding her in a hard embrace, but one hand slipped up to cup the back of her head, and she felt her heightened, aroused senses begin to respond to him.

His lips were demanding as he claimed her open mouth, but he was no longer trying to punish her, and she felt a familiar, insistent tempo begin to pulse through her body. She clutched at the lapels of his coat, no longer struggling in his embrace.

Then he let her go—so suddenly that she stumbled back and fell, landing in a heap on the wet grass.

She drew in a gasping breath and dragged a shaking hand over her mouth, more confused than ever by his unexpected action. He was standing over her, and she looked up at him, sensing rather than seeing his presence in the darkness. She could hear his rapid breathing, but she was almost beyond coherent thought or feeling.

At last he crouched down beside her. She felt his hand near her face and flinched away, unsure of what he intended.

'*Ne vous inquiétez pas,*' he murmured reassuringly, and his touch was gentle on her cheek. 'I'm sorry, *mon ange*. I was angry, but I didn't mean to hurt you.'

'I...' Angelica began, but she couldn't continue; she simply didn't know what to say.

'Get up.' Benoît gripped her arms and lifted her to his feet. 'You mustn't sit on the grass,' he said, wry amusement in his voice. 'You're going to be cold enough before this night is over without being wet through as well.'

'Why?' Angelica asked vaguely.

She was less interested in the implication of his words, than she was in what had just happened between them. How could he be so furious one minute and so gentle the next? Then she remembered what he'd said about her acting like a bitch in heat—or an army trollop—and her whole body burned with embarrassment and distress. Was that how he thought of her?

'I can't send you back on your own,' said Benoît reasonably, apparently unaware of her inner turmoil.

'Not with both the Gentlemen out and Sir William and his men no doubt playing their dangerous game of hide and seek. And I don't have time to take you home myself—you'll just have to stay with me.'

'No. I meant why did you. . .?' she began uncertainly.

'There isn't time,' he replied, briskly but not unkindly. 'Not now. I'm already running late. And with so many others apparently heading for the same beaches things may turn out to be more complicated that I'd anticipated. Dammit! Perhaps I ought to send you back. Dorcas knows her way home—'

'No!' Angelica protested instinctively. 'Please. . .'

'All right. Come on.' He made up his mind quickly and threw her up into the saddle almost before she was ready.

She fumbled for the reins as he mounted his own horse.

'Pull your shawl back over your head,' he said quietly. 'At least you had the sense to hide your hair,' he added with mild amusement. 'You might turn into a useful companion-at-arms yet!'

CHAPTER SIX

THEY arrived at the beach not far from the place Benoît had brought Angelica to that morning— although he avoided the lane they had used before.

He travelled quickly but cautiously, and Angelica was aware that he was alert for the slightest unusual or potentially threatening disturbance. She didn't try to talk to him. She kept Dorcas close by his side, determined not to do anything more to anger him. She desperately wanted time to think about what had happened in the shadows of the thicket, but at the moment it was better not to let her attention be distracted.

The open fields ran almost down to the beach. Only a line of trees at right angles to the sea offered any shelter. Benoît paused in the lee of the trees, where the dense confusion of brambles provided some shelter from both the wind and prying eyes, and swung down from his saddle. Angelica hesitated, then dropped down to join him. He'd soon put her back on the mare if that's where he wanted her.

The wind had momentarily dropped, but Angelica could hear the sea, crashing on the sands not far away. The tide was in, just as it had been nearly twelve hours ago when she had first come to the beach. She could feel the damp air on her cheeks and taste the salt on her lips, but her vision was limited by the lack of moonlight. Only the cold, pale stars twinkled in the distant heavens. She wondered if this was how it had been for her father, when he'd tracked and found Benoît so many years ago. She was suddenly glad she had come.

'Stand here,' said Benoît briefly, moving her into position with firm but not unkind hands. 'And don't let your skirts blow in my face.'

She did as she was told, although it was only when she heard steel striking against flint that she realised he was using her body as a shield. The light flickered so briefly she doubted if even someone watching for it would have noticed it, and then he covered it and stood up.

'What is that thing?' she asked softly, indicating the strange object he was holding.

She'd barely had time to see it, but she already had her suspicions about its use—Sir William had told her of such things.

It was made of two tubes of metal. A short, rather stubby vertical tube with a conical lid, and a longer, tapering pipe, which extended at right angles from the side of the first tube and which could be covered and uncovered at will.

'Spout lantern,' said Benoît shortly. 'Stay here.'

She heard his boots on the pebbles, then she saw his dim outline against the paler sea as he stood on the beach. She guessed he was signalling, but the spout lantern meant that the only light visible was directed out towards any waiting boats. No wonder smugglers used them. The penalties for being caught signalling out to sea were severe—and even innocently lighting a pipe on the beach could get a man into trouble if the wrong people saw him.

She waited, shivering and hugging her shawl tightly around her head and shoulders. The wind had picked up again and it tugged viciously at her skirts.

She could hear the roar of the sea, much rougher tonight than it had been during the day. Nothing happened for a long time, and she huddled against the mare's shoulder for warmth and comfort.

She couldn't believe where she was or what was happening to her. Nothing in her previous experience or wildest imaginings had ever prepared her for the events of this evening. She didn't know which was more unbelievable—the fact that less than an hour ago she'd seen a band of armed smugglers march within a few feet of her—or the strange and unprecedentedly intimate relationship she was developing with Benoît.

No one else had ever had such a profound effect on her behaviour, or so completely disturbed her peace of mind. She should be sleeping quietly in her bed now, not avoiding smugglers and riding officers on a black, windswept beach. What had he done to her that she could so unthinkingly abandon all modesty and decorum to follow him to an unknown destination?

She looked towards Benoît, and then beyond him, straining to pierce through the murky night and see what lay ahead for them. The stars above began to dance and blur before her overtaxed eyes; the shadows grew even darker and took on strange and alien shapes. She was no longer sure what was real and what was imagined. She gripped the comforting leather of the saddle, grateful for Dorcas's placid and solid presence. She had no intention of letting

Benoît discover how nervous this long wait was making her.

Then she blinked, and lifted her head, hardly able to credit that she'd just seen the signal. The light flickered again, and then the sea was dark once more.

Angelica left the horses and the shelter of the trees and stumbled down over the shingle to join Benoît. He turned sharply at the sound of her approach.

'It's me,' she said softly, and sensed rather than saw his relaxation of tension. 'Are they coming?'

'Assuming we haven't confused our signals,' said Benoît dryly. 'I'd hate to find we were the unintended recipients of several hundred tubs of brandy meant for the Gentlemen we saw earlier!'

'I know we're not smuggling,' said Angelica, shivering at the possibility he'd just raised, and wondering where the men they'd seen earlier had gone. 'But what are we doing here?'

'You astonish me, my lady,' said Benoît, and she heard the gentle mockery in his voice. 'When I've done nothing more questionable than offer you a glass of brandy you accuse me of smuggling, and when I'm standing on a moonless beach sending signals to an unidentified vessel you acquit me of the crime! Here!'

In the darkness, she realised he had shrugged himself out of his greatcoat, and was holding it around her shoulders. She slipped her arms gratefully into the sleeves and hugged it tightly about herself.

'I'd say I'm sorry you're cold,' he said softly in her

ear, his arms enfolding her from behind. 'But you shouldn't be here in the first place. How am I going to explain this to your father?'

'You won't have to explain anything,' Angelica protested, not sure what he meant.

The warmth of his body against her back was unbelievably comforting, and the soft caress of his breath against her ear sent a delicious tingle rippling down her spine. It was incredible that only a short while ago he had been rigid with fury at her.

'Papa won't know I followed you,' she murmured breathlessly as Benoît's lips brushed her cheek, devoutly hoping that she spoke the truth. 'All he wants you to do is rescue Harry,' she added rather incoherently.

'But what about you, my lady?' Benoît said softly, pushing her shawl back from her face.

'I want you to rescue Harry too!' she whispered, trying to maintain at least the pretence that they were having a normal conversation.

'I know.' Benoît began to explore the warm, delicate skin of her neck with soft, intimate kisses.

She gasped, and quivered responsively as glowing rivulets of pleasure radiated out from beneath his lips. Her eyes were open, but in the dark, lofty night there was nothing to see; she could only feel his arms around her, and hear his low voice reverberating through her body as he spoke to her, his mouth almost touching her skin.

'Is that all you want from me, *ma douce amie*?' he teased her, reaching across the front of her body to cover one of her hands with his as she clutched at his greatcoat.

'Of...course.'

She was still locked in his arms, the heat of his body burning through her back, his lips wrecking devastating delight beneath her ear. She was even beginning to forget why they were standing on the beach.

'Liar!' he murmured provocatively, biting gently at her earlobe. 'Besides, I might feel compelled to tell the Earl about this escapade myself.'

'What?'

She gasped with horror and tried to turn in his arms, but he prevented her quite easily. Fortunately she'd been too breathless to exclaim loudly, but it didn't stop him from admonishing her for her indiscretion.

'Shush!' he murmured infuriatingly, the familiar note of laughter audible in his low voice as he settled her comfortably in his embrace once again. 'Remember where we are! Besides, why not tell your father?' He returned to his thrilling explorations of her earlobe, his tongue running gently over the sapphire earring she had been in too much of a hurry to take off. 'Lord Ellewood might have some practical suggestions to offer about not wearing jewellery when tracking potential smugglers!'

Angelica drew in an indignant breath, but before she could speak Benoît lifted his head alertly.

'The boat's coming,' he said quietly, releasing her from his arms.

She looked out to sea. She couldn't hear anything beyond the familiar crashing of the waves, but she had no doubt Benoît was right.

'Go back to the horses,' he ordered, and went down to the tideline.

She started to walk up the beach, looking back over her shoulder, still not sure what to expect from the approaching boat. It was clear that Benoît was meeting someone, presumably one man who would ride the spare horse he had brought. But she still didn't know who the man was, although she was beginning to guess *what* he was.

She was still glowing from Benoît's embrace. The cold wind didn't seem so bitter any more. She smiled wryly. Twenty-four hours ago she would never have believed that she could care so little about whether Benoît was involved with a spy. But now she was far more concerned with how he felt about her, and how she felt about him. The man in the boat was just an unwelcome interruption to their conversation.

She hugged the greatcoat. She was much warmer than she had been. She reached the edge of the shingle and turned to look back at the sea. She could just hear the slap of oars on the water, and see the dark shadow of Benoît as he spoke to the men in the boat.

Then, somewhere to her right, she heard a man shout out. His harsh voice ripped through the peaceful, empty night—alien and frightening. His cry was followed by a pistol shot, raised voices and more shots.

Angelica jerked round in stunned amazement, staring blindly into the dark night. The noise was coming from further west. She blinked as she saw the brief flash as a pistol was fired. Her heart was racing in disbelief and alarm. She had almost forgot-

ten the men they'd seen earlier, but now the danger
from the smugglers had been made sickeningly real.
A full-scale battle was taking place between Sir
William and the smugglers only a few hundred yards
down the beach!

'Angelica!'

She'd been momentarily frozen with horror, but
at the sound of Benoît's voice she snatched up her
skirts and ran towards him.

As she did so, she was vaguely aware of someone
whistling—then Benoît seized her around the waist
and dumped her without ceremony in the boat.

Another man, no more than a faceless shadow to
Angelica, helped Benoît push the boat into deeper
water, then they were rowing out into the black void
of the Channel.

The boat rocked and pitched on the windswept
waves. Angelica was quickly soaked with seaspray,
and half-deafened by the thudding of her heart and
the crashing of the water around her. Her skirt was
already sodden from where it had trailed in the sea
as Benoît lifted her into the boat. Four men manned
the oars, with another at the tiller, and she huddled
as small as she could, trying not to get in their way.

She had been terrified when she'd first encountered Benoît, but now that real danger threatened
she felt more excited than afraid. She had no idea
what would happen next, or where they were
going—but she was with Benoît. She knew he would
take care of her.

She could hear low voices as Benoît talked to the
other passenger in the boat, but she couldn't distinguish what they were saying. This was the man

they'd come to meet. She wondered who he was, but instinct rather than the evidence of her senses told her that he was hurt and in pain.

The black bulk of the cutter loomed suddenly above them. Benoît gripped her arm.

'We're going on board,' he said quietly. 'Take off my coat, it'll get in the way. And take care as you climb up, there's no hurry now.'

'I'll be all right.' She stood up, swaying as the boat pitched, grateful for his steadying hands on her waist.

She slipped out of the greatcoat, then picked up the front of her heavy woollen skirts and held them clenched between her teeth. The creak of the wet wool in her mouth made her want to gag, but she knew it was safer than trying to spare one hand to hold them up and she daren't trip over them.

'Good girl,' said Benoît. 'Here.' He guided her to the ladder and she seized the rung.

It was a terrifying moment as she stepped out of the rocking boat, but she hung on grimly and then made the short climb. As she reached the top unseen hands seized her and helped her over the side of the cutter.

'Good evening, miss,' said a dry voice. 'This is an unexpected pleasure.'

'For me also,' Angelica replied, staggering slightly as the deck tilted. 'Thank you.'

She was grateful for her companion's roughly steadying hand, but she wished she could see him more clearly, and she felt very isolated now that she was no longer near Benoît.

She could only discern the dim outline of the man, just enough to know that he was of average height

and stocky build. He spoke with an unmistakable
Sussex burr and she guessed from his voice and his
stance that he was no longer young. She wondered
immediately if he had been one of Toby's cronies.

'What happened?' he asked sharply.

'I don't know exactly,' she said, not sure how
much she ought to say. 'There was a...disturb-
ance...further down the beach, then we came back
with the boat.'

'We heard shots,' he said grimly. 'Blunderbuss
Billy's busy tonight.'

He turned as a dark shape appeared over the side.
Angelica just had time to realise that Benoît was
carrying a man over his shoulder before her companion went to help lift him into the cutter.

'*Hell!*' The wounded man almost cried out as his
leg touched the deck and she heard his quick, hissing
intake of breath as he tried to suppress his agony.

'He can't walk,' said the stocky man, almost
dispassionately. 'I said he was foolish to try to land,
but he insisted. What are you going to do?'

'Can you land us this side of the Arun, on West
Beach?' Benoît asked crisply.

'Of course. But he still cannot walk, and no doubt
you sent the horses home. Besides—what of the
lady?'

'The lady is more than equal to the situation,' said
Benoît dryly. 'It's Adam I'm worried about. Get
under way, George, I don't want to waste time.'

George grunted, then Angelica heard him giving
orders to his crew.

Adam dragged in a groaning breath and Benoît

dropped on one knee beside him. Angelica joined them, feeling the rough decking beneath her hands.

'Is he badly hurt?' she asked anxiously.

'He took a sword thrust just before they left France,' Benoît replied curtly. 'I don't know the details yet. George, I need some light!'

'In the cabin. I'll not have a light showing on this boat tonight.'

They lifted Adam from the deck, and Angelica winced in sympathy as she heard his barely suppressed groan of anguish.

In the cabin light his face was grey and strained, but there was no fresh blood on the rough bandages around his thigh. His breeches had been slit open and a clean pad pressed over the wound, then strips of cloth had been wrapped around his leg over his breeches. Benoît looked at the dressing carefully, but he didn't touch it.

'As long as it hasn't started bleeding again, we won't interfere with it,' he said briskly.

Adam gave a choking laugh. Angelica guessed he was about the same age as Benoît, although the lines of pain on his face made him look older. He was a thin, narrow-chested man, although she suspected he was a great deal tougher than he at first appeared. His eyes were shrewd enough, and he was bearing his discomfort with fortitude.

'Your father was right, you should have been a sawbones,' he said hoarsely. 'Sorry, Ben. I didn't mean to cause so many complications. Although I hadn't expected such a turnout for my arrival either.'

His eyes rested with open curiosity on Angelica as he spoke. The shawl had fallen back from her hair and the sapphire and diamond comb glinted richly in the lantern light. Her cheeks glowed with fresh colour and her eyes were bright with interest and concern. She didn't seem in the slightest bit disturbed by the ugly stains on Adam's leg or the uncertainty of her current situation.

'Neither did I.' Benoît smiled faintly as his eyes rested briefly on the glittering comb. 'Adam, I am sure you will be charmed to meet Lady Angelica Lennard.'

Adam's eyes widened in surprise and appreciation.

'Ellewood's daughter!' he crowed in delight. 'Ha! Your sins are finally catching up with you!'

'As you say.' Benoît's smile broadened. 'My lady, may I present Mr Adam Kennett? If he hadn't lost the toss sixteen years ago, it would have been him, not me, who waylaid your father that night.'

'I'm pleased to meet you.' Angelica held out her hand to Adam without hesitation. 'I'm so sorry you're hurt.'

'I'm sorry to meet you in such uncomfortable circumstances,' Adam replied ruefully. 'But this is no place for you. I don't know what Ben was thinking of to bring you.'

'He didn't,' she said awkwardly, not daring to look at Benoît.

'She wants me to rescue her brother from Bitche,' Benoît explained, 'but she knows too much about my unsavoury past to trust me—so tonight she followed me to see what dark deed I was about to perpetrate. Next time I will know better than to wear a black cravat in her presence!'

Adam stared at Angelica in amazement, then gave

a crack of laughter which was cut short by a wincing stab of pain.

'Serves you right for being such a dandy!' he said gaspingly. 'Black cravat indeed! Well done, my lady! He needs taking down a peg or two sometimes—and so far the Lennards seem to be the only people who can do it. I'm *very* glad to meet you.'

Angelica blushed, avoiding Benoît's eye. Remembering everything that had happened that evening, she wasn't at all sure that Adam's enthusiasm was justified.

Adam stirred restlessly, his smile fading as he looked at Benoît.

'We'll be at West Beach soon,' he said breathlessly. 'Ben, you've got to take the news to London. I can't.' He hesitated, glancing doubtfully at Angelica.

'If I didn't think you could trust her, I wouldn't have told her your name,' Benoît replied instantly, taking Angelica completely by surprise.

'I guessed as much.' Adam closed his eyes for a moment. His face was pinched and, despite the fillip the unexpected discovery of Angelica's identity had given him, he was obviously weak and in considerable pain.

'Bonaparte's building a battlefleet in the Scheldt,' he said after a moment. 'There are ten ships of the line already in service, and more than that number being built at Antwerp and Flushing. I've seen them. If they aren't dealt with, they could pose a threat to England's security. You must tell the Admiralty, Ben!'

'I will.'

Angelica had been looking from Adam to Benoît and back again. Excitement, alarm and amazement had all flickered across her face as Adam spoke, but now she fixed her bright, glowing blue eyes on Benoît. He did not seem perturbed by Adam's news, but she was aware of the coiled, watchful tension which filled him. He was alert and intent on the business on hand, sure of his ability to overcome any obstacles. The black wolf was poised and ready for action.

'Wait,' he said briefly. 'Shield the light.'

He ducked his dark head through the low cabin door and went out on deck. Angelica unshuttered the lantern and looked at Adam. He smiled wryly.

'I nearly get myself killed bringing that information back, and all he does is snap orders at me,' he complained. 'I might have known I wouldn't get any sympathy.'

He winced, and reached down towards his injured leg.

'Don't touch it!' Angelica said quickly, catching his hand. 'We don't want it to start bleeding again.' She smiled encouragingly at Adam as he let his head fall back wearily on the rough pillow. 'It will only hurt more if you prod it!' she pointed out practically.

'I'm surprised you're not faint with disgust at the sight of me,' Adam sighed.

'I've seen worse,' Angelica replied quietly.

She tried not to think of the frightening picture her father had presented when they'd carried him home from the accident. She'd swallowed her fear and her nausea then because she'd had no choice. The memory had given her a few nightmares, and she never wanted to repeat the experience, but in general she wasn't squeamish. Adam's injury caused her anxiety only in so far as it was a danger to him.

She heard Benoît's footsteps outside and, at his command, she shielded the lantern as he came in. He glanced quickly at Adam, then looked at Angelica.

'Let me have the jewels,' he said abruptly. 'I don't think Martha intended you to wander round the countryside in them. They're hardly inconspicuous!'

'I forgot I was wearing them.' Angelica took off the earrings and passed them to him, then tried unsuccessfully to disentangle the comb from her hair.

After a moment he gave an impatient exclamation and pushed her hands aside.

'You have less control over your hair than any woman I have ever met' he said in exasperation.

'Martha put it up!' Angelica protested, submitting to his hands, but feeling particularly foolish because she knew Adam was watching them, a curious expression on his face.

'I know she did! Hasn't it ever *occurred* to you to experiment with a hairbrush for yourself?' Benoît retorted. 'There. Now, make sure you don't let the shawl slip. Ready, Adam?'

'As I'll ever be.' Adam allowed himself to be hoisted up in Benoît's arms.

Angelica followed them out of the cabin, blinking in the sudden darkness. Now that her eyes had become used to the light, the night seemed even blacker than before. Only the stars twinkled above them. The coastline was nothing but a dark blur beneath the paler sky. She remembered the battery on the east bank of the Arun, its cannon waiting to fire on intruders and she shivered. Were they sailing into an ambush?

'What if we meet Sir William?' she asked suddenly. Would the magistrate assume they were smugglers and shoot them on sight if he encountered them?

'He's the least of our problems,' Benoît replied. 'Stragglers from that disturbed band of Gentlemen would be far more dangerous—but I doubt if they'll have come this far east.'

Angelica bit her lip at the possibility, but she refused to admit she was nervous.

'Then we'll just have to make sure we don't bump into any,' she said stoutly.

Adam gave a grunt of painful amusement as Benoît lifted him over the side of the cutter and carried him down into the waiting boat.

'No one can accuse the lady of being faint-hearted,' he gasped.

'By no means,' Benoît agreed.

'Good-bye, miss,' said George, from beside Angelica. 'I'm sorry I could not offer you more hospitality. Perhaps we'll meet again under more comfortable circumstances.'

'I hope so.'

Angelica picked up her skirts and climbed down into the boat, not at all surprised when Benoît caught her firmly around the waist and lifted her the last part of the way. She settled herself beside Adam as the boat surged through the waves. The oarsmen were strong and impatient for their work to be over. It had been an unlucky and unprofitable trip for

them, though so far there had been no direct threat
to the ship or her crew.

When they reached the beach, Benoît lifted
Angelica out of the boat and carried her up onto the
sand, wading through the shallow water. Angelica
stood on the shore, tying her shawl more firmly
under her chin as she looked around nervously.
Dawn was still some hours away and the night was
as black as ever. She had good evidence now that
sometimes the shadows contained lurking danger,
and it was much harder than it had been earlier to
control her anxiety.

She strained to hear any unusual sounds, but all
she could hear were the waves rolling up the beach
and the wind blowing through the sand dunes behind
her.

She longed for the comfort of daylight, but she
knew that the darkness protected them as well as
potential enemies. She turned as Benoît came up the
beach towards her.

'This way,' he said in a low voice as he reached
her side, Adam slung over his shoulder.

Angelica followed him, careful to hold up her
skirts as they headed into the dunes. It was hard to
walk on the dry, shifting sands but, even burdened
with Adam over his shoulder, Benoît was still
moving quickly.

The wind blew up gritty, stinging sand in her face
and whipped her hair painfully in her eyes. She
slipped and fell to her knees, gasping for breath.
Then she tied her shawl tighter, scrambled to her
feet, and hurried after Benoît. Her skirts were a
nightmare of wet, dirty, clinging wool. The wind cut

through her riding habit and she no longer had the added warmth of Benoît's greatcoat.

She stumbled on, praying for the wind to drop, determined not to be left behind, or to force Benoît to wait for her. He had said that she would be equal to this, and she was going to prove him right. He had not asked for her presence on this trip, and she certainly wasn't going to give him cause to regret it.

The river wasn't contained between neat, high banks, and Benoît chose a route which swung quite wide of its main channel, avoiding as far as possible the worst of the marshy ground. Even so, Angelica found herself negotiating several streams of water which ran down into the river. Her skirts, legs and half-boots were soon plastered with mud. She staggered on, tripped over the uneven ground and pitched full-length in the quagmire.

She lay still for a moment, winded and almost grateful for the temporary respite, then pushed herself up onto her knees. She realised that Benoît had paused, and she sensed rather than saw that he was looking back at her. She gritted her teeth and shoved herself back onto her feet. If he could manage the walk burdened as he was by carrying Adam, then she could certainly do it hampered only by her riding skirts.

She caught up with him and they went on, neither speaking a word. She was aware of Adam's occasional hiss of pain, and knew his situation was far worse than hers.

At last they reached Littlehampton Harbour, and Benoît laid Adam down on the ground.

'Wait here,' he said in a low voice. 'I've got to find a boat to take us across the river.'

Angelica dropped on her knees beside Adam as Benoît went down cat-cautious to the water's edge.

The tide was going out; one or two boats were already beached above the waterline, and she could see the masts of ships and fishing boats against the sky as they lay at anchor in the harbour.

Adam drew in a deep, pain-racked breath and Angelica reached out to touch his shoulder comfortingly.

'It won't be long now,' she murmured, 'and then you can rest.'

Adam gave a sobbing gasp, quickly repressed, that could almost have been a laugh, but he didn't try to reply. Angelica supported herself on one hand as she pushed his wet hair back from his face, and waited for Benoît to return. She wondered exactly what he had in mind.

He came back very quickly and carried Adam down to a small rowing boat. He lifted Angelica into it and then rowed across the harbour. The fishing boats around them creaked and rattled continuously in the wind, but the oars of the rowing boat dipped almost silently in and out of the choppy water.

Occasionally Angelica saw a faint glint of reflected starlight in the wind-roughened black surface of the river, as Benoît negotiated the anchored vessels. She gripped the side of the rowing boat tensely, wondering whether there were watchmen on board the ships—and whether they would see and challenge the lone boat. But the harbour was dark and apparently devoid of any other human life.

At last the bottom of the boat grated on the shingle and Benoît lifted Adam out. Angelica climbed out before he could help her, uncaring that her skirts were trailing in the water. She was already so wet that it didn't make much difference; and she was growing sensitive to the fact that Benoît must be getting tired too, and that she didn't actually need to be lifted from place to place like a baby.

Benoît put Adam down in the shadows. Angelica knew without being told that once more they must wait for him. She crouched beside Adam, instinctively trying to make herself as small as possible, and wondered how he had been hurt. The French must have discovered he was a spy. Were they following him now?

She glanced nervously around the dark enshrouded harbour. Presumably Napoleon's agents would work very hard to prevent the information Adam had acquired from reaching London. If they found him he might be in considerable danger— along with anyone else who shared his knowledge. Angelica shivered at the thought. She must remember to ask Benoît a few questions as soon as she had the opportunity.

She heard quiet footsteps approaching, and lifted her head in alarm, instinctively leaning forward across Adam to protect him. Someone was coming. For an instant she was seized by panic—then she recognised Benoît, though how she could be so sure it was him in the dim light she didn't know.

She struggled quickly to her feet as he picked up Adam, and followed him to an isolated building that stood between the harbour and the huddle of buildings which was Littlehampton.

She just had time to realise it was an inn—she heard the sign creaking above her head in the wind although she couldn't see the picture—and then she was standing inside a darkened room. A lantern was unshuttered and she blinked around in the dim light.

They were in the taproom. No fire burned in the grate, and the room was uncomfortably furnished with a rough wooden settle, a table and a few stools; but it was dry and out of the wind. She sighed with relief, and looked at her companions.

The lantern was held by an elderly man dressed hastily in his nightshirt and breeches. She guessed he was the innkeeper. He nodded with curious politeness to Angelica, but most of his attention was on Adam.

'Bring him straight upstairs, lad,' he said to Benoît. 'Best get him to bed as soon as possible.'

Angelica followed them unquestioningly up the narrow, uneven wooden stairs. Her freezing, sodden skirts dragged around her legs and she was almost too weary to move. Benoît carried Adam into a small, back chamber and Angelica dropped into the only chair the room possessed.

She knew instinctively that they were safe—at least for the time being. They were out of the screaming wind and Benoît would take care of Adam. She thought she ought to get up to see if she could help him, but from what she could see and hear it didn't sound as if he needed any assistance.

The lantern light glittered and misted before her eyes. She had strained her mental and physical capacities to their utmost during the past few hours, and now that the immediate danger was over she was desperately tired. She leant back her head and closed her eyes. Disconnected thoughts and images of Benoît, smugglers, spies and the windswept sea swam through her mind—but none of them had any power to stir her emotions. She was too tired to think clearly or even to care what happened next.

She had no idea how long she had been sitting there before Benoît lifted her up in his arms. She murmured a wordless protest, but she didn't resist. Her arms and legs were far too heavy to move of their own volition. She didn't even open her eyes when he carried her out of the room and into another chamber.

He sat her down again, untied her shawl and began to unbutton the bodice of her riding habit.

'Come on, wake up!' he said, sounding amused. 'I want to talk to you.'

She blinked at him, trying to clear her tired, exhaustion-clouded mind.

'Yes,' she mumbled, lifting a heavy hand to scrub at her bleary eyes. 'Of course. We must. . .decide what to do next.'

Benoît grinned.

'I'll decide what we do next,' he declared firmly. 'And the first thing is to get you out of these wet clothes. Get up!' He pulled her briskly to her feet.

Angelica winced as her aching muscles protested. Then she tried to finish unbuttoning her riding habit with stiff, unresponsive fingers.

After a moment Benoît pushed her hands away with an impatient but tolerant gesture.

'I'll do it!' he said. 'How did you manage to get covered in so much mud?'

'I kept falling down,' said Angelica vaguely. 'I kept up with you though!' she added, on a note of triumph.

'I know.' Benoît pulled off her jacket and began to unbutton her skirt.

Angelica didn't protest. In the bizarre and unreal circumstances in which she found herself, the fact that he was undressing her had hardly registered in her weary brain.

There was a fire burning in the hearth of the spartan bedchamber, and a candle stood on the mantelpiece. But it was still dark and shadowy in the small room, and the draught from the warped shutters made the candlelight flicker unevenly.

'Will Adam be all right?' Angelica asked anxiously.

She was too tired even to think of asking where they were, or how Benoît came to know the innkeeper. She just took it for granted that he was one of Toby's friends.

'Yes, I think so,' Benoît replied. 'But he'll be weak and in pain for quite a while. He's sleeping now.'

He pushed the wreck of her riding skirt down her legs to her feet as he spoke. It seemed quite natural to Angelica to rest her hands on his shoulders to keep her balance as she stepped out of the sodden mass of wool. She was barely aware that she was standing before him dressed in little more than her muddy petticoats.

'What about the men who hurt Adam?' she asked,

voicing the fear she'd felt earlier in the harbour. 'Will they come after him?'

She looked up at Benoît as she spoke and saw that he was watching her thoughtfully.

'It's possible,' he said quietly. 'But there's a very good chance they won't be able to find him. George managed to elude pursuit in the Channel, and Adam's come from the Scheldt. No one would expect him to land this far west. That's partly why we arranged it so.'

Angelica was silent for a few moments as she absorbed this information.

'But if they know who he is, then they might expect him to come back to his home,' she pointed out at last.

Benoît smiled faintly, affectionate admiration for her reasoning in his dark eyes.

'That's the biggest danger,' he agreed. 'Adam isn't sure how much the French know about him. It's probably not a major threat, but the less attention we draw to his presence the better.'

'But he is safe here,' said Angelica, not in any spirit of doubt, but simply stating what she already believed.

'The landlord is an old friend of Toby's,' Benoît confirmed her earlier suspicion. 'He'll take good care of both of you.' He sighed. 'I've got to go to London,' he said, almost reluctantly.

'Is Adam's news bad?' Angelica asked anxiously, jolted by the realisation that Benoît would have to leave soon.

He slipped an arm reassuringly around her waist, drawing her towards him. She rested her hands against his chest as if it was the most natural thing in the world that she should be standing within the circle of his embrace.

He gazed at her for a few moments, a curious expression in his eyes, then he smiled.

'Twenty ships hardly constitute a full scale invasion threat,' he said lightly, 'but they should be dealt with, nevertheless. The sooner I've informed the Admiralty, the happier I shall be.'

'You'll go to London immediately?' Angelica asked, feeling bereft.

'At once.' He reached up to stroke her tangled golden curls, a regretful light in his brown eyes. 'You'll be safe here until I return,' he continued, after a moment. 'I can't take you back to Holly House now—even if you weren't too tired to ride it will be dawn soon. You won't have any reputation left if you're seen jaunting around the countryside at this hour looking like a gypsy!'

'I don't care about that!' Angelica protested vigorously.

'I do,' Benoît retorted. 'I'm going to have enough explaining to do on your behalf as it is! I must call on your father when I'm in London.'

'Oh, my God!' The colour drained from Angelica's face as she thought about the Earl for the first time in hours.

She slipped out of Benoît's arms and turned away from him. She'd hoped she would never have to explain to her father why she'd followed Benoît to the beach, but the events of the night had made it difficult to conceal her impetuous actions. In his current state of mind the Earl was unlikely to be sympathetic to her motives.

'Angelica? What is it?' Benoît put his hands on her shoulders.

'Papa—' Angelica said, and broke off, hugging her arms across her body.

Not once since his accident had she openly voiced her feelings about the changes in her father to anyone—even Martha. It seemed the ultimate act of disloyalty. But she needed to tell someone.

'Papa's not the same,' she whispered. 'If. . .if. . . ' She bit her lip, staring up into the dark corners of the ceiling as she blinked back tears. 'If Papa had been like he is now sixteen years ago you really would have ended in a gibbet,' she said in a rush, without turning round.

Benoît's hands tightened on her shoulders.

'His blindness has made him bitter?' he said quietly.

Angelica nodded mutely.

'I wondered.' Benoît sounded sad, but not surprised. 'Some of the things you've said. You're desperate to get Harry back, aren't you?'

'He's always so cheerful. . .optimistic,' Angelica whispered brokenly. 'Nothing I've done has made any difference.'

Then she finally responded to the steady pressure of Benoît's hands and allowed him to turn her into his embrace. She rested her head against his shoulder, trying not to give way to tears. There was no time for this conversation. Benoît had to go to London, and she had to stay and take care of Adam.

She felt Benoît stroking her hair and wished she

could prolong the moment. She longed to tell him everything that had happened since the Earl's accident. All the bitter recriminations, the angry words—the despair. But even now she could not bring herself to do so. She lifted her head and met Benoît's steady gaze.

'He's not. . .easy. . .to speak to,' she said with some difficulty. 'You must be prepared for many changes in him. I hope—' She broke off. 'It would be better if I could come back with you,' she said, 'but I know you must reach London as quickly as possible. Tell Papa I'm sorry.'

'Don't worry.' Benoît's arms tightened around her reassuringly. 'I'll explain everything to him. Lord Ellewood need never know you followed me tonight. I'll tell him that Admiralty business prevented me from escorting you home straight away—which is true. I *will* take you home as soon as I get back to Sussex.'

Angelica smiled: then she glanced down, biting her lip. She was grateful for Benoît's quiet assurance. She believed he probably could make things right with the Earl. But his words had forced her to think of the future, and she knew how hard she was going to find it to go back to a life in which he had no part. She would wait with the Earl for Benoît to bring Harry back to them—and then what? Would she see Benoît again? Or would he consider his promise to Lord Ellewood had been kept and sail away on the next tide?

'Angelica?' he said, softly questioning.

She summoned a smile and looked up at him.

'I'm sure you'll know just what to say to Papa,'

she said confidently. 'Benoît. . .' She hesitated, focussing her attention on one of his shirt buttons. 'I'm sorry for the problems I've caused you tonight,' she continued breathlessly, after a moment. 'But I'm not sorry I came. It has been an. . .adventure.'

'You haven't caused me any problems,' he said, and his voice sounded very deep. He sighed. 'I really must go,' he said regretfully.

He bent his head to kiss her, and Angelica lifted her hand to touch his face, feeling the rough stubble beneath her fingers because naturally he hadn't shaved.

Benoît had meant it only as a light, farewell kiss, but as his lips met hers a tide of strong emotion swept over both of them. His arms locked around her and Angelica forgot her exhaustion and all her anxieties as she responded to him.

The events of the night had been so fantastic that they bore no relation to anything she had previously experienced. The shabby inn room contained no reminders of her status or the conduct normally expected of her. There was nothing to inhibit her instinctive response to the man she loved.

And she did love him. He was her embodiment of life and adventure. There could be no other man like him. She could taste the sea salt on his lips, and her spirit soared with elation. The unquenchable vigour in his hard, masculine body was intoxicating: she pressed eagerly against him, unashamedly matching the intensity of his desire.

Benoît moulded her vibrant body with sensitive hands, rousing her to new heights of excitement. She murmured wordlessly, her slim fingers pressing into his shoulders in a strong, convulsive grip as he kissed her just below her ear. She lifted her chin, gasping with pleasure as his lips and tongue explored the soft flesh of her neck and shoulder.

Her petticoat was far more revealing than any dress she normally wore, but she felt no shyness as his lips continued their downward investigation. She quivered in his arms, new currents of delight pulsing through her as his kisses alternately scorched and soothed the tender, exposed curves of her breasts.

The small fire in the grate provided little warmth, but Angelica was burning with the sensations Benoît awakened within her. The cool air against her damp skin only heightened her arousal.

She did not protest when Benoît picked her up in a swift, urgent movement and carried her to the bed. He laid her down gently, and sat beside her, his hand resting on her waist. Her heart beat a tattoo of excited anticipation and she looked up at him with open trust and love in her eyes.

His black hair glinted in the candlelight, and she could see his lean face was tense with desire as he leant towards her. She lifted her hand to touch his cheek, glorying in her freedom to reach out to him so spontaneously.

He turned his head, catching her fingers between his lips and biting them gently. Then he slid his hand up from her waist to cup her breast. Angelica caught her breath, her eyes locked with his. More than anything she longed to feel his touch against her naked skin, with no barriers between them.

The electric moment lengthened almost unbearably; and then Benoît bent to kiss the hollow between her breasts.

Angelica arched her back instinctively, lifting herself towards him, He slipped an arm beneath her shoulders—but then he paused, his rough cheek resting gently against her soft flesh. She could feel his warm breath against her skin.

She put her hands behind his head, feeling the sticky salt in his hair, holding him against her. Her body was crying out with longing for him to continue his love-making. She had been swept along by the riptide of their passion, and she felt frustrated by his delay.

But then he drew in a deep, shuddering breath, and sat up.

'You're a dangerous woman, my lady,' he said unsteadily, a glimmer of wry amusement in his dark eyes, and she realised that he had been fighting to regain control of his raging emotions.

'I am?' she murmured, her eyes locked with his, a provocative smile teasing her lips as she stretched her neck and shoulders luxuriously.

She felt both disappointed, yet incredibly moved by his efforts to control his desire for her.

'Like playing with fire,' Benoît almost groaned.

He reached out to stroke her cheek as if he couldn't help himself, but he didn't kiss her again. She could sense the fierce struggle he was having to contain his ardour, and she was amazed at how desperately she wanted to tell him that his restraint wasn't necessary. Only a deep-rooted shyness and some remaining shred of decorum prevented her.

He sighed, turning his head to brush the soft skin

of her inner arm with his lips, sending rivulets of delight chasing through her veins.

'I always thought I was a man governed by self-discipline and reason,' he said wonderingly, 'but at this moment it would take very little to make me abandon both sense and duty. What have you done to me, my lady?'

'I don't know.' Angelica smiled mistily, unbelievably happy at his admission. Surely it meant he would *not* leave her when he had rescued Harry. 'What have *you* done to me, sir?'

'Nothing,' Benoît said quietly. 'I have never known such a passionate, high-couraged woman.'

He gripped her wrist gently for a moment, then he stood up, startling Angelica with the abruptness of his action.

'I will speak to your father as soon as I have been to the Admiralty,' he said more briskly. 'Don't worry, Angelica. I'm sure that when Lord Ellewood knows Harry is coming home, he'll feel more like his old self.'

'I hope so.' A shadow crossed Angelica's face as she thought of her father. She sat up. 'Benoît. . .?'

She felt confused. Not certain what was happening. One moment she was being carried along on the greatest surge of passion she had ever known—the next Benoît was calmly telling her he was going to visit her father. Was there a connection between those two things? Or. . .?

'I must go,' he said softly. 'Sleep well, *mon amour*. But make sure you put on the nightdress I obtained for you, and get *under* the covers before you do so.

Otherwise you will be extremely cold when you wake up!'

'Now you sound like my old nurse!' Angelica protested, her heart singing as she just realised he had called her his love.

Benoît laughed, sounding unbelievably light-hearted.

'If I didn't have to go urgently to London, I might throw caution to the winds and demonstrate some of the essential ways in which I differ from your old nurse!' he retorted. 'Good night, Angelica.'

He turned and went swiftly out of the room, leaving her alone in the glow of the firelight. She could hear the wind rattling at the shutters, and there was a cold draught blowing around her shoulders, but until that moment she hadn't noticed it. She turned her head to look around at the barely furnished room. It contained none of the luxuries she was used to, but it provided her with everything she needed—except Benoît.

CHAPTER SEVEN

THE day was well advanced when Angelica woke up. For a few moments she felt bewildered by her strange surroundings, unsure of what had happened the night before. She was only aware of an unspecified glow of happiness. Then she remembered.

It was hard to believe that it wasn't just a dream. Had she really done all the things she remembered doing? Most importantly of all, was she right when she hoped and believed that she meant as much to Benoît as he meant to her? She replayed their final conversation in her mind, reassuring herself as she remembered the expression in his eyes, the loving touch of his hands and those last few words he'd uttered before he'd left:

'Sleep well, *mon amour.*'

Benoît didn't say things he didn't mean. She smiled happily and pushed back the bedcovers, ready for the next part of the adventure.

The fire had long since gone out and the room was bitterly cold. She gasped, shivering convulsively, then winced as she sat up, because her muscles ached from her unaccustomed exertions of the previous night.

She climbed resolutely out of bed and washed as well as she could with the icy water in the jug on the wash-stand. Then she grimaced at her reflection in the tarnished mirror. She hadn't realised just how muddy and bedraggled she was until she saw herself.

Her hair was a tangled disaster, her stockings ruined, her petticoats damp and grubby, and the half-boots unwearable. The riding habit was in little better condition.

Benoît had spread it over the chair to dry, but it was still damp and unpleasant to touch. She beat out as much of the mud and sand as she could, but wearing it was an unenticing prospect. Unfortunately, she didn't have much choice. She flinched as the clammy wool touched her skin, then buttoned it up decisively.

At last she sat down and contemplated the wreckage of her hair. There was a comb beside the water jug. She picked it up and tried to drag it through her knotty curls. After nearly half an hour she finally managed to reduce her hair to some kind of order, but her eyes were watering from the discomfort and her arms ached from holding them above her head so long.

She let her hands drop into her lap and wondered what she was going to do now. She'd retrieved a few hair pins, but it was a mystery to her how she was going to put her hair up and make it stay up. She almost wished Martha was with her, but that was defeatist thinking. After all she'd accomplished the previous night, she wasn't about to let a little thing like doing her own hair stand in the way of her newfound independence.

She persevered until she'd achieved a result she wasn't entirely unsatisfied with, and then wondered what to do next. No one had come near her, and although she knew she wasn't supposed to draw attention to herself, she was very hungry. She was also concerned about Adam.

She got up and went to the door, listening to see if she could hear anything, then she opened it a crack. Voices floated up from the taproom downstairs, but the landing was empty. She slipped out of her room, down the corridor and into Adam's room like a wraith in her bare feet.

There were two men in the chamber and they both looked up sharply as the door opened. Adam was lying in the bed, his face pale and strained; Thomas the groom was sitting beside him on an upright wooden chair.

Thomas leapt to his feet as Angelica came in, then visibly relaxed as he saw who it was.

'Good afternoon, my lady,' he said gruffly, not sounding particularly pleased to see her.

'Hello, Thomas,' Angelica replied.

She had been momentarily startled to see the groom, but now she realised Benoît must have sent him to take care of Adam.

She walked over to the bed, her long skirts dragging across the floor.

'How are you?' she asked Adam, studying him carefully and a little anxiously.

'I'll do.' He smiled and held out his hand to her. 'I'm sorry you had such an uncomfortable time of it last night, my lady.'

In the background, Thomas snorted disparagingly, and Angelica saw a small smile flicker in Adam's eyes as he returned her gaze. She turned to look at the groom.

'That was a fine trick you played on me, your ladyship!' he said truculently, a scowl in his eyes. 'And Martha! A tricksy, meddling, deceitful—!'

'Oh, no!' Angelica protested instinctively.

'I'm not normally one to speak out of place,' the groom continued, as if she hadn't spoken. 'But I tell you to your face, my lady, I'll not be made a game of like this! Jaunting about the countryside as if you were in Hyde Park. And who do you think would have been blamed if anything had happened to you—that's what I'd like to know!'

Angelica flushed guiltily.

'I acted on the spur of the moment,' she said placatingly. 'I'm sure no one would have blamed you, Thomas.'

'Made a right fool of me, she did,' he grumbled, unappeased.

'Oh, no! I'm sure she didn't mean you to feel like that!' Angelica protested, realising that Martha's diversionary tactics had seriously hurt Thomas's pride. 'It was just. . .'

'Blind loyalty to you!' Thomas said grimly.

Angelica bit her lip. She had no idea how Martha really felt about the groom, and she didn't think it would be sensible to make false claims on her maid's behalf, but she did feel guilty about Thomas.

'In a right stew, she was, when the horses came home without you,' he said, with grim pleasure. 'Only way I managed to stop her following me today was to threaten to tie her up. And she still made me bring some things you might be needing!'

He gestured to a nondescript bag on the floor.

'Poor Martha,' said Angelica guiltily. 'I'm sorry, I didn't mean to give everyone such a fright.'

She lifted her eyes and looked at the groom as she spoke. Her luminous blue eyes were clear and sincere as they met his.

He grunted wordlessly.

'You'd best sit down,' he said grudgingly, offering her the chair. 'Though this is no place for the likes of you, my lady.'

Angelica laughed.

'I know you don't mean that!' she exclaimed. 'You're probably thinking that it serves me right!'

The groom looked at her for a few seconds, then he smiled, very grudgingly.

'When it's dark I can take you back to Holly House if you like,' he said. 'We can go out the back way.'

'What about Adam?' Angelica asked immediately, glancing at him in concern. 'Surely Ben—Mr Faulkener—sent you to look after him?'

Adam pulled a face.

'I can look after myself,' he said.

Angelica turned back to the groom, a question in her eyes.

'There's a nasty wind blowing,' he said immediately. 'I wouldn't want you to take sick on top of everything else, my lady. And Joe—that's the innkeeper—his wife died a while back. He hasn't time to keep coming up here.'

'In that case, I'll certainly stay,' said Angelica firmly. She didn't really have any desire to leave. Benoît had told her to wait for him here and that's what she intended to do. 'Only...' She glanced around, seeing the remains of some bread and cheese on a plate. 'I *am* very hungry,' she added. 'Do you suppose. . .?'

'Be my guest,' said Adam grandly. 'I haven't much of an appetite at the moment, I'm afraid.'

'I'll see what I can do,' said Thomas, and went quietly out of the room.

'You don't need to stay,' said Adam, when he'd gone. 'Thomas is just being overcautious. No one's going to bother me here. And even if they do,' he added carelessly, 'there's nothing you can do to help.'

Angelica had been eating the bread and cheese as quickly as she respectably could, but at Adam's dismissive words she lifted her eyes and looked at him steadily over a distance of some six feet.

'I hope I'd be of some use to you, sir,' she said coldly, a hint of unfamiliar imperiousness in her usually friendly voice. 'I'm not accustomed to allowing anyone ride roughshod over me—smugglers, magistrates, *or* French agents!'

She stared at him uncompromisingly. Her eyes were implacable blue sapphires, her back was straight and her carriage regal. Her bare feet, dirty riding habit and untidy hair did nothing to diminish the force of her personality as she confronted him.

Adam drew in a deep breath.

'My apologies, Lady Angelica,' he said after a moment. 'I did not intend to offend you. I should have known better. Forgive me.' He held out his hand to her.

'Of course.' She took it and shook it briefly. 'I

have a quick temper sometimes, particularly when I'm hungry,' she added ruefully. 'I didn't mean to be so overbearing.'

'You're a very unusual woman,' said Adam, looking up at her curiously. 'Did you really follow Ben just because he was wearing a black cravat?'

'Yes.' Angelica laughed a little self-consciously 'He said he was going to visit Sir William but I didn't believe him,' she explained. 'I'd wondered earlier how he disguised his white cravat when he went out smuggling—seeing as how all his other clothes were black—so when I saw him on the stairs and he was wearing a *black* cravat. . .I acted without thinking.'

'But it was a very acute deduction,' Adam observed, watching her shrewdly. 'My lady, I salute you. Ben's finally met his match! The future will certainly hold some interesting developments, I think.'

He grinned at Angelica's discomfiture, then tensed and turned his head as the door opened, but it was only Thomas.

'It's not what you're used to,' he said, putting a tray down on Angelica's lap, 'but it's the best Joe could produce—and I had to dodge my way up here, so no one saw me. I hope I haven't spilt any.'

'It looks delicious,' said Angelica warmly. 'Besides, I'm so hungry I could eat a hor. . .goat.' She changed her mind at the last minute as she remembered the groom's occupation. 'Thank you, Thomas.'

She ate the simple meal with relish. She would have been happy to stay and chat to Adam when she'd finished it, but she could see that talking to her was a considerable effort for him so she left him with Thomas and went back to her own room.

In her absence someone, possibly Thomas, had made up the fire and lit some candles. She opened the bag Martha had sent and found her maid had packed a warm, practical walking dress and shoes. She put them on and immediately felt much more comfortable. There was something very disconcerting about walking around in bare feet.

She spread out the riding habit before the hearth, hoping it might dry by the following morning. She hated the thought of wearing it again, yet she also felt strangely sentimental about it. She would have to replace it for Mrs Faulkener.

As she smoothed out the creases she heard the crackle of paper and frowned in brief confusion. Then she remembered snatching up James Corbett's letter the previous morning. She took it out of the pocket and flattened it out. The letter was even more battered and stained now than it had been before. The ink had smudged and run in the damp, but it was still readable.

She put it on the mantelpiece then sat down on the bed, wondering what to do next. She could hardly go back to bed so soon, and there was nothing else in the bare room to occupy her attention. She frowned irritably. After all the excitement of the past few days this enforced inactivity was almost unbearable.

There was a gentle tap on the door and she recognised Thomas's voice. She went over and opened it immediately.

'Excuse me, your ladyship,' he said sheepishly,

offering her a crumpled newspaper. 'I thought you might like something to read. An inn's a tedious place if you're on your own and you've got no taste for drinking.'

Angelica's smile lit up her face.

'Thank you!' she exclaimed gratefully. 'Is Mr Kennett asleep?'

'Yes, my lady.'

'Would you like to come in?' she offered impulsively. 'I'm sure you must be just as bored with this waiting as I am.'

'Well. . .' He hesitated, then glanced quickly up and down the landing. 'Very well, my lady.'

He came into the room and stood uncomfortably just inside the door.

'How long do you think it will take Mr Faulkener to get to London?' Angelica asked.

'He'll be there by now,' Thomas replied. 'Depends how long his business takes him when he'll be back. He's planning on being here tomorrow.'

'Yes, he said,' said Angelica. She thought of Benoît's business with the Admiralty, and with her father, and wondered which would take longer.

How would the Earl react to Benoît's news? She didn't want to think about that now. She was still basking in the glow of happiness left over from the previous night.

'You must have been with Mr Faulkener a long time,' she said brightly.

'I worked for his father,' Thomas replied, 'but I've known Master Benoît since we were both boys. I would have gone to sea with him, but my mother was a widow, and there were my sisters to think of. . .'

'Yes,' said Angelica abruptly, reminded once more of the Earl. 'There is always someone to think of. I'm sure you took good care of your family.'

'My sisters are married now,' said Thomas cheerfully. 'Ma lives with one of them. I could go with Master Benoît now. But I get seasick — and someone has to take care of Mrs Faulkener's horses.'

'I'm sure no one could do it better,' Angelica said warmly. 'I still haven't seen the tricks you've taught them. Mr Faulkener says you've taught Billy to count!'

Thomas smiled slowly, clearly gratified by her words.

'Ah, well,' he said. '*I* do the counting, Billy just does what I tell him. Pity I can't say the same for some I could mention!' he added, glowering. Martha's deception clearly still rankled. 'Well, I'd best be getting back to Master Adam,' he continued, before Angelica could think of a suitable reply. 'I'll be there if you need me, my lady, but I don't imagine there'll any trouble.'

'Thank you, Thomas,' said Angelica.

When she was alone again the room seemed even smaller and more cell-like than it had done before. She had sat reading to her father for endless hours, suppressing her thoughts of the world outside their walls. Now, in an unfortunate parody of those hours, she had to sit in a tiny, empty room with the sound of voices and laughter echoing up from the taproom below — with nothing to do but a paper to read.

She threw the newspaper on the floor. She'd done

enough reading to last her a lifetime. And Thomas's comment about his mother had excited her own insidious anxieties about the Earl. She had done everything she could to help him since his accident — but had she done enough? Was there any way she could have found that would have averted his terrible bitterness?

She had loved, admired and obeyed her father all her life; but Lord Ellewood had always been a proud and very private man, not given to sharing his emotions with his daughter. He had never been able to come to terms with his sudden dependence on others, and that made him so hard to deal with.

Her earlier mood of optimism faded, and it was a long time before she fell asleep that night. When she did, her dreams were troubled. Harry, her father, Benoît and even her mother advanced and retreated in a never-ending series of fragmented images. She woke up rigid with anxiety and almost too afraid to move — though she didn't know what had scared her. Surely she wasn't frightened of the people she loved most in the world?

It was a relief to get up the following morning. It was the first time she'd seen daylight for two days and the sight of the sunshine immediately restored her optimism. She couldn't imagine why she'd given way to such foolish worrying the previous night. She ate a hearty breakfast and even deigned to read the despised newspaper. It was nearly a month out of date, but since the news it reported was almost entirely local that hardly mattered to her.

She was engrossed in a story about the peccadil-

loes of some soldiers garrisoned at Horsham when
Thomas knocked on her door.

'My lady!' he whispered urgently, alarm in his
voice. *'My lady!'*

'What is it?' She snatched open the door.

'Sir William! He's downstairs, he's going to search
the inn!'

'What?' Angelica exclaimed, her heart thumping
in sudden alarm. She was remembering Benoît's
command that they do nothing to draw attention to
themselves.

'They wounded some men on the beach two nights
ago,' Thomas said breathlessly. 'And one of his men
was killed. Now he's heard there's an injured man
here—God knows who informed him—though I can
make a guess.' His expression darkened briefly.
'There's no time for that now. Sir William knows
Master Adam's in with us. He's been trying to catch
him and Master Benoît for years, I've got to hide
you both.'

'"In with us"?' Angelica queried quickly.

'The Gentlemen!' Thomas said impatiently.

Angelica suddenly realised that, although Benoît
might no longer be actively involved in smuggling,
his groom, landlord and a lot of his old friends still
were. Even more importantly, Adam had been the
one who'd led Sir William on a wild-goose chase all
those years ago while Benoît had been confronting
her father among the dunes of West Beach. And
Adam had come ashore secretly from a smuggling
vessel. If the magistrate discovered him wounded at
the inn, he might finally have the evidence he needed
to apprehend him for smuggling.

'God, what am I going to *do*?' Thomas groaned distractedly. 'You and Master Adam to hide and—'

'*Me!*' Angelica interrupted. 'Why. . .?'

'Your *reputation*, my lady.' Thomas wrung his hands together. 'The master will kill me if anything happens. . .and you can't even climb out of the window, there's a man outside. . .'

Angelica gathered her scattered wits together.

'There's no need to worry about my reputation,' she said firmly. 'Sir William is an old acquaintance. I'm sure I can deal with him.'

'But—'

'You go and take care of Adam. I'll speak to Sir William. Be quick,' she added crisply, as Thomas seemed rooted to the spot. 'Presumably Sir William knows you as well. You wouldn't want to bump into him on the landing!'

Thomas gave her a doubtful look, but he had no ideas of his own, and Angelica spoke with authority. The years spent running her father's household stood her in good stead. Although she didn't know it, she sounded very much like the Earl.

Thomas hurried back to Adam's room as Angelica picked up James Corbett's letter from the mantel-piece. Then she went to stand her ground at the top of the stairs. She could hear Sir William arguing with the innkeeper in the taproom below. The innkeeper was putting up a valiant resistance, but she knew he would soon be overborne. A few seconds later she heard Sir William thrust the old man impatiently aside and mount the stairs.

'Good morning, Sir William,' she said calmly.

At the sound of her voice he stopped dead,

halfway up the stairs, looking up at her in blank astonishment.

There was very little light on the landing and he couldn't see her clearly. All he was aware of was a tall, aloof young woman blocking his way. He certainly didn't recognise Angelica.

'Who the devil are you, miss?' he snapped, surprise robbing him of courtesy.

'I beg your pardon, Sir William,' said Angelica coolly. 'I'm sorry you don't know me.'

She moved slightly so that he could see her more clearly in the light from the small casement window.

'*Lady Angelica!*' Sir William gasped in disbelief. 'What the dev—? That is, my apologies, my lady. I had no idea the Earl was staying at this inn.'

'He isn't,' said Angelica imperturbably, although her heart was hammering with nervousness.

She was trying to imagine how her father would have dealt with the situation. She wondered briefly if she'd made a mistake in sticking to her original plan; but if she'd claimed that it *was* Lord Ellewood in Adam's room it would have been too easy to disprove her story.

'He isn't?' Sir William stared at her in confusion and dawning suspicion. 'I have heard no news of your marriage. Surely—'

'Certainly not,' said Angelica austerely, wondering if Sir William thought he'd discovered an elopement. 'No such announcement has been made. I am here on quite other business.'

'What other business?' Sir William demanded bluntly.

Angelica looked past him to his two henchmen staring at her with open curiosity on the stairs.

'It is a family matter, and one I am not prepared to discuss—certainly not in public,' she said repressively.

Sir William flushed angrily, but turned and dismissed his men with a jerk of his head. They retreated reluctantly down the stairs, though Angelica had no doubt they would remain within earshot.

Benoît had wanted to avoid a scandal, and now it seemed she was well on the way to making one—but she couldn't let Sir William discover Adam. Even if they could convince the magistrate he hadn't been involved in smuggling, it would be very awkward for the spy to be seen here. Angelica took her responsibilities seriously.

'Now, miss,' said Sir William grimly. 'Perhaps you will tell me what business brings you so far from home without the Earl's protection.'

'My father has not left home for more than eighteen months,' said Angelica rather bitterly. 'I am surprised you have not heard.'

'I am sorry, Angelica,' said Sir William more gently, startled by the bleakness in her voice. 'I called on him in town several times. I was told he was not at home.'

'I'm sorry. I did not know.' Angelica looked away, momentarily forgetting why she was confronting the magistrate at the top of the stairs.

'I will call on him again,' said Sir William. 'In the meantime,' he added briskly, 'I must warn you that you have chosen a most unsuitable place to conduct

your business. I have good reason to believe that
there is a wounded smuggler hiding in this inn.
Please step aside. I intend to search every room, and
I apologise in advance for any inconvenience I may
cause you.'

'I regret, I cannot allow you to continue,' said
Angelica resolutely, without moving from the top of
the stairs.

Sir William stared at her.

'You won't *allow*—?' he exclaimed explosively.
'My lady, I do not understand you! This is not a
matter of personal preference. There is a fugitive
from justice hiding here!'

It occurred to Angelica that, if Sir William always
wasted so much time making angry announcements
about his intentions, it wasn't surprising Toby
Faulkener had run rings around him. If Adam hadn't
been quite so badly wounded he and Thomas could
probably have dealt with the man beneath the
window and made good their escape by now. As it
was, she was just going to have to make sure Sir
William stayed on the right side of the door herself.

'Don't be ridiculous,' she said coolly. 'This is a
small inn and I have been staying here for several
days. I'm sure I would know if there was a wounded
man here.'

'I was told he was brought here late at night. . .'
Sir William had been thrown off balance by
Angelica's presence and he hadn't quite got his
argument together.

'Perhaps you were misinformed,' she said sweetly,
well aware of how exasperating the magistrate would

find her suggestion. 'I understand it's happened to you before.'

Sir William glared at her.

'Just what is your business here, my lady?' he demanded bluntly. 'I'll not have you make a game of me—or my office.'

Angelica hesitated, staring at him aloofly.

'It's a matter of considerable delicacy,' she said at last, with obvious reluctance. 'I could not confide in you without your promise not to repeat what I tell you.'

'For God's sake!' Sir William exploded. 'You don't have to coach me on matters of delicacy or honour, miss! What—are—you—doing—here?'

Angelica handed him James Corbett's letter without another word.

Sir William stared at it blankly for a moment, then squinted at it, holding it at arm's length as he tried to read it. The light at the top of the stairs was too poor, and Angelica stepped aside to let him go over to the small window, though she remained standing with her back to Adam's door.

At last sir William lowered the letter and looked at her.

'I had no idea' he exclaimed. 'I had not heard. Poor Harry! But—'

'Please send your men away,' Angelica interrupted. 'You have my word that there are no wounded smugglers in this house, Sir William. Someone had to bring me the letter,' she added softly.

She saw a measure of understanding dawn in his eyes, then he strode downstairs and she heard his strong voice dismissing most of his men.

She gave a deep sigh of relief, then glanced around as she heard Adam's door open a crack.

'My lady?' Thomas murmured questioningly.

'I think we're winning. Stay inside,' she said briefly.

'The master is going to kill me,' said Thomas with feeling. 'Now I really will have to run away to sea!'

He closed the door softly as Sir William came back upstairs.

'What's going on, Angelica?' he said, and from his tone it was clear he was determined to get to the bottom of things. 'Who is in that room? Does the Earl know you are here?'

Angelica hesitated. She had no desire to discuss her affairs on the open landing but, on the other hand, she was afraid to leave Adam's door unguarded in case someone else decided to investigate. She knew Sir William hadn't sent all his men away.

'Someone had to bring us the letter,' she repeated, to gain time. 'You can see it's had a difficult journey.' She paused. 'Anyone in a position to help Harry might be in considerable danger if Bonaparte learned their identity,' she said very softly and deliberately. 'I cannot let you or your men— especially not your men—into that room, Sir William. Your arrival has certainly complicated things for us. We were hoping to be as unobtrusive as possible. Now I dread to think of the rumours and gossip which will be flying around the countryside and perhaps coming to the wrong ears!'

'Dammit! My lady!' Sir William flushed angrily. 'I acted in good faith. If you knew you were conducting

such delicate business in this district you would have
done better to come to me in the first place. I *am*
one of your father's oldest friends even if he is no
longer prepared to receive me. And I hope I can be
trusted to keep a secret!'

'Oh, Sir William, I'm sorry!' Angelica stretched
out an impulsive hand towards him.

The magistrate had clearly been badly hurt by her
father's withdrawal—and now he was aggrieved to
have been excluded from news of Harry's fate.

'I have been so anxious these past few months,
particularly since we learnt about Harry, that I
haven't always been thinking straight,' she said
apologetically. 'I didn't mean to offend you—or to
be so rude to you earlier,' she added sincerely. 'But
your unexpected arrival with all your men frightened
me half out of my wits!'

'It wasn't obvious,' said Sir William dryly. 'You
reminded me very much of your father in one of his
more autocratic moments!'

Angelica blushed and bit her lip ruefully.

'I'm sorry,' she apologised again.

'Never mind, m'dear,' said Sir William gruffly.
'You've had a lot to contend with these past two
years.' He took her hand and patted it with rough
sympathy. 'But if the Earl didn't bring you here who
did?' he asked.

There had been no sound to alert Angelica, not
even a creak on the wooden stairs, but somehow she
knew he was there.

She looked past Sir William straight into Benoît's
dark, amused eyes. She had been desperately longing
for his support, and now her heart leapt with joyous

relief at his unexpected appearance. Despite the hard riding he must have done since they'd last met he was as elegant and assured as ever. His composure contrasted devastatingly with the magistrate's unfocused bluster.

Angelica's hand fluttered in Sir William's, and a brilliant smile lit up her face as she looked at Benoît. All the anxiety and tension were stripped from her eyes and she glowed with bright, happy radiance. Her warmth and pleasure seemed to illuminate the gloomy landing.

Benoît's expression had been watchful as well as amused as he'd mounted the stairs, but for an instant, as he returned her look, his eyes blazed with a passion to match her own. Then the familiar, wolf-wary gleam returned to his eyes, and he turned to face the magistrate.

'*My God!*' said Sir William, staring at Benoît in stunned disbelief. 'Not *you*, Faulkener?'

Benoît grinned. Angelica saw a flash of his white teeth in the poor light.

'Why not?' he asked mockingly. 'Don't you think I'm capable of protecting a lady?'

'Dammit! Faulkener!' Sir William growled. 'That's not what I meant. Although—'

'Although that would, in fact, appear to be the case,' Benoît interrupted smoothly. 'Forgive me, my lady.' He took Angelica's hand and kissed it gracefully. 'I had no idea you were going to have such an unpleasantly exciting time this morning.'

'Not. . .unpleasant,' said Angelica, trying to keep her voice steady at his touch.

She had spent a lot of time imagining their next

meeting, but it had never occurred to her that it would take place under the eye of the magistrate. She was acutely aware that Sir William was staring at them in open amazement, and she was desperately trying not to appear self-conscious.

'Sir William is an old friend of my father,' she continued. 'I could never find it *unpleasant* to talk to him, but the situation is a little *awkward*.'

'It is indeed,' said Benoît. He smiled faintly and squeezed her hand reassuringly. Then he turned to Sir William.

'You should have confided in me, Faulkener,' said Sir William brusquely, recovering from his initial surprise. 'Then none of this unfortunate business would have happened. I'd no idea you were acquainted with Lord Ellewood. But you've always been secretive and irresponsible!'

'That's not true!' Angelica burst out indignantly before Benoît could speak. 'He—' She broke off, biting her lip, as Benoît caught her eye.

'I think,' said Benoît deliberately, 'that we have spent enough time on this dark and draughty landing. We might proceed better with a little more illumination.' And he opened Adam's door.

He did it with so little drama that for a moment Angelica didn't even realise what he'd done.

'But—' she protested, as it dawned on her he was inviting Sir William to enter the room.

'After you, my lady,' he said, with unruffled courtesy. 'Sir William.'

'What game are you playing now, Faulkener?' said Sir William suspiciously, but he went into Adam's room without further protest.

Angelica felt as if the world had turned upside down. After all her efforts to protect Adam from the magistrate, she couldn't believe Benoît was just going to hand him over to Sir William! He must have some scheme in mind—but she couldn't imagine what it was.

Sir William took three paces across the room and stopped dead as he met Adam's strained expression.

'By St George!' the magistrate breathed, completely stunned. 'I thought you were dead, boy!'

'Just an unfounded rumour, I'm glad to say,' Adam replied, letting his head fall back against the pillow as some of the tension ebbed from his eyes. 'Although I came a bit too close for comfort this time.'

Sir William recovered from his first shock and strode over to the bed.

'What the *devil* have you been up to?' he demanded roughly. 'I heard you were going to try your fortunes in India—and then you took the fever. What did you mean by disappearing like that without a *word*?'

'Events. . .overtook me,' said Adam. 'I apologise for my lack of courtesy.'

'Damned improvident, reckless, thoughtless. . .' Sir William seized Adam's hand and held it very tightly.

Angelica stared at the magistrate in confusion. She was sure there were tears in his eyes, although he was doing his best to disguise his emotion beneath his customary blustering manner. She glanced at Benoît and saw that he was smiling. Thomas was looking both unhappy and uncomfortable in the furthest corner of the room.

'So you're the one who brought Angelica the letter about Harry!' Sir William exclaimed at last.

Adam hesitated. He looked pale and tired. Sir William's exuberance had pleased him, but it was also exhausting.

'He has just returned from France,' said Benoît quietly. 'It was a French agent who wounded him. You can understand why we didn't want to draw attention to his presence. I was going to take him to Holly House, but the Manor would be an easier journey for him—you could take the carriage along the sands at low tide.'

Sir William frowned.

'And what will you be doing in the meantime?' he asked bluntly. 'Getting Harry out of France?'

Angelica gasped. She hadn't expected the magistrate to be so acute. He glanced at her sardonically.

'They may have led me on some merry dances over the years, my lady,' he said dryly. 'But I've known both these idle scoundrels since they were in shortcoats. They'd never let a challenge like that go unanswered.'

'Well, we have a number of challenges at the moment,' said Benoît briskly. 'I suggest we start tackling them. Sir William, if you will be kind enough to organise Adam's departure for the Manor, I will take Lady Angelica back to Holly House. Perhaps you would collect whatever you need from your room, my lady.'

Angelica hurried to do Benoît's bidding. She was beginning to feel somewhat indignant that her efforts to protect Adam had apparently been entirely unnecessary, but she wasn't about to argue with Benoît in front of the others. Besides, the sooner they left, the sooner she would be alone with him.

It was another bright, windy March day, with a clear blue sky and a pale, glistening sun.

Benoît had come back to collect Angelica in his curricle, and she was able to watch the countryside pass by in reasonable, though chilly, comfort.

'Do you mean I did all that for nothing?' she demanded as soon as they were on their way. 'If Sir William is going to take Adam back to the Manor I needn't have tried to hide him at all!'

'I wouldn't say that,' said Benoît, grinning. 'You put up a spectacular defence. I was very impressed.'

'You were?' Angelica looked at him suspiciously, half afraid he was making fun of her. She felt almost shy in his presence, but that was ridiculous.

He glanced at her and smiled, and she felt her heart turn over at the warmth in his eyes.

'Yes,' he said. 'I was proud of you—though I dread to think of the rumours we'll soon have to contend with!'

'But if there was no harm in Sir William knowing, I might have saved myself the trouble,' Angelica protested, although her heart was beating a quick rhythm of happiness at his praise. 'And now I come to think of it—Thomas was terrified of Sir William discovering us! None of it seems to make any sense at all!'

Benoît grinned.

'Thomas's involvement with smuggling is rather

more recent than mine,' he explained. 'And he's
never had quite the same relationship with Sir
William that Adam and I had. It's hard for him to
believe that Sir William is not always a threat to our
interests. And it would have been unfortunate if
Blunderbuss Billy had gone stampeding into Adam's
room with half his men gawping behind him. It was
just as well you got him to send them away. He *can*
be discreet when he wants to be—but it doesn't
come naturally to him!'

'It doesn't, does it?' said Angelica, remembering
the magistrate's argument with the innkeeper, and
then his long debate at the top of the stairs with her.
'If that's how he normally goes about his business,
I'm not surprised he hasn't caught many smugglers!'

Benoît laughed.

'He was in a difficult position today,' he said fairly.
'Joe was one of Toby's cronies, so Sir William must
have been almost certain, even before he arrived at
the inn, that any smuggler it contained wasn't one of
the band he fought on the beach two nights ago.
That gang is far more vicious and violent than any
of Toby's old friends—and Sir William knows it. He
may even have guessed that Joe was betrayed by a
less scrupulous rival—but he had to be seen to act
on the information he received, even if he didn't
relish the task. He's usually behaves a little more
circumspectly!'

'I should hope so!' said Angelica forcefully. 'Was
it always like this, Benoît? I mean, Sir William seems
so fond of you and Adam, even though he admits
you led him a merry dance—yet we heard pistol

shots on the beach that night, and Thomas said one of Sir William's men was killed.'

'Toby always kept violence to a minimum,' said Benoît grimly. 'There have been a lot of unfortunate changes since his death. It may be time to do something about them. Too many men have died, and Sir William is getting too old for pitched battles through the countryside.'

'What do you mean?' said Angelica quickly, suddenly afraid for Benoît. 'What are you going to do?'

He glanced briefly at her, then his rather tense expression relaxed and he drew the horses to a standstill beside the road.

'Nothing at the moment,' he assured her. 'I was thinking aloud. Don't worry.'

'Don't *worry*!' Angelica exclaimed. 'How can I help it when. . .?'

He transferred the reins into one hand and reached up to touch her hair. Her pulse began to race and she caught her breath as she looked into his face. They had spent so long in the dark together that it was almost a shock to meet his eyes in the bright morning sunlight. There was so much warmth and admiration in his expression that she felt lightheaded.

'I'm sorry you had such a difficult time in my absence,' he said softly. 'If I'd thought for one moment that you'd be troubled at the inn I wouldn't have left you there. I should have had Thomas take you back to Holly House last night.'

'I wouldn't have gone,' Angelica whispered breathlessly. 'Benoît, it was real, wasn't it? I mean. . .'

He smiled and bent to kiss her.

As his lips met hers she closed her eyes, giddy with relief and happiness. She hadn't imagined any of it. The way he looked at her and the way he made her feel were both quite real. She twisted towards him, responding with her characteristic lack of reserve, and as usual it was Benoît who drew back first.

He laughed softly, stroking her sunshine-bright curls with teasing fingers. She gazed up at him, her wide blue eyes dark with glowing, undisguised emotion.

'Going anywhere with you is about as safe as carrying a live coal in my pocket!' he declared, a wicked gleam in his eyes. 'We *are* on the King's high road, my love. A little more decorum may be in order.'

Angelica blushed. Her lips were still burning from his touch and her body was throbbing with unfulfilled passion.

'Then you shouldn't have kissed me!' she said energetically, secure in the knowledge that he was teasing her.

'The temptation was irresistible.' He grinned, winding a golden curl idly around his finger, and sending a shiver of pleasure down her spine. 'What happened to your protestations of false modesty?' he enquired provocatively. 'Weren't you telling me only two days ago you had no intention of kissing me again?'

'I don't remember saying anything of the kind!' Angelica replied firmly, although a faint smile played on her lips as she spoke.

'What an adaptable memory,' he said admiringly.

'I have a very good memory,' she said placidly. 'What did the Admiralty say?'

'They thanked me for my time and effort,' Benoît replied wryly. 'I've a feeling it was old news to them. They have more than one iron in the fire. But the matter's in their hands now.'

'You mean Adam nearly got killed for *nothing*!' Angelica exclaimed indignantly. 'That's *wicked*!'

'That's war,' Benoît replied dryly. 'We shall have to see what develops.'

'I think it's disgraceful!' Angelica declared forcefully. 'Did they waste any thanks or sympathy for Adam?'

'He didn't do it for a reward,' Benoît said quietly. 'He did it because several of his French relatives died on the guillotine—and they weren't aristocrats. He hates the new regime more than most but I think he's had his fill of spying now. It goes against the grain with him. He's done some good work in the past, more than sufficient to earn him an honourable retirement. I doubt if he'll go back.'

'But you will,' Angelica whispered, feeling a shadow of fear, despite the bright sunlight.

'For Harry? Of course,' Benoît said calmly.

Angelica closed her eyes, finally confronted with the true magnitude of the task she had asked Benoît to perform.

She was bitterly torn by her love for her brother and her love for Benoît. She wanted to tell him not to go—but if she did that she was afraid she was sealing Harry's fate. She knew her brother would never wait patiently in a French prison. At the first opportunity he would make another escape attempt—and next time he might be killed.

She gripped her hands tightly in her lap, unable to speak, because nothing she could say would help. She knew better than to suppose Benoît would break his word because she was afraid for him. He would keep his promise to the Earl, and to her, no matter what it cost him.

She felt him cover her hands with his own, and opened her eyes, looking at him with a strained, tense expression.

'Don't be afraid,' he said softly. 'I will bring Harry safely back to you.'

'I can't help it,' she whispered. 'I am so frightened for both of you. I never saw the danger so clearly before. When I think how I tried to force you—if anything happened to you...'

'You didn't force me into this,' said Benoît gently.

He squeezed her hand reassuringly, then reached up to wrap a glowing curl around his finger.

'I made a promise to your father years ago,' he reminded her. 'Even if you hadn't brought the letter to Sussex yourself, I would still have rescued Harry. But I would never have met you.'

'I'm not sorry I came.' Angelica tried to smile. 'I just wish I could go to France with you.'

'I know.' He stroked her cheek. 'Waiting is always the hardest part. I've never relished it myself. But we will come safely home, don't ever doubt it.'

'I won't.' Angelica took a deep breath, trying to banish her anxieties. They served no useful purpose, and they only clouded the time she had with Benoît.

They had not discussed the future, but she felt more than ever now that they would share it.

'Did you see Papa?' she asked after a moment. 'Benoît, what is it?' she said sharply, as she saw a flicker in his eyes. 'Is Papa ill?'

'No,' he said instantly, 'far from it! But I didn't speak to the Earl—he'd left London before I arrived.'

'*What?*' Angelica could hardly believe it.

Her father hadn't left his town house since the accident.

'I understand that neither your letter, nor mine, reached him,' said Benoît. 'I don't know what happened to my messenger.' A flicker of concern glowed briefly in his eyes. 'Simpson's an old sailor. He's served with me for the past five years. He's utterly loyal. I hope he hasn't come to harm.'

For a moment Benoît's eyes remained clouded as he thought of his friend and servant, then he focused on Angelica's face. 'The Earl is at Holly House now,' he said quietly.

'*Here?*' Angelica gripped Benoît's hand convulsively. Not for an instant had she considered the possibility that the Earl might follow her. 'Have you spoken to him?'

'Not yet,' Benoît replied. 'I realised he was ahead of me when I was on the road. He probably arrived last night. He's come after you, and I thought the sooner he found you the better—so I didn't delay.'

'Oh, my God!' Angelica felt almost sick with anxiety and guilt.

What fear or anger had driven the Earl to leave

the security of his home after being secluded there
for more than eighteen months?

'He must be so worried about me,' she whispered.
'I should have gone home straight away. Oh, God!
What have I done?'

'He will surely understand you had doubts about
me,' said Benoît bracingly. 'As I remember, he is not
the kind of man to accept another man's opinion
without question. Your actions were entirely natural
in the circumstances.'

'I suppose so,' said Angelica doubtfully.

She was still stunned by the fact that the Earl had
travelled all the way into Sussex when he had refused
point black to go anywhere by carriage since his
accident.

'I never thought he'd leave the house again,' she
said wonderingly. 'I kept trying to make him go out,
but he wouldn't. Perhaps. . .' A smile suddenly lit up
her eyes. 'Perhaps his nightmares have receded and
he's no longer so afraid of the outside world. Perhaps
he didn't realise it until I came into Sussex. He used
to like visiting Sir William.'

'I mentioned his arrival to Sir William,' said
Benoît. 'I expect he will call later, when he has
arranged for Adam's transportation.'

'Yes. Papa would like that,' said Angelica eagerly.
'He's very fond of Sir William. Let's not waste any
more time, Benoît. Papa will be so pleased to know
you're going to rescue Harry.'

CHAPTER EIGHT

DESPITE her brave words, Angelica felt extremely apprehensive when the curricle drew up outside Holly House. She let Benoît help her down from the curricle, then lifted an instinctive hand to touch her golden curls.

Benoît smiled at her gesture.

'You've obviously been practising your skills,' he said humorously. 'I'm not sure what Martha would say, but to my untutored eye you look charming.'

Angelica blushed self-consciously.

'Thank you,' she said.

Then her smile faded, an expression of elusive sadness flickering over her face.

'I don't know why I'm concerned,' she said quietly. 'Papa won't see.'

She turned her head as Mrs Faulkener came out of the house to meet them. The Frenchwoman's expression was quite calm, but her eyes were strained and worried as she looked at Angelica.

'The Earl is in the library,' she said softly. 'His secretary is with him. They've been here since late last night. He is not. . .very happy.'

Angelica looked sharply at Mrs Faulkener, hearing the undertones of stress in her voice. She had a feeling it would take a great deal to ruffle the Frenchwoman, but the Earl had clearly succeeded.

215

'He's angry?' said Angelica flatly, needing no further explanation.

Lord Ellewood's displays of temper were never a pleasant experience for anyone.

'Yes,' said Mrs Faulkener simply.

Angelica pressed her lips together in a firm, resolute line, and walked into the house to confront her father.

The Earl turned his head sharply when he heard the library door open. The secretary leapt to his feet.

'Who's there?' Lord Ellewood demanded harshly.

He was a gaunt, ravaged shadow of the man who had once met Benoît on the seashore. He was still tall and rigidly upright, but his fair hair was prematurely white—and the darkened spectacles he wore could not hide the ugly scars on his face. There were deep lines around his mouth, his expression was hard, anxious and angry. His bitterness and frustration at what had happened to him were almost palpable, even submerged as they were by his more immediate fear for Angelica.

If he hadn't known who the Earl was, Benoît wouldn't have recognised him. Despite everything Angelica had said, he was momentarily shocked into silence by his old opponent's altered appearance.

'It's me, Papa,' said Angelica calmly.

'*Angelica!*' Lord Ellewood heaved himself to his feet. His secretary offered him a well-meaning hand and he struck it furiously aside. 'Come here!'

She went to him, stretching out her hands towards him. He groped blindly before him, found her wrist and seized it in a painful, vice-like grasp.

'Are you safe, girl?' he asked fiercely.

He was standing near the window; the scars on his face were livid in the bright sunlight as he turned his empty eyes towards her. He kept hold of her wrist in an almost brutal grip and ran his other hand rapidly up her arm to her shoulder.

'*Are you harmed?*' He shook her roughly back and forth in the ferocity of his anxiety.

'No, Papa!' Angelica cried out sharply, feeling a stab of pain at the bitter fear she had caused him. She reached out instinctively to reassure him. 'I'm quite all right.'

For a single heart-beat the terrible intensity of emotion in the Earl's face relaxed. It was possible to see in the ruins of his once handsome features the man who had chosen not to denounce Benoît—but then his expression darkened.

He released Angelica as violently as he had grabbed her; thrusting her away from him so forcefully that she stumbled back and would have fallen if Benoît hadn't caught her.

'I'm *sorry*—' she began—but the Earl's angry voice overrode her attempted apology.

'How dare you flout my orders?' Lord Ellewood snarled. 'Do you think I'm soft-headed as well as blind? What kind of daughter have I bred? A liar and a coward! Not worthy of the name she bears! By God! I'm glad to be spared the sight of you now!'

His lips were drawn back in an ugly grimace, his tone full of cruel, unmerciful contempt. His words had been intended to wound as deeply as possible—and they found their mark.

'No! *Papa!*' Angelica cried out in horror.

She had seen his rage before, many times, but this was the first time it had ever been directed entirely at her. She had known he would be angry with her, but she hadn't guessed he would be so unforgivingly, corrosively furious.

'Hargreaves!' The Earl turned his grim, sightless head towards his secretary.

'Here, my lord.' The young man leapt forward instantly, almost knocking over the wooden globe in his anxiety to obey.

'You are dismissed,' said Lord Ellewood harshly. 'Now that my daughter has returned—inadequate though she is—I no longer have any need for a secretary who connives behind my back and cannot be trusted to obey a simple order. *Get out!*'

Mr Hargreaves's face was bleached with shock and confusion. He opened his mouth to protest, turned to Angelica in mute appeal, then stumbled out of the room without saying a word.

'You can't do that!' Angelica protested hotly, appalled at her father's injustice. 'It was *my* fault, not his. *I* decided to bring the letter. You *can't* punish him for my fault.'

'He should not have disobeyed me,' the Earl said unrelentingly, his voice grating painfully on Angelica's ears. 'I will not be served by disloyal men.'

'But—'

'Silence!' Lord Ellewood roared savagely. 'I can banish Hargreaves—*your* disloyalty I must live with!'

Angelica stared at the Earl. Her face was drained of all colour, both hands were pressed against her mouth. She knew that her father's vengeful anger stemmed mainly from his fear for her and his overwhelming sense of helplessness—but that didn't make it any easier to bear.

She felt Benoît come to stand beside her and she glanced up at him, recognising the intent, watchful expression in his brown eyes. The wolf in him had been roused.

'My lord,' he said coldly, his quiet, even tones in stark contrast to the Earl's ungovernable ranting. 'I am sorry that you have had such a disturbing few days, but you have no cause to abuse Lady Angelica so. She did not intend to worry you—and her motives were unimpeachable.'

'Who's there?' Lord Ellewood flung up his head, almost like a hound sniffing the wind. 'Who are you?'

'Benoît Faulkener.' He approached the Earl.

The two men were much of a height: tall and broad-shouldered. But the Earl's body was wasted with pain and inactivity, his movements clumsy and awkward.

Benoît moved with the lean, controlled grace of a panther: silent, wary—and potentially dangerous.

The Earl stood listening tensely to Benoît's soft-footed approach, his hands trembling with furious, impotent energy.

Angelica caught her breath as she watched the two men. The difference between them revealed her father's ruin more brutally than ever. She could remember when he had been as assured and relaxed as Benoît.

'Yes, I should have guessed,' said Lord Ellewood

bitterly. 'I remember your voice. An arrogant, insolent knave. I should have known better than to take you at your word. *What have you done to my daughter?* Why wasn't she here when I arrived?'

Angelica gasped. The Earl had been so angry about her secretive departure from London she'd almost forgotten she had anything else to explain to him. The nightmarish situation was getting worse and worse, and she could think of nothing to say to abate her father's fury—no excuse for her behaviour.

But she was also growing angry herself, and she experienced a wild desire not to explain anything to the Earl. She couldn't believe he had treated Mr Hargreaves so cruelly, dragging him all the way to Sussex only to dismiss him at the moment of her arrival.

'Lady Angelica was quite safe,' said Benoît calmly.

His dark eyes were intent on the Earl's face. He was standing very still, poised and alert. There was a coiled, deadly spring of energy within him, but as yet he had made no attempt to engage the Earl's fury.

'Where was she?'

'This morning she was with Sir William Hopwood,' said Benoît evenly. 'Last night she spent the night at an inn in Littlehampton. I think the only hardship she had to endure was a certain amount of boredom. She has come to no harm, my lord.'

For a few moments the only sound in the library was the harsh, angry sound of the Earl's breathing. His chest rose and fell as he tried to master his seething fury. Angelica stared at him, white-faced; her hands were clenched together so tightly that her nails dug into her palms.

Even now, she could not imagine what it must be like for her father, unable to see where he was, or how many people confronted him, forced to judge their intentions and sincerity purely by the sound of their voices.

She knew that many blind people found ways of adapting to their handicap, but the Earl was not among their number. His memories of his former prowess were very vivid, and he was too bitter and impatient to learn new skills—yet he was also too young and too active to be content with a life spent confined within four walls. His anger seemed always to be roiling just beneath the surface, ready to scald anyone who inadvertently caused it to erupt.

'Have the carriage prepared,' the Earl ordered tautly. 'We are leaving. I want nothing further to do with this house or the people in it. I am sorry I ever thought of writing to you,' he added savagely.

'I'm sorry my messenger didn't reach you two days ago,' said Benoît equably. 'I replied to your letter immediately. Her ladyship also wrote to you to explain her delay. If you had received those letters, my lord, you would have been spared a great deal of needless anxiety. I have every intention of rescuing Lord Lennard.'

The Earl gave a brief, derisive, insulting laugh.

'Your fine words come too late,' he said scornfully. 'My son does not need the help of a presumptuous jackanapes! And I'll not leave my daughter in this house another minute! Your own actions betray you, cur! I should have had you flogged when I had the chance. Angelica! Order them to put the horses to!'

Benoît's eyes narrowed. He had been keeping a

firm grip on his temper, partly for Angelica's sake, and partly because he could imagine the torment the Earl must have been in when he didn't know where his daughter was. But there were limits to his tolerance.

'Whether you wish it or not, I will help Lord Lennard,' he said, an icy, dangerous edge on his soft controlled voice. 'I do not forget my obligations. Nor will I stoop to barter insults with you. You are free to leave when you wish—but Angelica can choose for herself whether she goes with you. I suggest you speak to her more courteously, my lord! Neither her love for you nor her loyalty can be questioned—*but I will not allow anyone to abuse her!*'

Angelica stared, wide-eyed at Benoît, some of her anxiety dissipating in pure astonishment. He was as furious as the Earl. His lean, dark face was rigid with barely-controlled anger, and she could sense the fierce tension in his whipcord body.

'*You* won't allow. . .!' The Earl's scarred face was black with uncontrollable rage. 'A swaggering dunghill cock! I'll destroy you! How dare you interfere! My daughter—'

'May shortly be my wife!' Benoît interrupted curtly. 'Your threats hold no fear for me, my lord. I will not compel Angelica to stay—though it might make it easier for her if I did—but she deserves better than to be forced to share the barren hell you seem to have made of your own life!'

Angelica's heart thudded with amazement, joy and distress. She had wondered if Benoît would ask her to marry him, but in the end there had been no proposal only a flat statement to her father. She was overwhelmed by an almost unbearable maelstrom of conflicting emotions as she glanced from Benoît's rigid face to her father's.

The Earl lifted his head, shocked out of his ranting fury into some deeper, darker emotion by Benoît's words.

'Angelica!'

She didn't immediately answer, and he stretched out a demanding, unforgiving hand in her direction.

'Come here!'

Angelica stared at his hand for a few, heart-stopping seconds. His gesture was terrible in its fierce, unmerciful authority. She took two, horrified steps backwards, away from her father, and looked up at Benoît. His expression was intent and uncompromising.

'Is that the life you want to lead?' he asked ruthlessly.

'I. . .' Her voice failed her and she shook her head in a desperate attempt to deny everything that had just happened.

'By God! You'll pay for this!' The Earl raged. 'A smuggling weasel to lay hands on my daughter! *Angelica!*'

He took an unwary step towards her, stumbled into the globe and lost his balance. He struggled wildly for a moment, then crashed to the floor. The globe landed partially on top of him. He cursed viciously and flailed at it, smashing his fist into the object which had betrayed him.

At the sight of her father, fighting with the globe like a madman, Angelica's composure finally broke.

She fled out of the library, wrenched open the front door and stumbled out of the house.

The Earl lay on the floor, his energy spent. He was angry, afraid — and humiliated. Above all else he felt humiliated, and his sense of degradation made him vicious. At that moment he was beyond reason. He felt the globe being lifted away from him and he tensed, ready to lash out, but nobody touched him. Benoît set the globe on its feet a safe distance from Lord Ellewood and walked out of the library without a word.

Lord Ellewood heard the door close. He lay still, his anger-crazed mind beginning to clear. He was not even sure if he was alone, but he could hear no sound except his own harsh breathing.

A log collapsed, hissing in the hearth and he turned his head sharply towards the sound.

'Who's there?' he demanded fiercely — but nobody answered.

At last his rigid muscles relaxed and he pushed himself up onto his knees, groping clumsily around him. He was in a strange room. He had no idea where any of the furniture was, or what obstacles lay before him.

His hand encountered a shard of glass, and he snatched it back. He had lost his spectacles in the fall and now they were broken, crushed by the heavy globe. His finger was cut and he sucked it painfully, a bitter, childish wreck of a once proud man.

But his pride would not allow him to remain huddled on the floor. They would come back, and he must be ready. He would get out of here — and then he would destroy the smugglers' whelp-turned-upstart shipowner.

He felt about more cautiously, and crawled across the floor until he bumped into the edge of a chair. He hauled himself up into it and dragged in several rasping breaths. His white hair was dishevelled, but his tragic, livid face was as set and unyielding as a teak mask.

Angelica ran blindly across the lawn, stumbling over her skirts in her unthinking attempt to get away from her father. She tripped and fell headlong, lying among the broken daffodils beneath an old oak tree. She'd been winded by the fall, and she made no effort to get up again. She rested her head on her arms and drew in deep, shuddering breaths.

Her father's unforgiving, uncontrollable rage had torn her apart. She hated to see him like this—a tragic mockery of his former self. Sometimes she thought it would have been better if he had died when the carriage overturned.

She closed her eyes, trying to calm her churning emotions, and slowly became aware of the sharp smell of broken daffodil stems beneath her arms. She could feel the damp grass beneath her cheek, and there was a robin singing a liquid melody in the branches of the oak tree above her. It all seemed quite unreal to her.

She didn't hear Benoît's footsteps, but she was instantly aware of his presence beside her. She didn't raise her head, but she felt his hand on her shoulder, then he lifted her to her feet.

She looked up at him, her eyes large and hollow

in her pale face. He returned her gaze quietly, profound, penetrating concern in his dark eyes. She was dimly aware of the tension in his lean body, but she was too preoccupied by her own feelings to pay much attention to his.

'I keep hoping things will get better,' she said wearily. 'But they won't, will they? The Papa I used to know has gone. You were right. He *was* a fine man. But now...' Her voice trailed away into hopelessness.

'Now he's had to endure more than three helpless days of worrying about you,' said Benoît, almost matter-of-factly.

Angelica was jolted out of her gathering despair by his unexpected comment.

'Are you blaming *me* for what happened?' she demanded, in surprised disbelief.

'No,' he said immediately. 'Come and sit down.'

Angelica resisted his guiding hand. She was staring at him with doubt, and a hint of rebellion, in her blue eyes.

'I wasn't criticising you,' he said quietly. 'I don't believe you have anything to reproach yourself with.'

'How generous of you!' Angelica snapped, swinging away from him, her latent anger with her father finding a ready outlet. '*You* are not the arbiter of my conduct. You have no *idea*—' She broke off abruptly, biting her lip.

She hadn't cried earlier, but now she felt close to tears.

Benoît looked at her searchingly.

'No, I don't,' he replied, more curtly than he usually spoke. 'Despite what you'd said, I wasn't prepared for such a profound change in the Earl. Are such episodes commonplace?'

'Not. . .exactly,' said Angelica unsteadily, turning slightly away from Benoît.

She reached out and touched the rough bark of the tree trunk, almost as if she was seeking comfort from its solidity.

After a moment Benoît covered her hand with his. She felt the warm pressure of his fingers and looked up, blinking back her tears.

'He *hates* his blindness,' she said, her words tumbling over each other as she finally voiced her anguish. 'He *hates* his helplessness, and he *loathes* being dependent on others. He has become cruel and vengeful. He lashes out at the slightest provocation. He's had more than a dozen valets since his accident! Poor Mr Hargreaves—' She broke off, her voice strangled by a sob.

'We'll worry about poor Mr Hargreaves later,' said Benoît firmly. 'Does he lash out at you?'

'Sometimes. Never like today.' Her voice caught on a sob as she struggled not to burst into tears. 'Perhaps he's right. I *was* a coward when I didn't tell him myself I was coming—but I couldn't face an argument with him.'

'Harry's safety was your priority,' said Benoît reasonably. 'You can't blame yourself for putting his interests first. You've put your father first for a long time.'

'He *needed* me,' she said brokenly.

She looked up at Benoît, her pain and sense of betrayal nakedly exposed in her blue, tear-filled eyes.

She had tried so hard to take care of the Earl since his accident. She had turned her back on her own life and friends when he'd made it plain he didn't want strangers around him. She had endured his impatience and lack of gratitude without complaint and in the end she had been desperate for Harry to return home to them.

Harry was always jolly and lively. Harry could cheer anyone up. She had pinned her hopes on the possibility that he might be able to conjure Lord Ellewood out of his black, despairing moods. She was miserably aware of her own failure to do so.

But now her love and devotion had been rewarded by anger and cruel recriminations. Her father's rage had been out of all proportion with her offence. How could he have accused her of such dreadful things? He'd even said he was *glad* he could no longer see her!

She could hear still hear his grating voice as he heaped reproaches on her stricken head.

Liar. . . Coward. . . Not worthy of the name you bear.

Was that what he really *believed*?

'How *can* he not know I did it for his sake, as well as Harry's?' she whispered bitterly. 'I've never been disloyal to him. *Never*! I thought—if only Harry came home. . .I knew it couldn't go on. It's been so. . .*killing*!'

'Yes, I see,' said Benoît slowly. 'What are you going to do now?'

'What do you mean?' Angelica swung round to face him, a startled question in her eyes as she wondered if he was retracting his earlier words in the library. 'You said. . .'

'And I meant it,' Benoît assured her softly. 'Although I hadn't intended to raise the subject in such a blunt way.' He paused, looking down at her with quiet intensity and she felt her heart skip a beat. 'Will you marry me, Angelica?' he asked, his voice very deep.

She gazed up into his warm brown eyes, seeing in them the love and support which she needed so much. She had never dreamt that he would propose to her under such circumstances. The joy and excitement she had anticipated feeling at this moment were inevitably muted by the situation—but not her love for Benoît. The burden of anxiety she had been carrying for so long seemed to grow lighter as she realised how willing he was to share it with her. She sighed with deeply felt happiness.

'Yes,' she said simply. 'Oh, yes. I will.'

Benoît smiled, his usually guarded eyes blazing with triumphant love. He reached out to take her in his arms and she felt the tension leave his lean body. She suddenly realised how difficult he must have found the scene in the library. His debt to the Earl and his desire to protect her from Lord Ellewood's anger must have torn him in two different directions—just as Lord Ellewood's black moods had been tearing her apart for so long.

She put her arms around him and hugged him fiercely, thanking him wordlessly for his understanding, his love and his support. His hold on her tightened, and for a moment she was content to stand within the circle of his embrace—but she could not forget her father, still waiting in the house. Until she had achieved some kind of reconciliation with Lord Ellewood she could not truly contemplate the future.

'What do you want to do?' Benoît asked at last.

'I don't know.' Angelica lifted her head and looked at him, seeing from his expression how well he understood her conflicting emotions. 'I'm not sure if I can face talking to Papa again right now,' she admitted with bleak honesty.

'He travelled all the way from London to find you,' Benoît reminded her gently. 'You said yourself he'd never left the house before—'

'Because he was *angry* with me!' Angelica interrupted bitterly. 'I'd hoped it wasn't so, but—'

'He was also afraid for you,' Benoît reminded her. 'His first words were to ask if you were safe. He's had no choice but confront his handicap these past few days, *mon aimée*, and that can't have been easy for him. I don't imagine he's had much sleep since you left either. When he's had time to calm down, you may find he's much more rational.'

'Perhaps.' Angelica bit her lip irresolutely.

She knew that there was probably a great deal of truth in what Benoît said; but she still felt hurt, betrayed and disappointed. There had been too many times when Lord Ellewood had spoken crossly to her when she'd only been trying to help. Too many times when he'd taken his frustration out on those around him, and she'd been helpless to intervene. Mr Hargreaves was only the last of a long line of people who'd suffered from the Earl's lack of tolerance.

All the small, daily frustrations and disillusionments of the past eighteen months melded together to create a core of revolt in her heart. She didn't want to go back to her father—to apologise, explain and try to make amends. She was tired of trying. It was his turn now.

She looked back at Benoît and he read her thoughts in her unguarded, almost defiant blue eyes.

She didn't have to go back to see the Earl if she didn't want to. She no longer had to explain anything to her father—and she could be as stubborn as Lord Ellewood when she chose.

Benoît smiled faintly.

'I've noticed a distinct family resemblance between you before,' he remarked dryly. 'If I were in your shoes, *mon amour*, I would feel angry and resentful—and very hurt. But it may still be worth trying to talk to him.'

Angelica sighed, glancing towards the house, wondering what her father was doing now. She knew Benoît was right. She had to try to make peace with the Earl. If she didn't, she would never forgive herself.

'Yes, I know,' she said. 'I'll talk to him.' There'd never really been any question that she would do so, but she'd needed a few minutes to collect her courage and her resolution. 'I was so surprised and pleased when you told me he'd left London,' she added, with resolute optimisim. 'Perhaps things *will* be different now.'

The Earl didn't know how long he'd been sitting in the library when he heard low voices in the hall. He had experienced a frightening kaleidoscope of emotions during his long, dark isolation, but now he was bored and impatient. He was used to being obeyed instantly—being ignored was a new experience.

He couldn't leave the library because he wasn't prepared to go stumbling around a strange house, his helplessness plain for everyone to see—but he hated not knowing what was going on. He didn't know where Angelica was. He didn't know what Benoît was doing and his volatile temper had begun to stir again.

He turned his head as the door opened.

'Who's there?' he demanded fiercely.

'Henry! *Old friend!*' Sir William strode across the room and seized the Earl's hand before Lord Ellewood could react. 'I'm so glad I haven't missed you. I came as soon as I heard you were here!'

He shook the Earl's hand warmly between both of his. The pleasure in his voice was unmistakable. If he was shocked by his old friend's appearance his cordial tones didn't betray it.

'William?' said Lord Ellewood, almost tentatively. He had forgotten Benoît's reference to the magistrate and he was taken completely by surprise by Sir William's arrival.

'"Blunderbuss Billy", more like!' Sir William gave a crack of self-deprecating laughter. 'Dammit! I was sorry to hear about Harry—though it sounds as if he's more than a chip off the old block. Gave the Frogs a good run for their money by all accounts!'

He pulled up a chair beside the Earl and sat down.

'How do you know about Harry?' Lord Ellewood demanded, frowning.

'Angelica told me. By George she's turned into a fine young woman,' said Sir William enthusiastically. ' Gave me a rare dressing-down for trying to discuss family business in public. I had no idea you knew young Faulkener. If anyone can get Harry out of France, he can!'

The Earl bit back a hasty retort. He wanted to deny all knowledge of Benoît, but he had sufficient control of his temper to realise that it wouldn't be wise. Whatever Angelica had been doing in Sussex over the past three days, she had been with Benoît Faulkener. It would not do her reputation any good if her father publicly denounced him.

'I met him several years ago,' he said shortly. 'Where did you see Angelica?'

'At the inn, in Littlehampton,' Sir William replied, sounding surprised. 'It's a pity you didn't send her to me, she would have been much more comfortable waiting for Adam at the Manor. *That* was a surprise, by God! I thought the boy was dead! You needn't worry about him though. I've got him safe at the Manor—and no Froggie agents will have a chance to pig-stick him there.'

'*Adam?*' A variety of unreadable expressions chased each other across the Earl's ravaged face.

'Young Kennett.' Sir William nodded vigorously. 'An excellent choice to bring you that letter. I take it you know its contents by now? Of course, Angelica wouldn't delay in telling you. But Adam's led me some fine dances over the years,' he continued almost indulgently. 'Do you remember that night we went hunting for smugglers? Adam told me in the carriage only today that he'd been the fox who led me so far astray. And you came back without your horse that morning. You never did explain how that happened! What days those were!'

'Yes.' Despite himself, the Earl sighed.

'Well, now that you're in Sussex, I'll be offended if you don't come to stay with me at the Manor,' said Sir William gruffly. 'Been trying to get you down here again for years!'

'You are very kind,' said the Earl, his tone unintentionally cold. 'But I'm afraid I must disappoint you. Angelica and I are returning to town immediately.'

'Nonsense!' Sir William exclaimed forcefully. 'You've only just arrived. Besides, I'm sure you'll want to talk to Adam. Get the news straight from the horse's mouth as it were! I wonder what Faulkener's got in mind? It's a pity Adam's so badly knocked up or they could have tackled it together.'

The Earl hesitated. He still felt extremely hostile to Benoît, and he was fiercely anxious to return to the security and familiarity of his own home. On the other hand, there was something unaccountably pleasant about the magistrate's explosive company. Apart from anything else, he still retained his remarkable ability to supply both sides of the conversation.

Besides, it was becoming glaringly apparent to the Earl that Sir William was almost as much in the dark about recent events as he was.

The magistrate believed that Adam Kennett—whoever the devil he was—had brought James

Corbett's letter to England. Whereas Lord Ellewood knew for a fact that that was not the case—so who was Kennett? And why had he apparently been injured by the French?

The Earl's hunting instincts were aroused. If Angelica wouldn't tell him the truth—he blocked out the thought that he hadn't given her much opportunity to do so—he would find it out for himself. They would see there was life in the blind old dog yet.

'I'd hate to disappoint an old friend,' he said, tacitly accepting Sir William's invitation.

'Good man!' Sir William bounded to his feet, landing an exuberant buffet on the Earl's shoulder.

'I'll have them prepare your gear at once. By heaven! This will be a day to remember!'

'I believe it will,' Lord Ellewood said, smiling for the first time in several days.

For the past eighteen months everyone he'd met had treated him as if he was not only blind, but also extremely frail. Sir William's thoughtless ebullience was oddly gratifying.

'*Papa! How could you?*' Angelica burst into the library.

Her cheeks were burning with colour, her eyes blazing with fierce, uncompromising anger.

'Angelica?' Lord Ellewood hauled himself instinctively to his feet.

'How *could* you dismiss Martha?' she demanded, her voice throbbing with furious indignation. 'How *could* you stoop to such a thing? To punish her for her *loyalty*! This morning you dismissed Mr Hargreaves for his *disloyalty*!'

'She has shown no loyalty to me,' said Lord Ellewood gratingly.

'She's *my* maid!' Angelica exclaimed passionately. 'Would you have had any respect for her if she'd betrayed *my* trust?'

'Respect?' the Earl snarled. 'She's a damned servant! As long as I pay her wages she'll obey my will! I will not tolerate defiance in *any* member of my household.'

Angelica stared at him, her chest rising and falling in quick, angry breaths. She could sense her father's volcanic temper was about to erupt, but she no longer cared. His treatment of Martha had goaded her beyond caution. The small spark of revolt she had suppressed earlier had now been fanned into blazing flames of rebellion by what she'd just discovered.

She and Benoît had returned to the house to find that Sir William was sitting with the Earl. Angelica had immediately decided to delay speaking to her father until he was alone. Benoît had agreed, and she'd seized the opportunity to go up to her bedchamber for a few moments of quiet reflection.

But Martha had been waiting for her, and one glance at her maid's face had been enough to tell Angelica that things were badly wrong.

Lord Ellewood had arrived at Holly House in the early hours of the morning, and he'd instantly had Martha hauled out of bed and dragged before him. He'd subjected her to an even worse ordeal than

Angelica had suffered later—and it had culminated in the maid's dismissal.

As far as Angelica could tell, Martha had remained stoically loyal to her mistress throughout, refusing to reveal more than the barest minimum of information. Angelica was bitterly aware of how much anxiety she had caused Martha, and she couldn't forgive herself for putting the maid in such an impossible situation.

But nor could she forgive the Earl for venting his fury on such a powerless victim.

'Then you may soon have no household left,' she said bleakly, the white heat of her anger dying as she confronted her father across the library floor. 'I understand you dismissed your valet before you left London. Today you have discharged Mr Hargreaves and Martha. You told me once I should judge a man's character on the way he is viewed by his servants not his peers.'

She paused.

There was no sound in the room except Lord Ellewood's rasping breath and the soft, measured tick of the clock. His head was flung up, his sightless eyes turned towards Angelica, but he did not speak. Though she did not know it, her words had struck a wounding blow. The Earl was already ashamed of his treatment of Martha, but he was far too angry to admit it.

Lord Ellewood had been alone when Angelica had thrown open the library door, but now she was dimly aware that there were people standing behind her. She ignored them. All her attention was concentrated on her father.

'I'm sorry I left London without telling you,' she said steadily. 'I'm sorry I exposed Mr Hargreaves and Martha to your wrath. I won't forgive myself for that. But, Papa, if I'd thought you would listen or understand, I would have *told* you why I had to deliver your letter myself—and if you'd told me what you must have known about Benoît I wouldn't have needed to.'

'*Told* me?' the Earl said harshly. 'Who the *devil* do you think you're talking to, girl?'

'I don't know,' said Angelica flatly. 'Certainly not the father I remember. Goodbye, Papa.'

'What do you mean?' Lord Ellewood's expression darkened. He was breathing heavily.

'I mean I will not be returning to London with you,' she said, with wintry finality. 'You will have to find someone else to sit in the dark and read to you while the rest of the world goes dancing by.'

She turned on her heel and walked out of the library without waiting for his reply. Benoît stepped crisply aside to let her pass. Sir William simply stared at her in open-mouthed astonishment.

'*Angelica!*' Lord Ellewood roared.

She put her foot on the first tread of the stairs and began to walk slowly upwards.

'*Angelica!*'

She didn't pause, or even look around. There was no colour left in her cheeks, but her lips were pressed resolutely together. She had made her decision and she would not be swayed—certainly not by Lord Ellewood's unreasoning anger.

'She will not come for such a summons,' said Benoît quietly.

He closed the library door and turned to study the Earl thoughtfully. Sir William was still standing silently, staring from one to the other with a mixture of bewilderment and appalled disbelief on his face.

'This is your doing!' Lord Ellewood accused Benoît savagely. 'You've polluted her mind with your insidious—'

'I've never been called insidious before,' Benoît interrupted coldly. 'If you believe I've turned Angelica against you, then you are mistaken. You seem to be doing very well without my help!'

'I'll *never* consent to her marrying you!' Lord Ellewood ground out.

He was shaking with fury, his hands clenched convulsively, but he had himself rigidly under control. He had no intention of humiliating himself again. He didn't risk taking even a single step towards Benoît.

'We don't need your consent,' said Benoît equably. 'Angelica is twenty-three years old. She can make up her own mind.'

'I'll disown her!' said Lord Ellewood wildly. 'She'll get nothing from me. Not a single penny.'

'She doesn't need your money,' said Benoît coldly. 'I am quite capable of supporting a wife. Your respect is much more important to her. Whatever she's done, she did out of love for you and Lord Lennard—but you've treated her worse than you did an insolent smugglers' whelp who held you at gunpoint!'

'Don't lecture me, sir!' the Earl blared. 'I will not leave Angelica in this house with you. Where's Hopwood?'

'H-here.' Sir William stumbled over his answer, too shocked to be coherent.

Lord Ellewood dragged in a deep, searing breath and then he hesitated. The library was filled with his fierce tension as he stood stock-still, battling with his powerful emotions.

He'd intended to order the magistrate to fetch Angelica back. He'd intended to drag her, kicking and screaming if need be, away from Holly House.

But he didn't.

He lifted his ravaged, scarred head like a proud old lion, and said with frozen dignity, 'It seems that my daughter will not be accompanying us to the Manor, William. I believe there is no longer any need to delay our departure.'

Sir William swallowed. He was still trying to catch up with events. He looked desperately from Lord Ellewood's rigid face to Benoît's wolf-wary, watchful expression.

'I'll see if the carriage is ready,' he said hastily. For once in his life he had no stomach for taking part in a melodramatic scene.

'You're still there,' Lord Ellewood stated flatly, as the door closed behind the magistrate.

'Yes, my lord.'

'Yes,' the Earl repeated, the single word dropping into the silence of the library like a stone.

Lord Ellewood listened with all his might, but even so he could hear no indication of Benoît's presence—not even his breathing. He might have been talking to a shadow—or fighting a shadow. No man could defeat a shadow.

'If I could still see, you would never get away with this!' he said savagely.

'If you could still see, you would *nevertheless* have asked for my help to rescue Lord Lennard,' said Benoît coolly, 'because I have connections which are not available to most men. But, if you could still see, you would not be so eaten up with frustration and envy that you're blind to the practical good sense of what you've done. Harry will be safe with me, my lord. So will Angelica—and you know it.'

'I have the promise of a smuggling cur for that?' the Earl jeered sarcastically.

'You have *my* promise,' Benoît said, a note of steely assurance underpinning his unemphatic reply.

'I believe your carriage is waiting. *Au revoir*, my lord. I am sure we will meet again.'

CHAPTER NINE

ANGELICA and Benoît were married the following afternoon by Special Licence. Angelica wore the same ivory satin gown she had worn to dinner at Holly House three nights before. She stood in a shaft of sunlight from the alter window of a small London church, her golden hair framing her face like a halo, and made her vows in a firm, confident voice.

There were no friends or relatives in attendance. But it didn't matter because, as Martha pointed out when she was dressing Angelica, the only person a bride really needs to be present at her wedding is the groom.

'You followed me all the way from London to deliver these letters?' the Earl demanded gratingly.

'Yes, my lord.' Benoît's messenger stood tiredly in front of Lord Ellewood. 'Captain Faulkener bade me deliver them directly into your own hand—but I was waylaid near Epsom.'

'Attacked?' said Lord Ellewood sharply.

'Yes, my lord.'

Simpson held his right arm stiffly, and there was a rough bandage around his head. The Earl could not see the man's hurts, but he could hear the cracked strain in his voice.

'What happened?'

'They knocked me cold and took my horse. I don't

remember much, but I was told they were searching me when they were frightened off. Otherwise I expect they would have taken the letters.'

Simpson fell silent. He was bone-weary and ached in every fibre of his being. He had discharged his duty, and now he longed for nothing more than a chance to lie down and sleep.

'And when you were fit to ride you carried on to London,' said Sir William, involving himself in the conversation for the first time, 'and when Lord Ellewood wasn't there you followed him back to Sussex, and then from Holly House to here. When you discovered his destination, didn't it occur to you that there was no longer any need to deliver the letters?'

'No, sir.' Simpson straightened his shoulders. 'The Captain gave me strict instructions. He would not expect me to fail in carrying out his orders.'

'Thank you,' said Lord Ellewood distantly. 'Your dedication to duty is commendable.'

He held the two letters between his fingers. They were creased and dirty, but the seals were still unbroken. He wondered if he had the courage to ask Sir William to read them to him. He put them in his pocket, fumbling a little as he did so.

'You poor fellow! You must be exhausted!' Sir William sprang to his feet as Simpson's shoulders slumped lower. 'Come with me.' He clapped the seaman on the back, making him stagger. 'You must have a good meal and a long rest before you go back to Holly House. Your master's not there at present, so there's no hurry. Your devotion deserves a fat reward. Be sure I'll tell him so when I see him.'

'Oh, no,' said Simpson, his speech a trifle slurred. 'The Captain knows I don't serve him for reward. We've been halfway round the world together. I'd never—'

His legs buckled under him, and he would have fallen if Sir William hadn't seized him.

Lord Ellewood sat quietly, listening to the magistrate bellow for his servants to bustle about and take care of Benoît's exhausted messenger. He was thinking of Angelica's bitter reminder that he had once told her the truest judge of a man's character was his own servant.

Angelica spent her wedding night at a coaching inn just south of London. Benoit normally stayed with his partner, Josiah Crabtree, when he visited the City, but he had too much tact to suggest such an arrangement on this occasion.

The busy inn suited Angelica perfectly. She was fascinated by the teeming life all around them. She stood at the window of their bedchamber, watching the lamplit arrival of a private coach in the yard below, delighted to be at the heart of so much activity.

She felt Benoît come up behind her. He slipped one arm around her waist and pulled the curtain closed with his other hand.

'*Ma chère femme*—' he kissed the graceful curve of her neck and shoulder '—you are supposed to save your attention for your husband on your wedding night—not a crowd of noisy strangers!' There was an unmistakable note of amusement in his deep voice.

Angelica caught her breath, relief as well as sensuous pleasure filling her at the touch of his lips on her soft skin. He had escorted her to London with such formal correctness she'd been afraid he'd been annoyed with her for forcing him into such a hasty marriage.

That hadn't been her intention when she'd walked out of the library the previous day. She hadn't thought any further than the fact that she could no longer allow her father to dominate her life. Lord Ellewood's cruelty to Martha had been the last straw.

It had been Benoît who had insisted they be married immediately. Angelica was aware that his decision had been prompted by a desire to protect her from scandal, but they had barely discussed the matter. She had been a preoccupied travelling companion, and he had been scrupulously punctilious in his dealings with her since they'd left Holly House.

She leant back against him, grateful to be enfolded once more in his embrace.

'Are you thinking about Lord Ellewood?' he asked softly, brushing her hair with his lips.

'Yes,' she admitted.

Her sentiments towards her father were confused. She felt angry, resentful, betrayed, sad, guilty—and liberated.

'When we go back to Sussex we'll call upon him at the Manor,' Benoît promised. 'I'm sure the breach between you is not irreparable.'

'No,' said Angelica flatly.

'Angelica—!'

'No,' she repeated uncompromisingly, slipping out of his arms and turning to look at him.

He returned her gaze, a hint of a frown in his dark eyes.

'What do you mean?' he asked quietly.

'I mean I will not go crawling back to him, begging his forgiveness, when it is he who should be apologising for his behaviour,' Angelica said stonily.

'I'm not in the habit of crawling anywhere,' Benoît replied dryly, 'and I certainly wasn't suggesting my wife should do so, but—'

'But what?' Angelica snapped. She hadn't realised how sensitive she was about the situation with her father until Benoît had broached the subject. 'Nothing's changed except we're married. If Papa was prepared to disown me rather than let me marry you, do you think he's going to be any more forgiving now I'm your *wife*?'

'I think that now he's had time for reflection, he may be more reasonable,' Benoît replied. He spoke mildly, although there was an underlying tension in his tone. 'I doubt—'

'That's what you said yesterday!' Angelica interrupted forcefully. 'And then it turned out that he'd dismissed Martha. He's not going to get any more reasonable—he's *not*!' Her voice cracked and she turned away to rest an unsteady hand on the mantelpiece, staring down into the fireplace with unseeing eyes.

The rift with Lord Ellewood was more painful for her than she was prepared to admit, even to herself.

'Lord Ellewood dismissed Martha in the middle of the night—before you'd returned to Holly House,'

Benoît reminded her sharply. 'You only found out about it *after* you'd already had one argument with him—and then you used it as a pretext to leave him.'

Angelica spun round to face Benoît, consternation in her fine blue eyes.

'Are you *blaming* me for what I did?' she demanded fiercely.

'No, *mon aimée*,' Benoît said equably. 'But I do want you to see things clearly—and I don't want this temporary estrangement between you and your father to become permanent.

'Lord Ellewood may already have been regretting his treatment of Martha, or he may not have been. We don't know, because when you confronted him in such a rage you forced his hand—just as he had forced yours earlier. You are both proud people. But I won't let you become locked in a spiral of anger which can only lead to increasing bitterness and pain for everyone. We will go back and see him.'

Angelica stared at him, doubt and disbelief in her wide blue eyes. She could hear the undercurrent of steel in Benoît's cool voice, and she knew he meant every word he said. She was far too overwrought by all the emotional upheavals of the past few days to give any rational consideration to his motives for saying it.

Her first, horrified reaction was that he was taking the Earl's side against her. Why was he so determined not to lose Lord Ellewood's favour?

'Why are you so anxious I make peace with Papa?' she demanded wildly, fear and suspicion in her eyes. 'Are you afraid he will indeed disown me? A penniless, disinherited wife would be a dreadful burden for an ambitious, but nameless, man—wouldn't she?'

The moment the words left her mouth she regretted them. She pressed her hands against her face, appalled at what she'd just said, her huge eyes locked on Benoît's rigid expression.

His jaw was set like a rock; a muscle twitched in his cheek and his eyes were narrow and dangerous.

'I should have left you with the Earl,' he said harshly. 'You clearly deserve each other. You could have traded insults to your hearts' content.'

'I'm *s-sorry*!' Angelica whispered, a stricken expression in her eyes as she reached out to him imploringly.

'Why did you marry me?' Benoît asked implacably, his eyes granite-hard as they locked with hers. He ignored both her outstretched hands and her pleading look. 'Why did you stay in Sussex an extra day?'

'What?' Angelica stared at him uncomprehendingly. She felt dazed and bruised. 'You know why.'

'Because you didn't *trust* me!' Benoît flung at her, with brutal irony. 'No, *ma douce amie*, that isn't good enough! You must have known you could trust me or you wouldn't have gone jaunting unchaperoned around the countryside with me. *Why did you stay after you'd delivered the letter?*'

He took two strides towards her as he spoke and seized her by the shoulders.

'*Why?*' He shook her, the strength of his grip making her wince, although she was not aware of feeling any pain.

'Because I c-couldn't bear to go back to London!'

Angelica stammered, dismayed by the blazing anger and suspicion she could see in his eyes.

She could feel the fierce, ruthlessly controlled rage which coursed through his whipcord body. He'd relaxed his grasp on her shoulders the moment she'd flinched, but his fury was no less disturbing because she knew he hadn't deliberately hurt her.

'That's it, isn't it?' He released her suddenly, as if she'd burnt him.

He turned on his heel and took a couple of hasty strides across the room, his hands clenched into fists. Angelica watched him, numb with shock.

'*Ma douce séductrice* indeed!' he snarled savagely over his shoulder. 'You knew the impact you'd made on me from the first and you decided to take advantage of it. I dare say it would have suited you better if I'd been a gentleman born and bred—but you were so desperate to escape an unbearable life that any half-way respectable man would have done!'

'No!' Angelica protested.

'No?' he taunted her bitterly. 'I've known experienced harlots pursue their quarry with more... hesitation...than you've used to entrap me. *My God!* What a fool I've been!'

He was still standing with his back to Angelica. He lifted an unsteady hand to run his fingers through his black hair. Then he leant his forearm against the bedpost and rested his forehead against it. His other arm hung by his side, his hand clenched into a fist. It was the first time Angelica had ever see him lose his composure so completely.

Her own hasty temper had been thoroughly

roused by his unfair accusations. Her blue eyes blazed with indignation. She opened her mouth to hurl a scalding rejoinder at him. But the bitter words died on her lips.

Her eyes were riveted on Benoît's rigid shoulders. Her anger drained away, to be replaced by a cold, hollow fear. She drew in a deep, shaky breath. They had been married only a few hours, yet already they were locked in a bitter dispute. Was this marriage a dreadful mistake?

For a few seconds she was overwhelmed by a desperate desire to escape: but then her shocked mind began to function again.

Benoît loved her.

She knew that with deep, wordless, instinctive certainty. The ferocity of his anger was a measure of how much he cared for her—and how much her cruel suggestion had hurt him.

In her own pain and confusion she had accused him of being a social-climbing fortune-hunter; and then she had inadvertently confirmed his apprehension that she'd simply used him to get away from the Earl. Perhaps he even suspected that her decision to marry the brickmaker's grandson was part of her revenge on the autocratic Lord Ellewood.

Benoît didn't lack self-confidence, but even he wasn't armoured against such a wounding slight from the woman he loved.

And he did love her. Angelica had never been so sure of it as she was when she gazed at his rigidly held shoulders and listened to his harshly controlled breathing. He was a guarded, cautious man, who had revealed more of his feelings to her than she suspected he had ever revealed to anyone before. She could not betray his trust.

'I stayed because I could not bear to leave *you*,' she said clearly, her heart pounding with quick anxiety as she tried to make amends for her unthinking, damaging accusation.

She walked over to him and reached out almost tentatively to touch his unresponsive back.

'I didn't know that—I didn't admit it to myself,' she continued, trying to speak steadily, although a pulse beating in her throat threatened to rob her of her voice. 'I told myself I was doing it for Harry's sake, because I didn't know if a smuggler could be trusted to rescue him. But it was for my sake I stayed, because I'd found...' She faltered and paused, trying to compose herself.

Beneath her hand she felt Benoît's tense muscles slowly relax, but he did not alter his position.

'I remember my first Season,' she said softly, gaining confidence. 'I had such high hopes, Ben. I thought I was going to find love and life—and perhaps even adventure—in the fashionable drawing-rooms and ballrooms of London.' She sighed, lost briefly in the past.

'It *was* exciting at first,' she continued wryly, 'but then I saw my friends get married. Sometime they found love, but mostly they didn't, and I thought—is this all there is? Will I have to chose between being a lonely spinster or a lonely wife? So I decided years ago I'd never get married unless I found a man I could love—and who loved me. I didn't care whether he was a prince or...or a *smuggler*.'

She slipped her hand through Benoît's arm and leant her cheek against his sleeve. His muscles were no longer rigid with tension and she felt a wave of relief wash over her as she realised he wasn't angry with her any more.

'I didn't have to marry you to get away from Papa,' she murmured, almost provocatively. 'Aunt Sarah in Bath has been sending me increasingly urgent invitations to visit her for nearly a year. She's a very high-spirited old lady, Harry's devoted to her. It was a difficult decision to make, but. . .'

Benoît turned round and slipped his arms around her waist. She looked up at him a little diffidently and saw a gleam of wry amusement in his dark, still shadowed eyes.

'That has to be the most long-winded, roundabout apology I have ever received, *mon aimée*,' he said, a hint of familiar humour in his voice.

Angelica was overwhelmed by a strange mixture of relief and nervousness; but she was too shy to reveal her feelings. She tried to hide them behind mock indignation.

'You *knew*, and you let me keep talking—!' she exclaimed.

'I was waiting to see if you'd ever manage to come straight out with the words, "I'm sorry. I love you",' he said softly. 'They stick a bit in that graceful throat, don't they, *ma chérie*?' He stroked it gently with sensitive fingers. 'I can't remember ever hearing you say them.'

Tears sparkled in Angelica's eyes.

'I do love you,' she said breathlessly. 'I love you with all my heart and soul, and nothing will ever change that. I'm sorry I said such a horrible thing to you. I know—'

His arms tightened around her and he stifled the rest of her apology with a kiss. She clung to him, trying to show him in her response to him how truly she meant what she'd said.

'I'm sorry too, *mon amour*,' he murmured a few moments later, his cheek resting against her hair as he held her against him. 'I know you didn't set out to trick me into marriage—I knew it even when I said it. It was just. . .'

Angelica lifted her head to meet his eyes and laid her fingers gently on his lips. Tears dampened her cheeks, but she didn't try to hide them. She smiled a little unsteadily.

'I gave you good reason to be angry,' she said softly, distress in her eyes. 'I've been so cross with Papa—yet the moment *I* felt hurt and confused I acted in exactly the same way. I lashed out at someone who loves me and wanted to help me.'

A sob caught in her throat and she swallowed, trying to suppress her tears.

'I'm not really as brazen as a h-harlot, am I?' she whispered anxiously, unable to conceal her own pain at the things he'd said to her.

'No!' Benoît exclaimed. 'No. I'm sorry, *mon aimée*! It was a cruel, unkind thing to suggest. Don't ever worry about it again.'

He smiled crookedly and stroked her cheek, brushing away her tears with infinitely tender fingers.

'Almost the first thing I noticed about you was the way your actions are guided by your heart,' he said softly. 'I think perhaps I am a little daunted, as well as captivated, by your openness. By nature I'm far more cautious and secretive. You will have to teach me to be less guarded, *mon amour*.'

Angelica gazed up at him, seeing his lean, dark face through a haze of tears.

She was remembering the inherent honesty with which Benoît had always treated her. Occasionally he had obscured facts, but only once had he deliberately misled her—and that had been about Adam's arrival. She didn't deserve his praise.

She bit her lip, struggling to control her overtaxed emotions.

Benoît smiled faintly, a quietly understanding expression in his brown eyes. He stroked the nape of her neck with gentle fingers.

'Ever since we left Sussex you have been so determined not to admit to any doubts—or reveal how upset you are,' he murmured. 'I do know, *ma chérie*, however insensitive I may have seemed. You won't have to face Lord Ellewood alone, I promise. I'll be with you. And we won't go to him until you're ready.'

Angelica gave a little gasp, and then the pent-up feelings of the past few days finally found release in a flood of tears.

Benoît held her comfortingly, stroking her hair and speaking softly to her until the first storm of emotion had passed.

Angelica let him support her, profoundly reassured and moved by his response to her. She could feel the firm texture of his coat beneath her cheek, and the relaxed vigour of his strong body against hers. His arms provided her with a haven and a source of strength. She knew with absolute conviction that from now on home was not a place, it was a person. Benoît was the only home she needed.

When the worst paroxysm of tears had passed, he guided her over to the bed and sat down beside her, one arm supporting her as she rested her head on his broad shoulder. She felt drained and exhausted, but so much better than she had done earlier. A crushing burden had finally become lighter.

She sighed, and accepted the handkerchief he offered her.

'Thank you,' she whispered, blowing her nose. 'I'm sorry,' she added a moment later with the first hint of humour she'd shown all day. 'A damp and overwrought bride is probably not what a man hopes for on his wedding night!'

Benoît chuckled and brushed her curls with his lips.

'I can think of worse things,' he said reflectively. 'And you are safely in my arms, *mon aimée*, even if you have just wept all over my best coat!'

Angelica smiled with weary contentment as she nestled within the circle of his arm. The nervous energy which had propelled her through the past twenty-four hours had finally burnt itself out. She was grateful for the interlude of quiet, gentle good humour.

'Adam's right,' she teased Benoît softly. 'You are a dandy! I thought so the first time we met. All you need is a gold ear-ring. . .!'

'You had me cast in the role of pirate from the

first!' Benoît retorted. 'I've told you before—I'm a respectable businessman.'

'Who gets woken up by smugglers in the middle of the night,' Angelica reminded him, lifting her head to look at him. 'Where *did* you go that first night I stayed at Holly House?'

'What a long memory you have!' Benoît remarked, grinning. 'One of Tody's old friends broke his arm escaping from Sir William,' he continued matter-of-factly. 'I learnt a lot from my father before I went to sea. They wanted me to set the bone for him. Being the trustworthy fellow that I am, you understand!'

'Respectable. . .trustworthy. . .I've married a paragon of virtue,' Angelica mused, a twinkle in her tired blue eyes.

Benoît smiled, but didn't rise to the bait.

'You look worn out, and pale as a ghost,' he said softly, stroking her dishevelled curls. 'Did you sleep much last night?'

'No,' Angelica confessed ruefully.

'I thought not. You must rest tonight.' Benoît kissed her lightly and stood up. 'I'll send Martha to you.'

'Benoît. . .Ben.' Angelica paused, gazing up at him with wide, dark-circled eyes.

He reached down to take her hand in his, lifting it to his lips.

'We've the rest of our lives together,' he said quietly. 'I know you're my wife, Angelica. I don't have to prove it at the first opportunity. Besides,' he added wickedly, 'as I recall, you find being jolted about in a carriage extremely traumatic. That was the reason you gave for staying at Holly House an extra day, wasn't it? I'm sure you need a good night's sleep just to recover from the journey up to London!'

Angelica woke slowly in the early hours of the morning. The room was shrouded in silky darkness, and at first she could see nothing when she opened her eyes. For a moment she felt confused, but then she heard Benoît's unhurried breathing and remembered they were married.

She hardly dared to move for fear of waking him, but she eased carefully over until she could look at him. He had opened the curtains before getting into bed—she thought perhaps he disliked being cocooned away from the sky—and she studied him in the dim light.

She could see his firm, slightly aquiline profile, and hear his slow, steady breathing. He had always been so alert and so forceful. It was strange to see him exposed and vulnerable in sleep. She could hardly believe that all she had to do was reach out to touch him. And he wouldn't even know.

She sighed soundlessly, and cautiously propped herself up on her elbow, scarcely daring to breath in case she woke him. He was brother to the wolf; she could not imagine her actions wouldn't disturb him, but his breathing continued slow and sure.

She couldn't help herself. She stretched out a single, tentative finger to touch the curve of his shoulder. He wasn't wearing a nightshirt, and she suddenly wondered if he was completely naked beneath the sheets. A tiny thrill of excitement tingled through her body.

His flesh was warm and firm beneath her delicate, questing fingers. She couldn't resist letting her hand glide gently over his collarbone. Her heart began to beat faster. She felt guiltily that she was stealing an illicit pleasure, but the temptation was irresistible.

A sunburst glow of joy flooded through her as she finally realised that she was, irretrievably, Benoît's wife. He was her husband, and she had a perfect right to reach out to him in the night.

Her touch was no less imperceptible, but considerably more confident, as she began to trace the contour of his muscular chest. She was so absorbed in her task that she was completely taken by surprise when he caught her hand in his.

'*Ma douce séductrice*,' he murmured softly, without opening his eyes.

'I thought you were asleep!' Angelica exclaimed, disconcerted. She tried to withdraw her hand, but he tightened his hold on it.

'I was. But you could rouse a carved stone knight from his tomb!' he retorted, a smile in his voice as he turned his head to look at her.

'Oh.' Angelica blushed in the darkness.

'Oh?' Benoît slipped an arm beneath her waist and drew her to lie alongside him. 'Were you hoping I wouldn't wake up?' he enquired teasingly.

'Yes. . .No!' Angelica replied, feeling flustered. 'I mean—'

She was acutely conscious of the feel of Benoît's lean, vigorous body through her thin nightgown. Her weariness of the previous evening had vanished. A warm, anticipatory excitement began to flow through her veins.

Benoît chuckled and lifted his hand to slip it beneath her heavy golden hair as she looked down at him. His fingers gently caressed the nape of her neck, and a quiver of pleasure rippled through her.

'I thought it was usually the Prince who was supposed to wake the Princess,' he murmured provocatively, 'and you haven't completed the spell, *mon amour*. If you really want to be sure. . .'

Angelica hesitated for a fraction of a second.

'You've tricked me like that before,' she reminded him huskily.

'The circumstances are not entirely similar,' Benoît said softly. 'You weren't my wife then.'

'And you never intended to tell me how you're going to rescue Harry, whether I kissed you or not!' Angelica exclaimed, with remembered indignation. 'It was an underhand, dastardly. . ..'

Her protests faded as Benoît allowed his hand to trace the curve of her back. She was still propped up on her elbow, half leaning, half lying against him, and she could feel the play of muscles in his arms and chest as he explored her warm, vibrant body.

'I thought the action provided its own reward,' Benoît teased her gently. 'I certainly found it more satisfying to kiss you than to discuss tedious rescue plans.'

'Because you have a. . .secretive nature,' Angelica gasped, as his fingers investigated the soft, sensitive skin of her throat, just below the neckline of her nightgown. She was finding it increasingly difficult to think coherently.

Benoît chuckled softly.

'I don't think that's why,' he murmured, and drew her head down until her lips met his.

She melted against him, her hair falling around them like a curtain in the darkness. She was lost in a world of delicious sensations. Her hand still rested against his chest and she could feel the firm, rapid beat of his heart. His mouth was warm and almost languid against hers. She realised they had all the time in the world.

When at last she lifted her head, her lips were swollen with tender passion and her whole body glowed with fiery anticipation. She could hear his quickened breathing, and feel the rise and fall of his chest beneath her hand. The desire to touch him more intimately was irresistible, and she let her hand drift inquisitively across his torso. She was in no doubt now about the lean strength in his virile body. She bent and pressed a kiss against his chest.

Benoît caught his breath, uttering a soft, wordless exclamation, and rolled her onto her back.

Her heart leapt in sudden surprise, but then she was overwhelmed by new sensations of pleasure. She slipped her arms around his neck and lost herself in another long, deep, infinitely satisfying kiss.

There were dark shadows all around them. She was excitingly aware of the gentle weight of Benoît's upper body pressing her firmly into the bed. She ran her hand down his arm, feeling his biceps tense at her touch. She felt utterly secure in his embrace.

He kissed her throat and she let her head fall back against the pillow, arching her body towards him. His hand rested lightly on her waist, burning through the fabric of her nightgown as his lips explored the hollow at the base of her throat.

Then he reached down and began to ease up the hem of her nightdress.

A wave of intense, almost heart-stopping expectation swept over her. She gasped, hardly daring to breath at the first, electrifying touch of his hand on her naked leg. He let his fingers slip sensuously across the tingling flesh of her outer thigh; trailing them over her hip until his hand came to rest lightly on her stomach.

Her heart raced. Her world had shrunk until it was contained within the murmuring shadows of the sturdy fourposter bed; yet at the same time she felt as if she were soaring in a lofty, star-filled sky.

She murmured incoherently. She was full of wonder at the glorious sensations which consumed her, yet she was hungry for even greater fulfilment.

She rolled slightly towards him, her fingers pressing convulsively into the muscles of his shoulders. She felt his hand move against her burning, excited flesh, curving around her side as he continued his upward exploration. The soft material of her nightgown seemed almost harsh when it brushed against her sensitised skin as Benoît pushed it aside.

She lifted her hips instinctively to make it easier for him, then caught her breath as his hand cupped her throbbing breast. She closed her eyes, surrendering entirely to the glorious sensations he was arousing within her.

His strong fingers teased her taut nipple gently, stimulating currents of desire which seemed to spring from deep within the centre of her body. She breathed in quick, erratic gasps, conscious only of Benoît.

He moved against her, gently nudging her legs apart with his knee. The pressure of anticipation within Angelica became almost unbearable in its intensity. She hesitated, a brief, last-minute nervousness tightening her muscles. She could sense the wild, fierce energy in his lean body, and it half frightened her, half exhilarated her.

'*Je t'aime,*' he murmured and waited, softly kissing the corner of her swollen mouth and stroking her breast almost soothingly.

She realised he was holding his desire in check with ruthless self-control and she was overcome with a rush of tenderness as well as love towards him.

She relaxed, no longer resisting him. He lifted himself until he was poised above her, his elbows braced on either side of her body. Her heart pounded with excitement. She was intimately conscious of the arousal in his lean, taut body. She wrapped her arms around him, delighting in the play of muscles in his strong back.

She felt a few moments of gentle questing, and then a sharp pain which almost made her cry out. She clung to Benoît, digging her fingers into his shoulders, turning her head briefly aside. He kissed her cheek softly, almost reassuringly. She sighed as an entirely new and seductive warmth began to radiate through her body, and turned her head to meet his kiss with eager, responsive lips.

Her whole world was filled with the feel, taste and scent of her husband. She was aware of nothing but her love for him, and the infinite joy and pleasure it gave her to be in his arms, completely united with him.

The tempo of his movements began to quicken. She was borne away on a rhythm of almost primal intensity. Golden fire pulsated through her body, exploding the shadows around them with glorious flashes of light. She seemed to hover breathtakingly on the edge of a precipice, gazing up at the bright stars in the dark void above, not knowing what lay beyond—and then the morning sun rose, enveloping her in swirling, glowing colours and warm, vivid, deep satisfaction.

It seemed a long time later when she sighed contentedly and stirred in Benoît's arms.

'Mon aimée?' he murmured softly.

'Mm.' She pulled herself up to press a kiss against his cheek.

Then she relaxed to lie half across him, her fingers laced together so that she could rest her chin on the backs of her hands as she looked at him. The first pale light of dawn was creeping in through the uncurtained window, and she could see him quite clearly.

His black hair was dishevelled, but his lean, hawk-like face was more relaxed and contented than she had ever seen it. He was watching her quietly as he stroked her hair. There was a hint of humour, as well as a question in his brown eyes, but the wolf-wariness she was so used to was completely absent from his expression.

She smiled, luminous happiness and profound satisfaction glowing in her blue eyes.

'So this is married life,' she said musingly.

'Does it meet with your approval, *ma chérie*?'
Benoît enquired softly, winding a lock of her hair
around his finger.

Angelica hesitated, a teasing reply on her lips.
Then her expression sobered as she realised her
answer was more important to Benoît than his light-
hearted manner made it seem.

'Oh, yes,' she replied, with heartfelt sincerity.
'Yes, my love, you know it does.'

She drew herself up so that she could kiss his lips,
her hair falling around them like a cascade of gold
in the morning light.

'And I thought you would be too tired after all
your exertions of the past few days,' said Benoît, a
few minutes later. 'That will teach me to underesti-
mate you, won't it?'

Angelica laughed and propped herself up on her
elbow. Benoît blew at an errant tendril of golden
hair which was tickling his nose.

'I could never be too tired for you,' she declared,
a reprehensible twinkle in her eyes. 'What are we
going to do now?'

'Within the next hour or so, or within the next few
days?' Benoît enquired, raising one black eyebrow
humorously.

'The next few days,' Angelica clarified her question. She had a very good idea of what was likely to
happen within the next few hours.

'Go back to Sussex.' Benoît caressed her shoulder
absentmindedly, but he was looking past her, up into
the shadows of the bed canopy.

'To see Papa?' Angelica asked.

'Partly.' He turned his head to meet her quiet

eyes. 'I must also see Adam and do something about that gang of smugglers which is causing Sir William so many problems.'

Cold ripples of fear crawled down Angelica's spine at his words, but she remained completely still, determined not to let him sense her anxiety. She knew he would do whatever he believed he had to do. It wouldn't help him if he also had to worry about her reaction to his plans.

'How will you go about it?' she asked, trying to sound matter-of-fact.

Benoît smiled lopsidedly.

'No words of warning or disapproval?' he asked quizzically.

'It wouldn't make any difference, would it?' Angelica said breathlessly. 'Besides, I tried so hard to persuade you to rescue Harry. I'm hardly in a position to complain now.'

'But you are worried.'

'I'm trying not to be,' she assured him. 'How could you tell?'

'When you're lying so close to me? It wasn't difficult.'

'Oh.' Angelica lowered her eyes, biting her lip ruefully. 'What are you going to do?' she asked.

'I'm not sure,' he said slowly. 'The role of poacher-turned-gamekeeper is new to me. It sticks in my throat a little to hand them over to be hung and gibbeted—killers though they are. We shall have to see.'

Then he turned his head and smiled at her.

'I won't come to any harm,' he said confidently.

'And think of all the adventures we'll have when Harry is safely home and you sail with me.'

Angelica's face lit up.

'You'll really take me with you?' she exclaimed joyfully.

'I'm not leaving you behind!' said Benoît firmly. 'I'm a very generous man. If I'm soaked to the skin in a torrential rain storm I shall expect my wife to be likewise cold and wet. No more living in idle luxury for you, my lady! You are going to learn at first hand the tedium of being becalmed in mid-ocean, the inestimable frustration of—!'

He caught his breath and rolled away from her as Angelica moved her hand purposefully across his lean stomach.

She blinked in surprise at his emphatic response to her action. She had simply intended to distract him from his mock-solemn list of the discomforts awaiting her. But then she guessed the explanation for his reaction.

'You're ticklish!' she exclaimed in delight, reaching towards him again.

'It's a base lie!' He grabbed for her wrist, missed, then gasped, his body jackknifing, as she ran her fingers provocatively below his ribs.

'No! It's true!' She started to laugh as he seized her hands and rolled her neatly onto her back. 'Now what?' She looked up at him challengingly as he held both her wrists in a firm grip.

'I'm not sure.' He grinned down at her, sunlight warm on his cheek. 'We could call a truce.'

'Oh, no!' She shook her head gleefully, her hair spread out wantonly across the pillow. 'After all the times you've made fun of me, all the times you've seemed so cool and sophisticated and in control— and all I had to do to get my own back. . .'

She tried to pull her arms out of his grasp, a wicked expression in her blue eyes. He resisted her attempt to escape without difficulty.

'Don't worry, *mon amour*. . .' he transferred both her wrists into one hand, a hint of laughter in his voice '. . .you have always had far more subtle methods of wreaking your revenge on me.'

'So you've said before,' Angelica murmured, as he bent towards her, his lips brushing hers. 'But I'm sure none of them are quite so satisfying. . .'

'Positive?'

'Mmm.'

'*Angelica!*' The only reason Benoît didn't leap completely out of bed was because he was too tangled in the bedclothes.

She laughed uninhibitedly, feeling deliriously happy and unbelievably lucky.

'You're not safe to be near,' Benoît growled, keeping a wary distance, although there was an answering gleam of humour in his brown eyes. 'Very well, my lady, two can play at that game.'

He dragged back the bedclothes in one swift gesture and it was Angelica's turn to gasp. She reached out to pull down her nightgown, but he caught her hand.

'It's only getting in the way,' he said softly, the laughter in his eyes replaced by a far more intense emotion. 'Sit up.'

Angelica did so, feeling shy as she allowed him to draw it over her head and toss it away.

'*Ma belle,*' he murmured huskily, and kissed her shoulder.

'I'm going to have to practise my French,' she said unsteadily, as they sank back onto the bed.

She was truly naked in his arms now, and in the morning light there were no comforting shadows to hide them. But she didn't need to hide from Benoît. He was her husband and he loved her. Her brief moment of shyness passed.

'I shall take pleasure in teaching you, *mon aimée,*' he replied lightly, and then stiffened as she laid her hand on his ribs.

'Don't you trust me?' she whispered, meeting his eyes.

'No!' But he didn't try to stop her as she slipped her hand delicately over his side towards the flat plane of his stomach.

'I trusted you.' Their eyes were locked together and a smiled tugged at the corners of Angelica's mouth as she continued her deliberate caress.

'I know,' Benoît half groaned.

She could feel the tension in his body as he exerted all his self-control not to jerk away from her hand.

'It can't be that bad,' she teased him, exhilarated by the power he was allowing her to have over him. 'I haven't done anything to make you jump.'

'It's not what you've done—it's what you might do!' he retorted. 'I didn't expect my wife to startle me half out of bed on our wedding night.'

Angelica giggled.

'And you don't want me to do it again?' she said provocatively.

'I can think of more rewarding ways to pass our time,' he replied softly.

Angelica hesitated. Her hand still rested gently beneath his ribs. She had no real intention of tormenting him, but she couldn't help relishing the fact that she had finally found a way of turning the tables on him.

He chuckled.

'Make up your mind quickly, *mon ange*,' he recommended. 'We've a lot to do today. But before we begin. . .'

She moved her hand carefully around his body to his back and he exhaled with relief.

'I thought we'd already begun,' she murmured, her eyes gleaming wickedly as she rubbed his back in slow, sensuous circles.

'My error,' said Benoît hoarsely. 'You're quite right, *mon amour*, we have!'

EPILOGUE

June 1809

THE tide was coming in. Lord Ellewood could hear it. He stood on the beach and listened to the waves rolling up the sand. He could hear the seabirds screeching overhead, and feel the hot June sun scorching his scarred cheek—but he could only imagine the glitter of sunlight on the sea.

The Earl had remained at the Manor House for more than three months, a difficult and uncomfortable guest for both Sir William and his household. He had shown no inclination to go back to London, yet he had refused point-blank to receive Angelica on the two occasions she had attempted to see him. The first time she had come with Benoît; the second time she had come alone. That had been more than two months ago.

The relentless passing of the lonely days gnawed at Lord Ellewood's soul. He had hoped that Angelica would make one more attempt to see him, but she had not—and he was too proud to go to her. The days passed, but time seemed to stand still. Until Benoît and Harry returned from France, life could not begin again for any of them.

Lord Ellewood lifted his head to taste the sea breeze. He didn't know what he was doing on the beach; he only knew he had been driven by a deep, compelling need to come back to the sea. He had ordered a frightened servant to bring him—but he had forbidden the man to follow him down over the pebbles to the sands.

Now he stood by himself, a stiff-backed, solitary figure, braced against a gale which did not blow; and wondered bleakly if the waiting was as agonising for Angelica as it was for him—and if his son would ever return home.

He clenched his fists together in anger, frustration, and shame. He was bitterly ashamed of his behaviour over the past two years—but it was hard to bow his head and make amends. The harsh, discordant cries of the seagulls suited his mood. The hot summer sunshine on his cheek seemed incongruous. There was no harmony left in his life.

He heard boots crunching on the pebbles behind him and swung round furiously on the approaching servant. Dear God! Did he no longer have any authority even over a groom?

'I told you to stay away from me,' he snarled viciously. 'I'll summon you when I want you!'

'You already did,' came Benoît's cool, soft voice. 'Four months ago. Good afternoon, my lord.'

Lord Ellewood was shocked into silence: plunged back sixteen years to the last time Benoît's voice had come to him out of the darkness on these beaches.

The Earl had not been able to see his opponent then, and he could not do so now—but this time no dawn light would reveal Benoît's features to him. It was the final, damning confirmation of all he had lost, and everything he would never be again.

He held his body rigid, tense with conflicting emotions, as he struggled to master himself.

'Harry?' he grated at last, his anxiety for his son finally overriding every other concern.

'Is safely home,' said Benoît calmly. 'He's a brave, resourceful lad. I'm sure he'd have managed without my help—but it didn't hurt to expedite things a little.'

The knots of fear slowly eased from Lord Ellewood's muscles and he sighed, his square shoulders slumping slightly in pure relief.

'Where is he?' he demanded. 'Why hasn't he come to me?' A new spark of fear ignited within him. 'Is he injured?'

'No. He's with Angelica,' said Benoît equably.

Lord Ellewood's expression darkened.

'Have you turned my son against me—as well as my daughter?' he asked acidly.

'I've turned no one against you,' Benoît replied coldly. 'Certainly not Angelica. How many times do you intend to rebuff her before your pride is assuaged, my lord? Or have you indeed disowned her?'

'Damn your—'

'*No!*' Benoît's icy voice sliced across the first rumblings of Lord Ellewood's anger like a knife. 'Save your curses. They earn my contempt—not my respect. Did you lose your backbone as well as your eyes when the coach overturned?'

The scorn in Benoît's tone, even more than his words, stabbed straight to the Earl's heart, striking with the freezing, bitter intensity of a winter frost, completing the work Lord Ellewood's self-disgust had already begun.

The Earl dragged in several painful, sobbing

breaths. He no longer felt the hot summer sun blazing down on his body. He was lost in a black, barren world of his own. His darkest, innermost fear had been hurled in his face with uncompromising directness by a man he could not help but respect.

For two years he had been driven by rage; but now he had worn out his anger, and he had nothing left with which to replace it. For a moment he felt utterly desolate.

But Benoît's words had had the force of a challenge. And Lord Ellewood suddenly realised that the cost of refusing to meet it was more than he was prepared to pay. He released his breath in a long sigh. His inner battle had left him empty and drained of emotion.

'You must despise me,' he said tonelessly.

'No,' said Benoît quietly. 'I pray to God I will never be set the same challenge.'

'Are you not the one who told me—on this very beach—that you'd rather try, and fail, than live knowing you'd never had the courage to try at all?' Lord Ellewood asked sharply. 'No wonder I've earned your contempt.'

'I was young and arrogant,' said Benoît, a hint of apology in his tone. 'I wouldn't have the gall to repeat those words now. Will you walk with me?'

'Do I have a choice?' Lord Ellewood enquired, with a flicker of resigned humour. 'The field is yours, sir. It's time I attempted to preserve my dignity at least.'

He allowed Benoît to take his hand and tuck it through his arm, and they began to stroll along the tideline. They were much of a height and their strides were of similar length. The Earl found it surprisingly easy to keep pace with his companion.

'I think you'll find you've retained more than that,' said Benoît quietly. 'It wasn't for your swordsmanship I respected you sixteen years ago.'

Lord Ellewood drew in a sharp breath.

'Angelica must hate me,' he said bleakly, with uncharacteristic openness. The events of the past few minutes had shaken him out of his usual reserve.

'No. She never even came close to doing so,' Benoît replied, without hesitation.

'I thought she would come again, but she didn't,' said the Earl, following his own train of thought. 'I thought she would come again. . .and next time I would have—' He broke off. 'Next time isn't good enough in this uncertain world,' he said bitterly. 'I should know that by now—if you delay, next time may never come.'

'It will come,' said Benoît, with the quiet assurance Lord Ellewood remembered from sixteen years before.

They paced on in silence for a few moments, then the Earl roused himself from his introspection.

'Harry's safe, you say?' he said gruffly, although he didn't doubt Benoît had told him the truth.

'Angelica says he's thinner than he was, but otherwise he's completely irrepressible,' Benoît replied humorously.

'But he didn't come to find me,' said Lord Ellewood flatly. He had been hurt by that omission. 'Does he also despise me for what I've done? If I were in his shoes—'

'I asked him to wait,' Benoît interrupted equably.

'I had an axe of my own to grind first, my lord. But have no doubt—Harry is as eager to see you as Angelica.'

They took several more steps in silence.

'What do you want of me?' the Earl asked discordantly.

He felt raw, and painfully exposed to the contempt he was sure Benoît felt towards him. It was a measure of his real courage that he had accepted the need to have this conversation at all.

'I want nothing,' said Benoît quietly. 'Angelica would like to have her father back, I think.'

The Earl stopped walking abruptly. He turned his ravaged face towards the sea, away from Benoît.

'I've re-employed Hargreaves,' he said harshly, after a very long silence.

'I know,' said Benoît. 'So does Angelica. She's very happy.'

'*Stupid!*' Lord Ellewood exclaimed suddenly, referring to the absent secretary. 'He should *never* have let her outmanoeuvre him! But he never failed me before, and I can't hold him entirely to blame. She's as stubborn as a mule!'

'It's a family characteristic,' said Benoît mildly. 'Do you still blame Angelica for what *she* did?'

'She disobeyed me!' said Lord Ellewood gratingly.

'You prize obedience above all other virtues?' Benoît enquired softly.

'*No!* Damn you!' Lord Ellewood snapped. 'But in my daughter. . .'

'You left her with the impression that I was a disreputable smuggler,' Benoît pointed out. 'You must have known it wasn't true. Angelica had no difficulty finding me, and I've only owned Holly House for the past three years! In the circumstances—knowing as little about me as she did—it was inevitable she would want to confirm my integrity. You'd have done exactly the same thing in her position.'

Lord Ellewood swallowed a hasty retort.

'I didn't want her to get foolishly romantic notions about you,' he said grittily, almost as if he were speaking against his will. 'A rich, handsome, adventurous shipowner—she's been desperate to travel for years—and far more restless over the past few months.' He grunted sardonically. 'My petty-mindedness backfired on me, didn't it?'

'She was certainly very suspicious of me when she arrived,' said Benoît reflectively. 'Practically the first thing she asked me was whether the brandy I was offering her was smuggled.'

The Earl gave a crack of unexpected laughter.

'She must have inherited her tact from me,' he observed dryly.

He hesitated, then reached into his pocket and drew out two letters which he held out towards Benoît.

'My lord?'

'You recognise them, I'm sure,' said the Earl ironically. 'Your messenger delivered them to me on the day you were married. Poor fellow rode himself into the ground to get them to me. Take them.'

Benoît did so, noticing that the seals were still unbroken.

'I couldn't bring myself to ask William to read them to me, and there was no one else,' said Lord

Ellewood distantly. 'I want to know what Angelica said.'

'You could ask her.'

'No! I want to hear what she wrote to me then,' said the Earl harshly.

'Very well.' Benoît glanced shrewdly at Lord Ellewood, then broke the seal and quickly scanned the letter. He smiled faintly, and began to read aloud.

'Dear Papa, you will be glad to learn that I have safely delivered your letter to Mr Faulkener. I arrived yesterday afternoon, when he was away from home, but his mother made me very comfortable while I waited for him. She remembered you from your previous visits to Sussex—'

'Determined to make it sound like an ordinary social call!' the Earl interrupted scornfully. 'As though that could make it any better.'

Benoît grinned and carried on reading.

'When I met Mr Faulkener I was relieved to discover that, to all appearances, he is a very respectable gentleman—'

'Ha!' the Earl exclaimed.

'I am sure he has both the ability and the means to rescue Harry. He has indeed agreed to do so. Unfortunately, he will not tell me when or how he intends to set about it. I confess I am a trifle disturbed by his reticence because we do know so little about him—'

'Hoist by my own petard,' said Lord Ellewood fatalistically.

'However, I did have the great good fortune to see your old friend Sir William Hopwood this morning, and he appears to be well acquainted with Mr Faulkener. It seems a pity to leave before I have taken this opportunity to discover more about him, so I will return to London tomorrow. I am sorry that I left without discussing my plans with you, but we had an uneventful journey yesterday and Martha and John Coachman have taken good care of me. With all my love, Angelica.'

Benoit folded the letter and put it back into Lord Ellewood's hand.

'Thank you.' The Earl weighed it for a few seconds in his fingers. 'I would have been infuriated by her impertinence if I'd received this in London,' he remarked.

'I don't think that was her intention,' Benoît replied quietly.

'No. I know.' Lord Ellewood returned the letter to his pocket. 'William hasn't said anything about meeting her at Holly House before their encounter in Littlehampton,' he said curiously.

'They didn't meet face to face,' Benoît explained, smiling faintly. 'She overheard Sir William accusing me of being a dastardly smuggler and a traitor to England into the bargain. That's why she stayed in Sussex. She thought I might sell Harry back to the French. And why she followed me when I went to meet Adam.'

There was a further silence while Lord Ellewood absorbed that information.

He could hear the waves lapping gently on the sands beside them, and he could remember the glittering expanse of the beach that stretched out before them. There was a little less pain in that memory now than there had been.

'No, that's not why,' he said at last. 'I know my daughter better than that, and I believe I know you better than that. She didn't think you were a traitor. But it doesn't matter now, she's your wife.'

'Yes, she is,' said Benoît.

'You'll take better care of her than I can,' said Lord Ellewood harshly.

'I'll take care of her,' said Benoît quietly.

'Where is she?' Lord Ellewood demanded.

'About a hundred yards away.'

'*What?*' The Earl was very shaken.

'You don't think she'd have let me come alone, do you?' Benoît asked quizzically. 'She and Harry both. We followed you from the Manor, but I wanted to talk to you first. They've been waiting with the horses.'

'My God!' Lord Ellewood drew in a deep, unsteady breath. 'I didn't expect that. Harry as well, you say? My God!'

'They'll come when I signal to them,' said Benoît. 'And I'll do that when you give me the word.'

'No more ambushes, hey?' Lord Ellewood tried to inject a note of liveliness into his voice. 'That seems to be my destiny on these beaches, doesn't it? To walk in darkness and run blindly on my fate.'

'Not necessarily,' said Benoît calmly.

'My God! I hope if you and Angelica have children they inherit *your* tact!' Lord Ellewood exclaimed forcefully. 'Why don't you just tell me I've made my own darkness these past two years?'

Benoît chuckled.

'That *would* be impertinent, wouldn't it?' he observed. 'I think your own children are getting rather impatient, my lord. May I. . .?'

'Yes, yes,' said Lord Ellewood hastily.

They began to walk back along the beach. The Earl listened intently for sounds of Angelica and Harry's approach. Then he heard quickly running feet.

'Angelica?'

'Papa.' She flung her arms around him.

Lord Ellewood hesitated fractionally, then embraced his daughter stiffly. It was still so hard to unbend.

But it was even harder not to respond to her. He felt her sunny curls beneath his harsh cheek, and suddenly he was hugging her so tightly she thought her ribs might crack. He had been afraid he might never hold her in his arms again.

'Harry's home, Papa.' She lifted her head to look at him.

The Earl grunted, not trusting himself to speak. He lifted his hand almost tentatively, and felt the tears which stained her cheeks.

'Of course he is,' he said gruffly. 'Do you really think I'd entrust my son's life to an incompetent jackass? Well, where's Harry, by God?'

'Here, sir.' Lord Lennard came forward, grinning broadly.

His likeness to Angelica was unmistakable. His unruly curls were almost angelic in their golden fairness, and his blue eyes were as clear and lucid as hers. But his debt to his father was also clearly apparent. He was thin-faced and sallow from months of hardship, but there was no doubting the determination in his firm jaw, or the vigour in his long-limbed body.

Lord Ellewood gripped his son's shoulder fiercely.

'Good lad,' he said roughly. 'You've seen some sport since you were last home, I'll be bound. You must tell me all about it.'

'Yes, sir!' said Harry enthusiastically.

'I look forward to it.' The Earl shook Harry back and forwards a couple of times to emphasise his words. Then he turned his attention back to Angelica.

'No more books for you,' he said abruptly. 'No more books for me, either. I've been talking to Adam Kennett. He plays a damned good game of chess! He won't tell me how he managed to get himself wounded, but he *has* told me about the tricks Faulkener's groom teaches his horses. So I was thinking—how hard can it be to ride along an empty beach?'

Angelica stared at her father in amazement, then turned to look at Benoît. He grinned.

'I'll talk to Thomas immediately, my lord,' he promised.

'Good! We've wasted enough time,' said Lord Ellewood briskly. He hesitated. 'I've been following your husband's career for years,' he said gruffly to Angelica. 'You've made an excellent choice, girl.

I'm proud of you! Harry!' he continued before Angelica could respond.

'Yes, sir.'

'Walk me down the beach,' the Earl commanded. 'I want to hear all about *your* adventures now!'

Angelica turned to Benoît as her father and brother strode away. Tears of happiness and relief sparkled in her eyes as he took her in his arms.

'I'm so happy,' she whispered. 'After all these months of waiting, you've come home—and Papa...' her voice was temporarily suspended. 'I didn't mean to cry,' she murmured, leaning her head against his broad shoulder.

Benoît smiled, stroking her golden curls gently.

'I'm not complaining, *mon aimée*,' he said softly. 'I think my impatience to get home was greater than Harry's! I've never left a wife behind before. It's an experience I intend to avoid in the future!'

Angelica gave a watery chuckle.

'I'll hold you to that,' she assured him, and sighed contentedly, happy simply to be in his arms.

The past few months had been very hard. She had done her best not to worry about Benoît and Harry, but it hadn't been easy.

And all the time she had known her father was only a few miles away, enduring exactly the same anxiety, but refusing even to speak to her. There had been so many occasions when she'd longed to talk to him; but she hadn't visited him a third time because she hadn't been able to bear the possibility that he might reject her yet again.

But now she was here on the sunlit beach with her husband, and the Earl had said he was proud of her.

She lifted her head and looked at Benoît. His brown eyes gleamed with the familiar half-teasing, wholly loving expression as they smiled into hers. His black hair glinted in the sunshine, but his lean, watchful face was relaxed and unguarded. The wolf within him slept.

She touched his cheek with gentle fingers, then slipped her arms around his neck, drawing his head down to hers.

'I am so glad you're home,' she murmured. 'I missed you so much.'

He kissed her gently, and then with growing passion. The blue sky arched above them, and only the lightest of summer breezes tugged at Angelica's skirt. It was hard to remember how bleak and desolate the seashore could be—and the pitched battles which had been fought here.

'Hmm,' said Benoît rather hoarsely, some time later. 'I think I've mentioned before the hazards of going out in public with you, my lady!'

Angelica started to laugh from pure joy, and a second later he was laughing with her. He picked her up and swung her exuberantly round on the shining sands, while seabirds rose, protesting, above them.

'Faulkener!'

Benoît set Angelica down on her feet again and they turned to see Lord Ellewood striding towards them. Angelica tensed instinctively. It was a long time since she had seen her father move so purposefully, but then she saw Harry was grinning and she relaxed.

'Faulkener!'

'Yes, my lord,' Benoît responded, his hand still on Angelica's waist.

'William's been telling me tales about a villainous gang of smugglers that were terrorising the countryside a few months ago,' said the Earl energetically. 'He said he found it impossible to obtain any solid evidence against them. Everyone was too frightened to talk. Then one day the three ringleaders vanished and the whole thing fell apart.'

'Really, my lord?' Benoît said politely.

He drew Angelica back to lean against him, slipping his arms loosely around her waist from behind, and looked at the Earl over the top of her head.

'So I understand,' said Lord Ellewood briskly. 'Hopwood's been going around in a state of thwarted curiosity for the past three months. He almost came to blows with Kennett the other day when Adam swore he didn't know anything about it!'

'Dear me,' said Benoît mildly. 'Why should he suppose Adam knows anything about it?'

'Because you're as thick as thieves?' Lord Ellewood suggested dryly.

He laughed suddenly, startling and delighting Angelica because it was so long since she'd seen her father in such a good humour.

'Now you're back, you can indulge *my* curiosity,' he said pleasantly. 'In lieu of asking for permission to marry my daughter. What the devil *did* you do with those murderous brutes, Faulkener?'

Angelica twisted in Benoît's arms to glance up at

him. A twinkle of shared amusement passed between them, then Benoît glanced from Harry to Lord Ellewood and grinned.

'They suffered the same fate you once suggested for me, my lord,' he said matter-of-factly, but with a hint of amusement in his voice. 'I had them pressed into the navy.'

GET 4 BOOKS AND A MYSTERY GIFT

Return this coupon and we'll send you 4 Mills & Boon Historical Romance™ novels and a mystery gift absolutely FREE! We'll even pay the postage and packing for you.

We're making you this offer to introduce you to the benefits of Reader Service: FREE home delivery of brand-new Mills & Boon Historical Romance novels, at least a month before they are available in the shops, FREE gifts and a monthly Newsletter packed with information.

Accepting these FREE books and gift places you under no obligation to buy, you may cancel at any time, even after receiving just your free shipment. Simply complete the coupon below and send it to:

MILLS & BOON® READER SERVICE, FREEPOST, CROYDON, SURREY, CR9 3WZ.

No stamp needed

Yes, please send me 4 free Mills & Boon Historical Romance novels and a mystery gift. I understand that unless you hear from me, I will receive 4 superb new titles every month for just £2.99* each postage and packing free. I am under no obligation to purchase any books and I may cancel or suspend my subscription at any time, but the free books and gifts are mine to keep in any case. (I am over 18 years of age)

H6JE

Ms/Mrs/Miss/Mr _____

Address _____

_____

_____ Postcode _____

Offer closes 30th April 1997. We reserve the right to refuse an application. *Prices and terms subject to change without notice. Offer only valid in UK and Ireland and is not available to current subscribers to this series. Readers in Ireland please write to: P.O. Box 4546, Dublin 24. Overseas readers please write for details.

You may be mailed with offers from other reputable companies as a result of this application. Please tick box if you would prefer not to receive such offers. ☐

Historical Romance™

Coming next month

THE RAINBOROUGH INHERITANCE
Helen Dickson
YORK 1709/10

Miss Lucinda Howard had had several skirmishes with an unknown gentleman, who clearly had no pretensions to the name, so when he claimed to be the Earl of Rainborough she had no hesitation in denying the possibility. Then he arrived at her home, truly the Earl, to propose to her elder sister Henrietta. Laurence had inherited debts, and a wealthy marriage was the only real solution, but Henrietta loved another. Lucinda thought she would not see him again—but she had reckoned without the machinations of her aunt Celia!

THE LAST GAMBLE
Mary Nichols
ENGLAND 1820

Miss Helen Sanghurst had had too many shocks, discovering after her father's suicide that he had gambled away her inheritance. It was some relief to find she had a guardian, even if it meant travelling from London to Scotland. Needing some peace, she was bent on travelling alone, but coach travel was risky and Helen was secretly thankful for the protection offered by Captain Duncan Blair, also travelling north. That didn't mean, however, she was going to reveal her identity to a stranger, no matter how attractive...